THE FEW

C. L. NAIDITCH

1

"You should be careful, you know. They will come."

Troy Hubbard looked at his friend, derision evident in his expression.

"You believe that nonsense they're spouting on the alternative news? None of that will ever happen."

Carson Jacobs smiled, then sobered.

"Easy for you to say. You think your family connections will save you. I'm not as convinced. You know, I've already seen it happen. They took Jimmy last week."

"Jimmy? *Our* Jimmy? Who took him?"

"Of course, our Jimmy. Do you know any other Jimmys? And it was one of those squads. You know, the ones created by the new leader. The leader you thought was going to fix the world. Yeah, right. Only thing he's fixed is his tie. And why does he even wear one, anyway? No one has worn a tie since mid-last century."

Troy laughed. "You're having a day, aren't you? You make it sound like the enforcement squads are against us. They're not. They're protecting us. And what do you even know about fashion trends from last century?

Come to think of it, what do you even know about last century? We're not allowed that information. It's for our own good. You know it is. Why waste time on that useless crap? Today and the future is all that's important. And we're making sure our future is bright and beautiful. No conflict. Unity. All united. Everyone agrees that's best."

Carson ignored the fashion comment. He didn't want to admit that he still accessed the historical archives. It was risky to do so. The most recent decree declared such activities illegal. Most anything other than listening to and studying the prescribed dogma was illegal. And the current leadership was intent on destroying all records of anything from the past. It was almost as if they wanted everyone to believe there was no past. Only today. Maybe yesterday, or last week. At most, the last two years, when the leadership changed. But nothing earlier. Carson was surprised the archives hadn't already been obliterated. But then again, there were those who made it their life mission to protect them. Carson knew they were, in fact, risking their lives to do so. He didn't think he could be so brave.

Based on his comments, it appeared Troy had bought into the-past-is-bad thinking one hundred percent. Carson knew better. One had to be committed. And careful. Extremely careful. One never knew who was trustworthy. But there were ways to access past historical records. There were always ways.

He'd known Troy since they were in diapers. Best friends? Such a term was used easily. But he no longer trusted Troy. They were from different worlds. And Carson knew, if push came to shove, Troy would discard Carson as easily as discarding a tissue he'd used to blow his nose.

"Protecting us? You think they're protecting us? From what? Some non-existent threat of aliens? And I don't mean space aliens, so stop laughing. I mean other people. People different than who the leadership thinks is acceptable. People from other countries, cultures, religion, or family beliefs. Is that who you think you're being protected from?"

"Careful, Carson."

Carson heard the warning in Troy's voice and took a deep breath.

"Troy. Jimmy was part of our circle. We stood up for each other. Now he's gone. Where, I don't know. And I've tried to find out. I really have."

"Leave it. I'm sure he's fine. They probably just relocated him to one of the settlements. He's better off there. With his own kind."

"His own kind? His own kind? What does that mean?"

"You know what it means. Jimmy was different. Sure, he was a nice guy and all, but he wasn't like us."

"Why do you keep talking about him in the past tense? Do you know something? Tell me if you do!"

Carson watched Troy carefully. He noted his friend didn't look him in the eye. Nor did he look remotely comfortable, shifting from one foot to the other.

"Troy? You do know something! What is it? Please tell me."

"You're better off not knowing. Just believe me when I say Jimmy is where he should be."

"I don't understand."

"Look. I don't know the details. I only know what I overheard my dad say. He didn't know I was listening. He was talking to one of his people. Jimmy was placed in one of those holding camps for people of," Troy hesitated, then said the rest in a rush. "People of undetermined gender."

Carson paled. "Undetermined gender? But Jimmy is a guy. How undetermined is that?"

"We both know Jimmy didn't start out as a guy. Leave it Carson. It's dangerous to talk about such things. The new administration is determined to recognize only two genders. There's no room for any other thought or belief. It's better to just accept that reality. I need to go. Dad wants me to shadow him at work this afternoon. I can't be late."

Troy turned and walked away without another glance. Carson watched him go. A feeling of dread seeping deep into his bones.

2

Marcus Hubbard greeted his son with a smile. He was proud of the boy. Now in his early twenties, Troy was on the cusp of inheriting a future full of opportunities. He'd been a good student. Sometimes a little over-concerned about things that shouldn't really concern him, but Marcus had diligently guided him into the correct mindset.

"Are you ready, son?"

"Ready for what, exactly?"

"We have a meeting with the Leader today. Quite an honor for you. You're also going to meet some of his most trusted advisers. People known for their expertise in all the major topics."

"Like what?"

Troy was still thinking about his conversation with Carson. He hadn't fully transitioned into his father's world, yet.

"Don't be obtuse, son."

"Sorry. I was thinking of other things."

"What things?"

Troy heard the intensity of his father's voice. He knew his father wouldn't be happy he'd been talking with Carson. Lately, any time Troy talked or interacted with any of his old friends, he'd been subjected to a lecture on the difference is social and economic status. The need to maintain an appropriate persona. Troy wasn't completely sure what that meant, but he had a pretty good idea. He didn't want to go there today and quickly deflected the question back towards the day's agenda.

"Am I dressed appropriately to meet all these people? Can you give me an idea of who everyone is?"

Reassuring his son regarding his apparel, Marcus named several people. Troy recognized most of them. One would have to be living in a cave not to. They were the elite of the elite. People who controlled the country's law enforcement, finance, environmental, health, scientific, and cultural agendas. All were extremely rich. All wanted to be richer. And more powerful. Part of him was impressed his father was considered a peer of these people. Part of him understood that if one wasn't part of this group, one was considered expendable. A cog in some unnamed machine that was discarded if, or when, it broke. He pushed that unwanted thought away and focused on his father's words.

"I've asked that you be considered for a position in the Leader's administration. I know you're young, and others are telling me you're too young. But I think I've convinced them that we need to groom the next generation now, so that our work can be carried on. If we don't, I fear those that are resisting will gain traction and at some point, convince others unhappy with their current situations to rise against us. We can't allow that."

"But isn't that the whole point of being able to vote for the leader you think best represents your interests?"

"The common people don't know what's in their best interest. It's up to people like us to tell them."

Troy opened his mouth to protest but closed it without comment. He didn't want to antagonize his father and get into an argument. Sometimes he wondered what had happened to the man who used to reach out to those less fortunate. Who wasn't concerned about backgrounds or ideologies. Who saw only need and tried to alleviate it. The man standing before him was no longer that person. Troy tried to think of when and how the change had come about. He couldn't. Had it been so gradual as to not be noticeable? Or had Troy simply chosen not to notice?

"When do we leave?" Troy asked.

Marcus glanced at his expensive watch. "Now. We must clear security at the House. Best we aren't the last ones to do so. I don't think I need to say it, but I will. Keep your mouth shut and your eyes forward. Don't look around like some idiot tourist and for all our sakes, don't get chatty."

Troy nodded. He remembered when the building used to be called the White House. It was where the President lived. The new administration refused to use the term 'White House' or even 'President'. Now it was simply 'the House' and 'Leader'. Troy supposed it was part of the effort to reprogram the population's thinking. Get them to forget old terms, old expectations. But not change things so much as to cause a revolution.

He was surprised his dad had used the term 'tourist'. Tourism implied visitors. No one was allowed to visit or tour the House anymore. He remembered there were tours when it was still called the White House. School children often had field trips for the very purpose of seeing their seat of government. He also remembered being jealous of those classes that got to go. It seemed his never did. He was either a year too early or a year too late to participate. Considering the times, he thought it a bit ironic that he was now going to see inside the place.

School field trips today were to local churches. Not just any church, though. Only those that preached what the Leader declared appropriate. A lot of it was rather extreme in Troy's mind. He'd never read the Bible. He doubted most people had. It was just one of those books that had been around forever and supposedly everyone knew what it said. He figured he had as good an understanding of it as most people. And that understanding was more about love and forgiveness than what was being preached now. The current messages seldom mentioned love or forgiveness. Unless it was directed towards the Leader. He knew that. He listened to them every Sunday.

His church and others like it were the only ones still sanctioned and active. People were required to attend them on Sundays, unless they had an authorized exception for work. But not any type of work. Only that work considered essential. Healthcare and energy production came to mind. Troy thought there might be a couple more, but mostly, all businesses were required to remain closed on Sundays. The day was to be used for prayer. Or, if you didn't like that word, meditation was an acceptable alternative.

Indoctrination. That's what Carson called it. Troy felt almost a physical pain at the memory of Carson's words. He shut down his thoughts immediately. He looked at his dad.

"I'm ready. I won't let you down."

Marcus smiled. "I know you won't, son. I can always count on you."

3

Carson scurried down the alley between the two old, abandoned buildings. He wasn't completely sure but thought surveillance didn't penetrate here. You couldn't say that anywhere else. Cameras were on every corner and building top. What wasn't covered by the physical cameras you could see, was picked up by drones. The drones flew nonstop, day and night. They were high enough that unless you had binoculars intently focused at the sky, you simply didn't see them.

But the surveillance consisted of more than tracking one's movements on the streets. All communication devices automatically sent copies of any message, typed or voiced, to the governmental department in charge of monitoring such things. Like the drones, most people forgot the existence of this. It wasn't like you could see the copy being made and sent off. It was invisible to the device user. And for most people, out of sight was out of mind.

Not for Carson. It had taken a lot of careful collaboration with others who thought like him to learn the ways of avoiding detection. Nothing was one hundred percent, but those who made the effort could shield at least half of their movements and communications. If caught, however, the penalties were strict. Often excessive. The tolerance for flouting this societal expectation of total compliance was near zero.

There were those who wouldn't be punished, of course. Such people always existed in any form of government. But Carson knew the current government, and he had a hard time even thinking of it as a government, took this particular issue seriously. Very seriously. It wanted to know what its citizens were up to at all times.

Reaching the end of the ally, Carson looked both ways before pressing his body against the wall and sliding around the corner into the open doorway ten feet from him.

"Anyone see you?"

Carson jumped at the voice that came out of the darkness.

"Jeez! You nearly gave me a heart attack!"

He heard a soft chuckle. "You're late. Any trouble?"

"No. I was talking with a friend and lost track of the time."

"This friend happen to be the Hubbard kid?"

Carson was glad for the darkness. It shielded his shock. He answered hesitantly.

"Yes. Is that an issue?"

"Not at all," the voice was mild in tone. "In fact, it ties in nicely with your new assignment."

"New assignment?"

"Yes. We want you to keep an eye on Hubbard. Report his activities. Let us know his intentions when he starts his new position."

"What are you talking about? He doesn't have any position. And, as far as I know, he hasn't applied for anything. It's not like there's a massive number of open jobs these days. Nearly forty percent of the workforce is idle. You know that. How they manage to continue to survive is beyond me. Especially with higher costs of goods and all the cuts to services that's taken place."

"You do it. We all figure out ways. But we know that Hubbard is about to join the current administration."

"What? When? Which sector? And how could you possibly know that?"

"Accept that we do. It's anticipated he'll be entering either the environmental or health sector. Considering the state of both, having an inkling into the proposed actions could be invaluable."

Carson thought about that. His contact was right. The current state of both the environment and the health system was dire. The large corporations, with minimal checks on their operations, managed to increase the toxicity of the land and water almost tenfold in the past year alone. Pollution-caused illnesses had tripled. Incidents of certain diseases couldn't even be statistically calculated. If you were lucky, you died quickly. If you weren't and managed to enter the health care system, you died a slow and painful death. And no one seemed inclined to change either situation. The environment was getting worse, as was healthcare.

Carson was convinced that the people who thought they were fortunate enough to be accepted into care were used for human experimentation. Oh, not the cut them up and study them kind of experimentation. No. This was more about studying the environmental affects on human systems. In some ways it made sense. How could things be fixed unless one knew what was causing the problems? But the dark side was that knowing what caused the illnesses could lead to creating more of the same. To cull the herds, so to speak. Harsh, Carson knew, but he wouldn't put it past the current bunch of people in control. Those who weren't like them were expendable. Carson knew he fell into the expendable group.

He'd read somewhere in one of his sources that the male sperm was degrading. Something to do with the Y chromosomes. Initially it was thought the process would take thousands, if not millions, of years to fully manifest. But recent indications were that it was happening at an accelerated pace and there was a full-out effort to find out the cause and reverse the process. Preferably stop it before it began.

He presumed the ultimate fear was a world filled with women. It was hard to contemplate that could even happen. Particularly considering that women were considered almost more expendable than the social classes lower than his. Almost. After all, they still needed babies to be born, and although huge strides had been made around what was called test-tube babies, it was nowhere near replacing nature's way of reproducing a species.

He remembered learning about the X and Y chromosomes in his biology and health classes in school. How the combinations decided whether you were born a boy or a girl. Sometimes, things went a bit awry and people ended up with rare, odd combinations. Extras of one or the other chromosome, which created some interesting results. He'd thought it fascinating at the time. He'd even considered pursuing medicine or something related, like dedicated research into such topics. When they had to dissect reptiles and small rodents, he quickly changed his mind.

But today's school system was radically changed. Those subjects weren't taught to the general population anymore. In fact, he was pretty sure that most couldn't even name body parts correctly. And even if they could, they were prohibited from speaking the anatomical words.

Those who knew them, like Carson, were careful to never use them. Instead, unless referring to arms, legs, or the head, bodies were described using vague terms. Like 'down there' or 'upper torso' or 'privates'. Never penis or breasts or uterus. One of his older acquaintances told him the vague terms were used in the old days by those uncomfortable saying the real names. But it was a voluntary choice. Now, the real words were considered sinful.

He gave a small shake of his head to clear his thoughts and spoke hesitantly to his contact.

"You want me to spy on my friend?"

"Don't be dramatic. It's not spying. Simply engage him in conversations as you already do. From time to time slip in questions that we'll feed you. Report back the answers you get. That's it. It's not like we're asking you to sneak around and follow him."

Relieved but still concerned, Carson accepted what they were asking seemed reasonable. But he supposed that depended somewhat on the questions they wanted him to ask. He hoped they wouldn't put a strain on his relationship with Troy.

On the other hand, he'd noticed Troy had been withdrawing from him a bit. Perhaps his father was pressuring him. Carson hoped not. Even though his trust in Troy was eroded, and their world views were getting further apart, he admitted to himself that he would miss Troy if their contact ceased.

"OK. I'll see what I can do."

"Good man. You'll have to be careful. You can't come on too strong or you'll scare him off."

"I know how to communicate with my friend."

"Be cautious who you call friend."

Carson heard a door close softly and he knew his contact had left the building by an alternate route. The man's last words repeated in his head. He realized they could be applied not only to Troy, but to the man he'd just conversed with.

4

Troy was overwhelmed. He lost count of the number of people shaking his hand, patting him on the back and congratulating him. He wasn't even sure what the congratulations were for. Presumably something to do with his dad putting his name forward for some position. He supposed it would be good to have a job. Especially with so many people out of work. But in his heart, he knew he wasn't qualified for anything they might assign him to.

He saw his father and wandered over to him, weaving his way through the well-wishers.

"Dad, I don't understand what's going on. Why is everyone congratulating me?"

Not immediately answering the question, Marcus commented on the quick appearance and disappearance of the Leader. Then he looked at Troy with both worry and pride.

"You've been accepted as an aide to the head of the health sector. Quite the honor. More than I hoped for or expected."

"But I know nothing about health services, health care, health in general."

"Doesn't matter. You'll learn."

"But—"

"Later, Troy. For now, just go with it. Express your appreciation. Memorize names, faces, and positions. This is your meal ticket, boy. Don't screw it up."

Marcus walked away, calling out to one of the men on the other side of the room. Troy was surprised at the harshness of his dad's tone. It sounded like his dad was mad at him or something. Troy couldn't remember doing anything that would make his father mad. His shoulders drooped a bit, and he turned to reenter the fray of people milling about when a hand clamped down solidly on his shoulder, and a deep voice spoke in his ear.

"There you are, my boy. Been hard to get close to you. Too many suck-up well-wishers monopolizing you. Welcome to my team."

Troy turned and looked into the blue eyes of the man who ran one of the biggest sectors in government. It took him a second to grasp the man's name from his memory.

"Mr. Darwin. A pleasure to finally meet you. Thank you for this opportunity."

"Call me Francis, kid. Darwin is kind of creepy, if you know what I mean. Considering I'm head of the health sector."

Troy had no idea what the man was talking about, and it showed on his face. Francis Darwin laughed.

"Never mind. It's an old joke. One your generation wouldn't get."

Troy just nodded. If it was a joke, he figured it wasn't important.

"I'm embarrassed to admit that I have no experience in, or particular knowledge of, the health sector."

"No worries, son. I'll teach you what you need to know."

"You're a scientist, or doctor, then?"

"No, neither one. Although I've read and written plenty of science and medicine-related articles. So, I feel I have a good handle on what I need to know."

Troy was about to question that opinion when some innate caution silenced him. He figured it wouldn't do to challenge his new boss on credentials.

He remembered the general sense of disbelief when the Leader announced his picks for key positions. Many said the people were totally unqualified. He'd asked his father about it and had been told not to discuss it outside the home. And his father himself had refused to discuss it at all. Shortly after that, the news simply stopped reporting or commenting on it, and people moved on to other things.

"I'm looking forward to learning all I can." Troy hesitated. "Am I to start tomorrow?"

Darwin laughed again. "Quite the eager beaver, aren't you. Take the rest of the week for yourself. You can start on Monday. Be at the office by eight. Someone will help you with the necessary paperwork. You know where to report?"

Troy was about to admit that he didn't, when he was told someone would meet him at the main door of Building H. Troy knew where that was. He and Carson had passed it often on their meanderings. He opened his mouth to confirm but was interrupted.

"I must go. Glad to have you on board. I'm sure you'll be as supportive as your father has been."

With that, Francis Darwin walked away. Troy watched him go, wondering what he'd meant about his father.

5

Jimmy sat on his cot. You couldn't call it a bed. It lacked even a mattress. He looked at the rows of them, neatly arranged. He figured they must be surplus from the military. The military that was once respected and feared throughout the world. He'd contemplated joining at one time. Then, as attitudes changed and the cultural wars became more intense, he'd changed his mind. But he remembered his astonishment at how quickly that mighty military had been dismantled.

Less than two years. Who could have guessed? Shortly after the Leader had assumed full power, he'd begun the process, primarily because the military commanders refused to follow what they considered to be unconstitutional orders. Their outright confrontation resulted in the Leader's speedy actions to completely dissolve the various branches. Jimmy was sure the Leader had been frustrated at how long it actually took, but in the end, he'd accomplished what he set out to do.

The main military was gone and smaller enforcement squads, those who expressed full loyalty to the leader, were created. They consisted of military as well as state and local police officers.

Those who backed him said his methods would ultimately make the country stronger, more efficient. Those who disagreed, assuming they were brave enough to express their disagreement, said he was destroying everything and anything associated with the old. That if allowed to continue, there would simply be no country. At least not one remotely comparable to that which had risen to world leadership.

Then again, the rest of the world had its own issues to deal with. Many of which the Leader had deliberately caused.

Jimmy pulled his thoughts away from the larger setting and focused them back to his current circumstances. He knew where he was. He'd heard such places were being set up, but he never imagined he'd be swept up into one. He realized now how silly he'd been. Of course they would have snared him at some point. He was right up there on the most-wanted list. Most detested, actually.

He'd forgotten. Been too comfortable. Granted, there'd always been prejudices to navigate. But overall, society had moved on to worry about things other than how an individual chose to live their personal lives. Even if not completely accepted across all social groups, he'd found his niche and been happy. He should have paid more attention.

He heard a bell ringing in the distance. Sighing, he stood. Time to line up for his latest treatment.

He grimaced. Treatment. He wouldn't call it that. He'd call it torture. If he were honest, he felt worse every day he was here. Not only was his body changing due to the treatments, his mental health was fast deteriorating. Assuming no fatal physical side-affects, he knew his body would ultimately absorb and accept what was being done to it. His sanity? He wasn't so sure.

He was already noticing the changes. Only two weeks in and he was experiencing loss of body hair, tenderness in areas he shouldn't feel tenderness in, and a voice that was coming out a higher tone than what he was used to hearing.

Worse, he'd noticed some slight bleeding the last time he'd used the toilet. All changes associated with the administered treatments. Bad enough they'd stopped his current therapies. Over a longer time period, the changes would have happened by just that action alone. But someone had decided administering the opposite, in higher than advised doses, would be the quicker course of action to gain desired results.

He felt his very essence being forcefully ripped from him. He wondered if he could survive it. He wondered if he even wanted to.

6

Troy followed the young woman to a back office and spent the next hour or more filling out paperwork. He was surprised at some of the questions asked. They seemed intensely personal. Invasive.

His father had warned him. Had even told him how to answer certain inquiries. Confused, Troy simply nodded his head. Now he better understood. What he didn't understand was why he was doing this all on paper. Why not use the computer that was sitting idly on one of the desks? When he'd asked, the woman murmured an answer Troy couldn't hear and she refused to repeat it.

Indicating to the woman he'd completed his tasks, she came over, gathered up the papers, and put them in a drawer. Then told him to follow her. She led him to a large, brightly lit room. He looked around with interest. Then confusion. There were upwards of twenty desks in the room, but only one person. He was seated in a corner tapping on the keys of a computer.

At least he's using it, Troy thought. About to question his guide, she cut him off before he could verbalize the words forming in his head.

"I'll leave you to it, then. David will show you the ropes."

She turned and left without another word. Troy stood awkwardly at the door. The man in the corner looked up. Troy saw he was close to his own age.

"Don't just stand there, dude. Come on in. Join the party. I'm David. What's your name?"

Dude? Troy almost laughed at the totally retro term. Who even said that anymore? Obviously, this David guy.

Troy stepped forward and weaved his way through the desks to David.

"I'm Troy. Pleased to meet you, David. What's with all the empty desks?"

Troy held out his hand, but David ignored it.

"Budget cuts. I'm the only one in this department. Well, now it appears there's two of us. Pick a desk. Doesn't matter which one. But I suggest you check to see if the computer works before you make the area your home. Most of them don't."

"What do you mean?"

"No one to keep things running. The department that services the computers is emptier than ours. As in, there isn't a department to keep computers running."

"I don't understand."

David laughed. "How'd you complete your new hire stuff?"

"Filled out a bunch of forms."

"On paper, right?"

Troy nodded.

"Yeah. Someone figured out it was easier to hide things by using paper. Paper has this combustible component to it. Know what I mean? Can't be hacked into like computers and can easily just," he hesitated, then snapped his fingers, "disappear."

Troy sank onto a chair from a desk opposite of David. He processed what he'd just heard.

"But how does anything get done?"

"At our level? It doesn't."

Troy frowned. "I—"

"Yeah, I know. You don't understand. That's the point. We're not supposed to understand."

David shifted topics. "Who's your dad?"

Troy was confused and showed it. "What does that matter?"

"It matters a lot. My dad is head of the environmental sector. I was put here to be groomed."

David made air quotes as he spoke the last word.

"Groomed?"

Troy remembered his father using that word.

"Yeah. Groomed. As in, mold us into little mini-thems. The bigwigs. The rich hot-shots who manipulate everything simply to make themselves richer. But that's just the line they feed us to keep us in check. They have no intention of turning the reins of power over to the next generation any time soon. If ever."

Troy didn't know how to respond. He wasn't even sure David expected a response. He realized David hadn't pursued his question on who Troy's father was. Troy decided to distract by asking his own question.

"How long have you been here?"

"Six months. Or, maybe longer. I've lost track."

"What's your primary responsibility?"

David laughed until he started choking. Clearing his throat, he indicated he had no primary responsibility. In truth, he had no responsibilities.

Other than to show up every day and collect his wage credits at the end of the week.

"Wait. In the time you've been here you haven't been asked to do anything? You haven't been trained to do anything? But you're being paid?"

David shook his head at Troy's first two questions and nodded at the third.

"Then what do you do all day?"

David smiled and rotated his monitor so Troy could see the screen. "When I'm not trying to hack into the existing system, I play video games. The former provides endless challenges. The latter entertainment."

7

Carson wandered along the street, not caring whether the cameras picked up his movements. He was one of many using the physical movement of walking to idle away the day. There were few alternatives. Most on the streets had nowhere else to go. Loss of employment had led to loss of homes. Sold possessions financed basic needs. Until there was nothing left to sell. Or no one able to buy.

Those who rebelled against their circumstances were quickly dealt with. One often didn't see them again. Assuming one was even paying attention to such things. Other, more lucky ones, managed to get day work. Mostly hard labor. Harvesting crops. Or clearing garbage. Maybe working in a factory for a few days to a few weeks. Nothing long term. No opportunities to advance. It didn't matter if you had degrees from prestigious universities in your past. You either performed the tasks that were needed at the time, or you went without.

Carson remembered many of the types of jobs currently offered used to be filled by people who had come to this country with a dream to better their circumstances. Often the roles they filled were ones his fellow citizens thought beneath them.

Whether arrival was legal, or illegal, was no longer even a conversation point. It didn't matter. Those people were all gone now. Or almost all gone. Carson didn't want to contemplate what became of those who hadn't left of their own accord, or who had been physically removed from the country. It was better not to think about such things.

He slowed to look into the window of a small café. One of the few businesses still open on this block. He was surprised to see several people inside. But when he looked closer, he noticed how they were dressed. These were the group of people often called the Essentials. People who had the needed skills to keep essential systems running. They weren't the elite. Far from it. But they also weren't part of the masses who needed to be watched and controlled.

Carson glanced down at his clothing, shrugged, pushed open the door and stepped into the establishment. He heard a soft buzzing sound and assumed it was a door alarm, similar to the old bells that used to jingle. A young woman behind the counter looked up and studied him. Others in the room ignored him.

Carson was surprised to see a woman. *Must be the owner's daughter,* he thought. *Otherwise, she wouldn't be allowed to fill a position a man would usually be in.*

Carson mentally smirked as he assumed it was the owner's way of not having to pay wages. He glanced at the prices listed on the large menu behind the woman and realized he couldn't afford even a cup of coffee. But he wasn't here for the coffee. He glanced around the room, his eyes focusing on a young man who sat at a corner table with a small electronic tablet in front of him. He moved in that direction, aware the woman was watching him intently. He stopped next to the table.

"May I join you?" he asked in a soft voice.

The man looked up, startled. Then, recognizing Carson, quickly motioned for him to take the chair opposite him.

"What are you doing here?"

"Looking for you."

"Why?"

"I need information."

The man waited. The silence stretched.

"I can't help you."

"You don't even know what I want."

"Doesn't matter. You shouldn't be here. We shouldn't be seen together."

"Afraid I'll tarnish your image?"

The man grimaced. "That's not fair."

"Nothing is fair these days. You know that as well as I. The only difference between us is you happened to study the correct subject in school. It's placed you in your current position. But I hope you remember, nothing is permanent. What is essential or accepted today may not be tomorrow. We're all at the whim of those who think they're superior to us.

Things we never thought would happen. Could happen. They have happened. We're nothing but slaves to those with money."

"That's a bit extreme."

"Is it? Is that what you now believe? Or is that the persona you project to remain in a protected class? You always were easy to manipulate."

The man frowned.

"You probably get a free pass for Sundays. When's the last time you had to sit through one of those sermons?"

At the man's head shake, Carson continued.

"Yeah, I thought so. You know what they preach? Oh, they couch it in pretty terms. Well, not always, but the message is that the white man is supreme. But not any white man. Only a certain few. The rest of us are no better than all those they've been trying to get rid of. The brown, black, and whatever color they use, as well as those who love differently, identify differently. Anyone who doesn't think and believe as they do.

Women are almost in a worse state. They're literally considered property, again. Like they were way back in what seems like prehistoric days, now. Zero rights. Simply an extension of the man they're partnered with. And if they're not partnered, then the male head of household controls them. I'm surprised they're even allowed out in public. I know some who would like to change that." Carson paused, "And this is the world you serve."

"It's not that bad. You're exaggerating. Like you always do. Like you always did. Even back in school. Always stating things in terms that were overblown."

Carson looked at the man he'd shared several years of schooling with. They'd never been friends. Well, not like he and Troy. And Jimmy. They'd gotten along. Helped each other through the tough subjects. But Carson knew he'd made a mistake coming here. Asking for the man's help. It was clear the man was unwilling. And now Carson was concerned he might be reported to the authorities. Assuming the man had those kinds of connections. On the other hand, one really didn't need any special connections. There were anonymous hotlines that could be used.

Feeling slightly sick to his stomach, Carson brought the conversation to a close.

"Maybe it was a mistake asking you for help. I thought—. Well, never mind. I'm sorry. Truly I am. I didn't think what position I might be putting you in. I hope I didn't endanger you. Don't worry. I won't seek you out again. And I wish you all the best. But seriously. Watch your back. Things aren't always as they seem. And they change daily. OK? You'll be careful?"

The man looked at him for a long time. Carson thought he saw pity in the man's eyes. But he maintained a relaxed posture, and that gave Carson hope. Before standing, Carson reached out and briefly touched the man's forearm.

"Take care."

As he turned to walk away, he heard the man say very softly, "You, too."

Carson exited the café and hurried down the street. Not so fast as to draw attention, but he wanted to put distance between him and the storefront. He was glad he hadn't articulated what information he'd hoped to get. He felt that, alone, was enough to keep them each safe. He wasn't paying attention as he rounded a corner. A hard collision found him on his back. It took him a minute to comprehend the situation.

"You all right?" a voice asked.

Carson looked up and saw a barrel-chested man reaching down to help him to his feet. The man had a familiar look about him. Not a 'I-know-this-guy' look. No. Something else. Then it hit Carson. A shot of pure terror raced down his spine.

This guy was an enforcer. Carson knew it as certainly as he knew his own name. Tentatively he took the man's hand and was quickly pulled to his feet.

"You should be more careful," the man said. But he looked intently at Carson.

Carson briefly met the man's eyes then looked away. With a mumbled thanks, Carson nodded and started to move forward. But the man was speaking again.

"No, really. Be more careful. You could get seriously hurt."

"I understand. Thanks again."

Carson picked up his pace. He knew a true warning when he heard one.

8

"How was your first day?" Marcus looked closely at his son. The boy looked tired and stressed.

"Different."

"Different? How so?"

Troy sighed. "Dad, I'm really tired. Not much in the mood to talk. Not very hungry, either. Do you mind if I skip dinner?"

"Why don't you take a tray up to your room. You can eat it later, if you feel like it."

"Good idea. Thanks for understanding."

Troy went to the buffet and fixed a plate for himself. As he did so, he glanced at the variety of food being offered. It was way too much for just the two of them. He knew the servants would eat some of it after they'd finished. And the rest would be donated to one of the many shelters that existed. Doing so made his father feel benevolent. Troy pushed down the thought that it wasn't benevolence, but arrogance.

Giving food away showed just how rich his father was. Reinforced an image of superiority. There were people who barely managed to survive a day. And here he was, choosing personal favorites from several options.

He swallowed down the nausea that rose. He spared a brief thought for his friend Carson. While not at the very bottom, Carson's family wasn't that far removed. He hoped Carson was able to enjoy a decent meal tonight. Maybe he should think about packaging up some extra supplies and taking them over. But he knew that would create issues he wasn't willing to face. *Best leave things as is,* he thought.

He finished preparing his plate and headed towards the stairs.

"Thanks again, Dad. I'll see you in the morning?"

"I have an early meeting."

"Then I'll see you when I get home. Goodnight. Have a good tomorrow."

Marcus watched his son trudge up the stairs, carefully balancing his plate of food. Even after the boy reached the top and turned down the hall out of sight, Marcus stood there. He had an uneasy feeling. He felt for his phone.

Marcus listened to five rings before his call was answered.

"Marcus, my man. What can I do for you?"

"Francis. Thanks for taking my call."

"Absolutely," the voice was cheerful. Marcus thought it sounded a bit forced.

"Everything OK? Am I interrupting?"

"No, not at all. Everything's fine. But it's unusual for you to call."

"I'm sorry. I just thought I'd check up on my boy. He looked beat. You working the poor lad too much? It's only his first day, you know. And this is his first real position."

"The lad did fine. He's a great asset. You should be proud of him."

Marcus felt a surge of relief. Against his own internal urge for caution, he pushed forward.

"Where did you end up placing him? What department?"

"He didn't tell you?"

"He was so tired he went straight to his room."

Francis laughed. "That's great to hear. Oh, not that he's tired, but that he didn't reveal where he was placed. We caution everyone to keep placements quiet. We've found that it helps shield people from those who would try to use them. Influence them. Know what I mean?"

Marcus didn't, but wouldn't admit it.

"Anyway, stop worrying. Your boy did fine. Look, I've got to go. We'll catch up sometime soon, right?"

"Right," Marcus echoed, then realized Francis hadn't heard it because the man had already disconnected. The uneasiness returned.

Across town, Francis stared at a blank wall. He'd often thought a nice painting should be hanging on it, but he'd never found anything he liked. Well, that wasn't completely true. He hadn't felt remotely inspired to look for anything.

The phone call he just took disturbed him. He hoped Marcus hadn't clued in that he had no idea where the boy had been placed. He didn't care.

It wasn't like the lad was going to learn or do anything. He'd only brought him on to appease the Leader. Same as that other kid. The environmental sector's offspring. He couldn't remember their names. Father or son. Nor did he care about that, either. Right now, all he cared about was staying in favor with the Leader. He'd seen what happened to those who didn't.

Francis looked at the pile of papers on the table next to his chair. Medical research. Studies on all kinds of things, many of which served no purpose than to line the pockets of those who wrote the papers. He picked up a report and glanced at it. Something to do with vaccine injuries. He tossed it back on the table. Old news. He picked up another report. This one had been spiral bound. *Woohoo,* he thought, *fancy.*

He flipped through it. It was full of graphics and statistics. Just thinking about trying to interpret the data was enough to give him a headache. No way was he going to read it.

He glanced at the title. *Pesticides: The Influence on Fertility.* He chuckled as he put it back in the pile, thinking that someone in the environmental sector, where the report should also be, would probably read it. Or, maybe it went to agriculture. He could never remember if that was its own sector, or part of the environmental one. No matter. He wasn't going to waste his time with the report.

He was about to pick up another report when he glanced at the title again. He wondered how such a project had even been funded. Doubtful it had come through his sector. He made sure to fund only the things the Leader thought important.

And while Francis fully admitted to himself that the Leader wouldn't know what projects were important enough to deserve funding, he would never say such a thing to anyone else. Even thinking it could be considered treasonous. He was glad that, with all the surveillance the administration indulged in, they had yet to figure out how to read peoples' thoughts.

He sighed. He knew he should go through the reports. But he simply didn't feel like it. He stood and walked to the side table against the wall and reached for his favorite alcoholic beverage. Not pausing to consider the wisdom of his actions, he poured himself a large amount and took the glass with him to his bedroom. He'd watch some mindless movie while he sipped his drink. If he was lucky, he'd be asleep soon.

9

Troy ate his dinner. He had to admit, the food was good, and he was hungry. He hadn't had much lunch. Really, just a bowl of soup. He and his new colleague, David, had spent the afternoon trying to hack the health sector system.

Not sure it was a good idea; he was less sure when David told him it was rumored the system contained information from past administrations. Information that had been deliberately kept from the public. Troy couldn't decide if he was annoyed, or relieved, they hadn't made any progress on David's quest.

He wanted to call Carson, but didn't want to officially establish a record of the call. He thought it ironic that the Leader had promised he would do away with the censorships he declared were established by the previous administrations. He'd gone on and on about how those administrations had destroyed the peoples' freedoms. And to a point, he had removed some of the regulations that impeded free expression.

But his replacements were worse. Far worse. And Troy couldn't understand how people had let all the cameras and surveillance processes be put in place. Did they not realize how much freedom they'd given up? And it wasn't as if all the monitoring had made people safer, even though that had been the justification for the systems. If he were honest, Troy would admit the population was less safe now than at any time in the recent past.

But Troy wasn't ready to be honest. That would require a mind shift he knew wasn't healthy. He'd tried to warn Carson to be careful. He worried his friend would cross a line that shouldn't be crossed. Informants were everywhere. And there were those who thought murder perfectly acceptable if it served the current agenda. They didn't see it as anything other than support of their Leader. All else be damned. It didn't even matter if the current agenda contradicted itself.

As he thought about it, he understood that those who supported the Leader did so not because of policies. If it were about policies, they'd realize how much worse off they now were and do something about it.

No. They followed the Leader because of some misguided need to feel important. Part of something bigger than them. A way to justify their feelings of being ignored, victimized, or whatever else they could come up with. Although Troy didn't think they'd ever been truly victimized. Not like those who were now being targeted. They just enjoyed being vocal about their perceived injustices.

He put his fork down and looked at his plate, surprised he'd eaten everything on it. The observation distracted his thoughts, and he was glad. He'd been wandering down a dangerous path. Better he think of other things. Acceptable things. Where he'd been going was against everything his father had spoken to him about. But he realized it was exactly where Carson's mindset was. And that thought re-ignited his worry that Carson would be targeted.

It wasn't just people like Jimmy who were being targeted. Although he felt a bit ashamed about it, he admitted that he wasn't as concerned about Jimmy as Carson was. Jimmy had made choices. Choices not currently considered appropriate. That Jimmy was now reaping the consequences of those choices was something Troy pushed aside. All for the greater good. That's what they said during the Sunday messages. Troy had to believe it was true. He wasn't brave enough to believe otherwise.

Troy stood and began undressing. In his t-shirt and underwear, he crawled into bed and pulled the covers up to his chin. He wondered what tomorrow would bring. He didn't wonder for long. His mental exhaustion caught up with him and he was soon fast asleep.

The next morning, he arrived at the office with two minutes to spare. He felt disoriented, his thoughts in complete disarray. David picked up on his anxiety.

"Whoa, dude. Chill. It's not like anyone is keeping track of our comings and goings. And in any event, you got here before the clock struck the hour."

Troy half-smiled at David's use of the word dude. He was getting used to it.

"Easy for you to say. You're already here. Probably been here forever."

David shrugged. "Maybe a half-hour. But that wasn't my choice. I come in with my dad. I get here when he gets here. If he has an early meeting, then I'm here early. If it were my choice, I'd be racing in here every day like you just did. I see no purpose in spending more time here than I have to."

Troy didn't respond, simply walking to the desk he'd chosen and sitting down in the chair. After he'd pretended to arrange things to his liking, he turned back to David.

"What's on the agenda today?"

"We actually have something productive to do." David lifted a stack of papers, then put them back on his desk. "We're to read these reports and recommend which studies should continue to be funded."

Troy looked doubtful. "We're to recommend funding? Isn't that something the big boys usually do? In fact, isn't there some department that's supposed to look at all government spending?"

"Yes. But apparently, they're too busy playing golf, or counting their wealth, or spending government money on things that personally benefit them. Can't be bothered with real work."

"That's a bit harsh, don't you think?"

"No. I don't. It's the truth. You'll figure it out yourself if you stay here long enough."

"If you feel that way, why do you stay?"

David deflected the question by divvying up the stack of paper on his desk. He got up and walked to Troy's desk, dropping an eight-inch-thick pile of reports.

"Happy reading. We'll switch when we get through our piles, then talk about what we've read."

He walked back to his desk, sat, picked up a report and began reading. Troy shrugged and grabbed the first report on his pile. As both young men focused on their task, the silence stretched.

Three hours later, David spoke. "You hungry? Want to go to the cafeteria and see what slop they're serving?"

Troy smiled at David's description of the cafeteria food. Yesterday, he'd thought it passed muster. Barely. He wasn't quite sure what was being offered. He thought it something plant-based or manufactured in a factory somewhere.

While it looked like recognizable food, he admitted to himself it certainly didn't taste like anything he'd call fresh or organic. But it supposedly was healthier than the alternatives. Alternatives that involved slaughtering animals.

He put down the report he'd been reading and stood. "I could eat."

They left their area and followed the hallways until they found the cafeteria. Only three other people were seated in the room. A buffet of covered dishes gleamed in the lights hanging above it. The two made their way towards it. David lifted two covers and looked at the contents beneath.

"Looks kind of gross. But I guess it's this or nothing."

He put one of the covers down and grabbed a plate, asking Troy to spoon some of the congealed mess onto it. Troy barely kept from gagging as he did so.

"You really going to eat that?"

"I'm sure it tastes better than it looks." David cheerfully replied.

Troy wasn't as convinced. He glanced around, hoping he could repeat yesterday's choice of soup. He didn't see that option available. Sighing, he moved down the line, looking under each cover, hoping for something that presented as appetizing.

He finally found a rice dish and decided to take his chances. But he wasn't brave enough to scoop up whatever was mixed in with the rice. Instead, he pushed that aside and ended up with two spoons of rice on his plate.

"That's it? That's all you're going to eat?" David looked incredulous. He'd added a few more choices to his plate.

"If I need more, I'll come back for seconds."

They chose a table away from the others in the room. As Troy pushed his rice around, David began eating in earnest.

"How's it taste?" Troy asked.

"I've had better."

"How can you even eat it?"

"Gotta eat to stay alive."

Troy watched him, then asked, "Do you find it strange that the food offered here represents probably everything the health sector is supposedly against?"

David's fork hesitated on its path to his mouth. "What do you mean?"

"I've read some of Francis Darwin's earlier writings. He was all for organic, real food. All against highly processed and lab-made meats."

David looked at Troy intently. "How did you get access to that material? I thought it had all been scrubbed from the internet and removed from library depositories?"

As Troy opened his mouth to respond, David interrupted.

"No, don't tell me. I don't want to know. And if you're smart, you won't mention what you just said to anyone else. You hear me?"

Troy looked confused. "But—"

"No. Not another word. I'll say this only once. Follow the money. That should tell you everything you need to know."

David looked around, as if checking to see whether anyone was close enough to hear their conversation. Apparently convinced all was well, he continued eating.

Troy watched him for a few seconds. Then got up, walked over to the trash container, scraped his plate, and put it in the used-dish area. Without returning to the table or acknowledging David further, he exited the room.

10

Carson sat on the steps leading to his front door. He watched as three young children argued. He judged their ages to be around ten. They were using tablets, and he assumed they were engaged in a group video game of some sort. It appeared the girl was winning, and the two boys were not happy.

"You obviously cheated!" one of the boys yelled.

"Did not! You just don't have the skills you need," the girl replied.

"You're lucky we even let you play! You're just a girl. Everyone knows girls are stupid. That's why they're not allowed to do anything by themselves anymore." The second boy jumped in.

"Girls are better than boys! I just proved it. And you can't even lose without accusing someone of doing wrong. You're the stupid one. It's just like my mom told me. Boys are stupid and grow up to be stupid men! You're stupid. You'll be a stupid man."

Carson hid his grin. She gave as good as got. Maybe better. But ultimately, he knew the boys had a point. Women were treated as second-class, no, third-class citizens now. The more vocal argued they always were treated as such.

But now was different. Now, so many opportunities and choices had been taken from them under the guise they were being protected. Hardly any were able to work a job outside the home. The few available jobs were reserved for men.

Most women working did so because it was a family business and there was no money to pay wages to outside workers. So, while one could argue the woman was working, Carson knew it was just another form of controlling them. Slavery, really.

"She's got spunk. I hope it doesn't get crushed. She's young. There's still hope things will turn around."

Carson turned to the person speaking. A woman about his age, maybe a year or two older, was standing a slight distance from his steps, watching the interplay.

"Do you know her?" Carson asked.

"She's my little sister. The youngest in our family. She hasn't learned, yet, that it's useless to fight back. I hope she never learns it."

"Isn't that wishing her a troublesome future?"

"Maybe. But this new leadership can't last forever. Maybe by the time she's of the age where she understands how things work, things will work differently."

"You're brave to say that out loud."

"Not really. What can they do? I'm simply exercising my freedom of speech." She laughed. "That's a good one, isn't it?"

She studied Carson. "I'm Shannon. I've seen you around. I've noticed you don't always follow the path most walk."

Carson wasn't sure what she meant by that. He wasn't sure he wanted to know. But curiosity got the better of him.

"Carson. And what did you mean by that?"

"That you don't follow the path? You don't. I've seen you avoid the surveillance cameras. That's a dangerous game to play. You know those in power disapprove of such behavior. Why do you do it? Is it just a game to you? A way to personally fight back? Or something else? Something bigger?"

"You ask a lot of questions."

"You aren't answering them."

Carson looked at her. Really looked at her. There was something vaguely familiar about her, but he couldn't pull it from his memory. Then it hit him.

"You were the senior class president when I was in my second year of high school. I remember you. Someone started some kind of trash talk campaign against you. The whole school took sides. A few went a bit extreme."

Shannon joined him on the steps. "Which side did you take?"

Carson smiled. "Yours. I was surprised at how you fought back. Even then, attitudes were changing. Females were supposed to be seen. Not heard. And definitely not leading."

Shannon laughed. "Fun times. Hard to believe where we are today. Who'd have believed things could change so quickly?"

Carson chose not to pursue that line of conversation. Instead, he asked, "You live in this neighborhood?"

Shannon gestured with her head.

"Three doors down. It's just my mom, my two sisters, and me."

She nodded towards the group of kids. No longer arguing, they were fully engaged in their game again.

"That little spitfire over there is the youngest. My other sister is fifteen. She's the compliant one amongst us. I think she just got tired of fighting."

"Where's your dad?"

Shannon was quiet for so long Carson was about to apologize for his question and tell her to never mind.

"We're not sure. He was removed from his job shortly after the new Leader took over. Then, one day he just never came home."

"You think—"

"We don't know."

Shannon's voice was harsh. Carson understood the message. Don't ask. Don't speculate. Leave it be.

"I'm sorry," he murmured.

They were quiet for a moment, watching the three younger kids who seemed to have no issues, now. Carson broke the silence.

"How are you all getting along? Have you enough to eat?"

Shannon looked at him. He thought he saw pity in her eyes. He wasn't sure why she should be pitying him.

"How does your family get along?"

"My dad works. We manage."

"Aren't you afraid your activities will jeopardize his job?"

"My activities? What do you mean?"

Shannon just looked at him, saying nothing. Carson used all his willpower to not fidget under her gaze.

When it was clear he wasn't going to respond, Shannon stood.

"Have it your way. But if you need—" She hesitated, then continued. "As a woman, no one pays attention to me. It's almost as if I'm invisible. That can be very useful. You might want to remember that."

She stood and descended the steps, calling for her little sister as she did so. Carson watched them walk in the direction Shannon had earlier indicated.

He mentally replayed her last words. He realized she was asking to be recruited to his cause. His cause? Even he wasn't sure he had a cause. Then again, what else could he call his recent agreement to pass along information gleaned from conversations with Troy? He knew whatever he learned, and passed along, would be used to further the resistance against the current Leader. He wondered at the ultimate outcome.

11

"How do you feel?"

"How do you think I feel? Awful." Jimmy replied to the medical specialist.

"Can you describe what you mean?"

"I can. But I'm not going to. You and your kind are well-aware of what you're doing to me. I won't give you the pleasure of detailing how it's killing me."

"Killing you? Don't be so dramatic. And what do you mean by my kind?" The medical specialist was busy recording Jimmy's blood pressure and other vital signs.

"I'm not being dramatic. I feel like I'm dying. Slowly. Torturously. What I don't understand is why. Why is this being done? My decisions affected only myself." At the other's raised eyebrows, Jimmy continued. "It's true. Tell me how my life choices changed how you live your life?"

"That's not the point."

"What is the point?"

"Your choice of lifestyle is just plain wrong."

"Says who? You and your kind. That's who."

"My kind, as you call it, is the majority opinion. It's why we put the current Leader in office. He believes the same."

"The Leader believes whatever caters to those who want to help him control the population. And right now, those who want to control the rest of us. Yes, your kind, are the most vocal. But you're not the majority. Don't think you are. And this all-wonderful Leader? He only wants to increase his own wealth at our expense. Yours and mine. That's all he cares about. That and power. You think you're helping to establish a society sanctioned by whatever deity you worship. You aren't. Y'all have declared yourselves the deity. And your petty little grievances are driving you to destroy our society. Not make it better."

"Quite the speech. Quite the dangerous speech."

"You going to tell on me? To whom? And what more can you do to me than what you're already doing? Death is not a threat to me."

"There are worse things than death."

"I know. I'm currently experiencing it."

The medical specialist laughed. "Things could be worse. Far worse."

"Sure. Whatever. Are we done here? Can I go back?"

"You may."

Jimmy stood and walked toward the clinic door, but the words that followed him chilled his blood.

"Be careful who you express your views to. I'll ignore what I heard but know there are others who won't. And those others aren't always who you think they are. Similar lifestyles don't necessarily create similar viewpoints."

Jimmy closed the door quietly behind him. He experienced a moment of light-headedness and took time to steady himself.

He thought about the people he'd met in this settlement. People like him, who had made choices like his. They were all experiencing the side-effects of the treatments received. He'd bonded with a few. Or at least he thought he had. But now, the words of the medical specialist rang in his head. He was no longer sure who he could trust.

He wished he could talk with Carson and Troy. They'd always supported him. They hadn't questioned his choices or acted in any way that gave him pause to think they wouldn't continue to support him.

He wondered if they even knew where he was. There'd been no time to notify anyone. He'd been swept up in a cleansing movement conducted by an enforcement squad. They'd claimed he had violated several laws, but never actually named any specifics. He'd tried to resist, but they'd given him something that rendered him unconscious. When he awoke. He was here.

Having no way to communicate with the outside world, he was starting to wonder if there still was an outside world. The hormone treatments weren't the only thing he was subjected to. Mind-numbing, continuous broadcasts about right and wrong choices constantly filled his days. Friendships between the residents were discouraged, but most disregarded that edict, quietly forming relationships to counter the mental and physical hardships they experienced daily.

Jimmy reached his barracks and found his cot. He noted three others on the opposite side of the room. He ignored them and crawled onto his cot. Pulling his blanket over his head, he tried to shut out his current environment and create a happy place in his mind. Focusing on one particular event from his childhood, he finally drifted to sleep, a slight smile curving his lips.

12

Troy was sitting at his desk reading when David returned. He didn't acknowledge his co-worker, nor did David acknowledge him. After about twenty minutes, David broke the silence.

"You seeing anything in your stack that's interesting?"

Troy looked up. "Describe interesting."

David laughed. What tension that was in the room dissipated. "I'm reading stuff about animal husbandry. I suppose if I were of a different mindset, I might find it titillating. But mostly I find it boring and just a little disgusting."

Troy spun his chair around. "Why do you say that?"

"You should read the report. Well, I guess you will. Are you through with your pile, yet? Ready to switch?"

"Not yet. I'm reading something here about pesticides and their influence on fertility. Human fertility. Specifically male fertility. Now that I think about it, I wonder why they didn't include effects on female fertility in the study."

"Probably a separate study. What's it say?"

"You'll read it for yourself, but essentially, we're all going to die."

David laughed again. "That's a bit dramatic. Besides, we are all going to die. It's not a question of if. Never has been. It's always a question of when. And how, I guess I should add."

"True. I should have phrased that differently. I think this is saying that at some future date, humans simply won't be born. No, scratch that. They're saying male humans won't be born. Apparently, something is happening to the Y chromosome. And the kicker is that while they think this has been happening for several years, now they think something is accelerating the process and rather than speaking in terms of hundreds, maybe thousands or millions of years, they're talking a decade or two. Maybe less."

David sat up straighter in his chair. "That must be frightening for those who are totally invested in a patriarchal society."

Troy smirked. "I guess. But could you even imagine a society consisting of only women? Sounds like some sci-fi movie plot. I wasn't a great biology student, but seems to me, I remember men are needed to make babies."

David looked at him. "You didn't pay much attention in class, did you? Men aren't needed. At least not the way you're thinking." He grinned. "Only their sperm is needed. And that can be taken and frozen for future use. Long after there are no men around, assuming there's even the remotest possibility of that happening."

Troy could barely speak; he was laughing so hard. "What? You think men will be corralled like livestock and subjected to that animal husbandry crap you're reading over there?"

David wasn't laughing. He was skimming the report in his hand. Troy sobered.

"David?"

"Let's switch stacks. Not everything. Keep what you haven't read. Just give me what you've already read, and I'll give you what I've finished."

"But I've only read a couple reports. They're rather dense with statistics."

"Have you finished the one you just mentioned?"

"Yes. I was on the second read-through."

David stood and walked to where Troy was. He held out the report he'd just read in his left hand while motioning with his right he wanted the one in Troy's hands. They exchanged papers and David went back to his desk. Troy watched him for a few seconds, then shrugged his shoulders and looked at the report in his hand. It didn't look remotely interesting. He sighed as he opened it and began reading.

Two hours later, as they were wrapping things up for the day, David asked Troy's opinion on the article.

"I must agree with you. It's rather boring and disgusting. Why do we even need to study such stuff. Just let nature take its course."

"But that's the problem. Our environment has become so polluted and toxic that nature is losing the battle. At the rate those in power are proceeding, it will be surprising if anything survives the next decade."

"That's a little extreme, don't you think? Besides the rich must also live in this environment. You think them so stupid as to destroy the very thing that makes them money?"

"You forget. They can afford to clean where they live. Create small enclaves of freshness in an otherwise dirty world."

When Troy looked to object, David continued. "Think about it. Where do you live? Do you worry about the water you drink or the food you eat? No? Ask yourself why that is. Now think about someone you know that lives in a different neighborhood. Ever ask them how they feel about what their choices are at the grocery store? Or how much it costs them? Admit it. You're one of the privileged few. Just as I am. I'm probably better off, to be honest. My dad works for the Leader. Your dad is an advisor and/or colleague of those in the administration. While that's an important role, it isn't the same."

Troy was silent, thinking about what David had just said. It was true. He never thought about what he ate or drank at home. And the more he thought about it, the more he realized he seldom indulged in anything that wasn't prepared at his home.

Carson would occasionally look envious when he talked about what he'd had for his meals. But he'd never thought about why. Or what, exactly, Carson and his family did for food. He just assumed it was the same as him, except Carson's mother prepared the food rather than a house servant.

And as for the differences between their fathers' status, he had to again admit David was right. His father was entrenched in the administration. Protected. Unless he did something stupid. Whereas Troy's dad was just to the outside of the truly inner circle. Close enough to garner several advantages, but not fully protected like those he socialized with.

David was studying Troy. "Starting to realize some unpleasant realities?"

Troy shrugged, refusing to outwardly confirm anything. "You ready to go? Do we need to lock up these reports?"

"Nah. Who'd want them? They're safe enough sitting on our desks."

David walked to the door. "I'll see you tomorrow. Another exciting day of reading."

Troy watched him leave, then followed behind at a slower pace. He reached the front door of the building in time to see David slide into the back seat of a long black car. He took a left and began his walk home.

His dad met him at the door as he came up the walk. Troy realized his dad, still dressed in a power suit, was on his way out.

"How was your day?" Marcus asked.

Troy smiled. "Nothing to write home about. Where are you going?"

"I have a meeting with some finance people. We're working on the cryptocurrency issue."

"Cryptocurrency?"

Marcus looked slightly exasperated. "Don't you keep up with the news? The Leader wants to make cryptocurrency the legal tender of the country."

Troy was confused. "But isn't that what our cash and electronic transfer system is?"

"Old news. Who wants to handle dirty bills and coins? And keep track of the physical inventory? Cryptocurrency is the future, son. You should know that I've already invested heavily in it and have set up a couple of different accounts for you, also."

"But—"

"I don't have time now, Troy. We'll discuss it later."

Marcus patted Troy on a shoulder as he passed him on the step. "Your dinner's in the oven. Cook had to leave early."

Troy watched Marcus hurry towards the street, timing his arrival perfectly with the taxi that pulled up next to the curb. His dad slid into the back seat without another glance in Troy's direction.

As the vehicle pulled away, Troy murmured to the empty space around him, "Her name is Beth, not Cook."

He turned and entered the large house. Loneliness and depression settling on him like a shroud.

13

Carson met Troy at their usual corner as arranged. He hadn't seen his friend for over a week, Troy's new position keeping him unavailable during the days. Carson missed hanging out with him and was glad they were finally getting together. He had lots of questions. A few that weren't his, but he chose not to analyze that part of it.

Carson got to the meeting place first and glanced around, taking in the lack of people as well as the cameras mounted on the streetlamps and corners of buildings. He had an urge to make an obscene gesture at one but managed to control it. *Wouldn't do to get picked up by the morality police,* he thought as he half-smiled to himself. He heard his name and turned to see Troy hurrying towards him. They exchanged a quick fist-bump, then fell into step beside each other.

"How's it going? How's it feel to be part of the working class?" Carson asked.

Troy smiled. "I'm not sure I like that classification. But it's different. Not what I expected."

"What do you mean?"

"Well," Troy hesitated. He was unsure what he could and couldn't talk about. No one had told him what he did was secret, but no one had encouraged him to discuss it, either.

"What?"

"Well, there's only two of us. The other fellow, a guy named David, says it's the budget cuts and implementation of efficiency measures. But I don't see how a whole department can run with just two people."

"Two of you! How strange. What department are you in?"

Troy hesitated again. Then admitted working for the health sector. But he didn't say which specific department. Carson noted that omission but didn't comment on it. Instead, he casually asked how Troy filled his days.

"That's the thing," Troy was starting to warm up to the topic. "There really isn't much to do. No one assigns us anything or tells us what we're supposed to be doing. The computer system isn't functional. At least I don't think it is. David says the folks who are supposed to maintain it were all let go in the efficiency purge. But get this," Troy paused and laughed, "David has been trying to hack into the system since he's been there. No success, yet, but it doesn't stop him from trying."

Carson glanced at Troy. "Why is he trying to hack into it if it supposedly doesn't even work?"

"David says it has all the archive files. What happened in previous administrations. A history book, if you get my drift. He says he's curious."

"Curious about what?"

"I don't know. All kinds of stuff, I guess."

"Who is this David guy? Do you know?"

"Yeah. That's even more interesting. He's the son of the guy who runs the environmental sector. You'd think he'd be over there, shadowing his dad. But he was put in the health sector. I'm starting to wonder if it's the dumping ground for unwanted relatives. You know?"

"Why do you say that?"

"We're not doing anything. We just goof off all day. No one seems to care. Yet they pay us. How does that even jive with an efficiency mentality?"

"You really don't do anything?"

"Well, the last couple of days we've been reading these research reports. David says we're supposed to recommend if the studies get continued funding or get shut down. Kind of weird, don't you think? Two kids with no background in any of that making those kinds of decisions?"

"Maybe they're just using you to weed out the really ridiculous stuff and someone else will actually be making the decisions."

"Maybe." Troy didn't look convinced.

"What kinds of stuff are you reading? Anything interesting?" Carson was curious. He also knew his contact would be interested in this information.

"Not sure I'm supposed to talk about it. But mostly, it's stuff about the environment, how it's affecting reproduction, that kind of stuff. Boring, really."

"Why would the health sector be reading about environmental issues. Shouldn't that be in their sector?"

"You'd think, right? But then again, the environment affects our health. We all know that. Maybe those that are doing the studies are trying to show the connections so that something will be done about the pollution we're experiencing."

Carson laughed. "Wishful thinking. These billionaires running things don't care about anything but making more money. Now, if the studies show a way that they can manipulate markets to make more money, sure, they'll do something. Will they do the right thing?"

Carson laughed again and didn't bother answering his own question. But Troy looked thoughtful.

"How does your family get along? Does your dad make enough? Do you guys get enough to eat, are you able to heat your home, keep the lights on?"

Carson stopped. When Troy kept walking, he hurried to catch up.

"Why on earth are you asking such a thing?"

Troy noted a slight aggressiveness in Carson's voice. He kept his light.

"Something David said. About he and I being privileged and protected."

"You are. Can't believe you sound like it's a new concept to you." Carson said flatly.

This time Troy stopped. Carson took five more steps then also stopped and turned to face Troy. He stared at his friend in silence.

"You think I'm privileged?" Troy asked hesitantly.

Carson indicated with his head for Troy to continue walking and waited for Troy to reach him before turning and continuing forward. He let the silence stretch.

"Carson?"

Carson took a deep breath and let it out with a whoosh. "Troy. You and I have always overlooked the differences in our circumstances. We've never let it get in the way of our friendship. But face it. You've always been in a protected class. More so now with the new Leader. Your dad is part of the inner circle. That makes you part of the inner circle. The rest of us? We just try to get by. We adjust. Are we happy? Not really. Can we do anything about our situation? Again, not really. Sometimes there's nothing to eat. Or what's available isn't worth eating. You realize that the markets my mom shops at contain the leftovers from the markets your kind shop at? Sometimes the food is okay, or almost ready to be thrown out, or moldy, or," Carson hesitated, "or simply not fit to be used. That's how the rest of us live. We're at the mercy of whatever new scheme the billionaires want to try. Doesn't matter if they think it's a good idea. To them, the only criteria is will it make them more money.

But all that aside, we've managed to maintain our friendship. Let's focus on that."

Troy had stopped again, and Carson with him. They stood facing each other. Troy wanted to protest that his father really wasn't part of the inner circle, that he wasn't any different from Carson.

But in his heart, he knew the truth of Carson's words as they related to the two of them. Yet he wasn't ready to fully embrace them. If he did, he'd have to admit that the same differences existed between him and David, even if on a different level.

For the first time, Troy was understanding the complexities of the current society they lived in. He felt stupid for not seeing it sooner. But still, there was a part of him that refused to accept all that Carson was saying. So much of it went against what his father had told him. And his father had no reason to lie to him. He was silent so long that Carson vocally nudged him.

"Troy?"

"Just thinking. What you said was a lot to take in. Maybe a bit extreme?" Troy's voice ended in a higher pitch, indicating a hopeful question. Carson gave him the out he was looking for.

"Perhaps I got a bit carried away. Forget about it. Let's not allow it to come between us. We've been friends forever. That's what's important, right?"

"Right," Troy was quick to agree even as he remembered his father's less-than-enthusiastic support of their relationship.

Carson shifted his stance. "Look, I should probably get going. It was great to see you. Want to get together this weekend?"

"Yes. I'd like that. But I'll have to let you know. Not sure if my dad has anything planned. I'll text you, OK?"

"That works."

Carson started to walk back the way they'd come but stopped after a few steps. He turned to Troy.

"Forget what I said, OK? It's not worth getting worked up about. But I do have a favor to ask, if you can do it."

"Sure. What do you need?"

"Can you find out where Jimmy is?"

Without waiting for a response, Carson turned and continued walking. Troy stood there, watching his friend walk away. Hearing Jimmy's name caused many feelings to surface. Feelings Troy was not able, or willing, to process. He glanced around to get his bearings, then set off on a course perpendicular to what Carson took.

14

Carson shut off the television. The news had been talking about cryptocurrency, something Carson neither understood nor cared about. He did wonder if the few dollars in his pocket were going to be worth anything tomorrow. But he always wondered that.

More and more places were refusing to take cash. Some of the smaller family-owned establishments were willing to barter, but most retailers now insisted on the use of electronic payments. While there were still a wide variety of systems available to access the electronic world, Carson noted that many were being phased out. The people were being forced to use a select few. He figured it wouldn't be long and there would only be one system available. Everyone was told it was the most efficient way to move forward. Carson knew it was the most profitable to someone in power and had nothing to do with efficiency. Still, who could fight it? And the worst part was, it cut a large swath of the population out of the equation. Carson wondered how those people would survive.

But he didn't spend a lot of time on the issue. His own survival, and that of his family, were the primary focus for him. His dad's salary met their basic needs. Barely. Carson managed to supplement that by hustling odd jobs and participating in his own bartering network.

He thought it amazing how quickly the economy had changed. People who'd wanted the Leader, said he would fix everything that was wrong, were finding out that things weren't getting fixed but were being made worse. Not for everyone, of course. But for most. *Be careful what you wish for,* he thought. *You'll likely get it. And then what?*

He glanced at the clock on the wall. He had to meet his contact in another hour. It would just be coming up on dusk. That meant the infrared cameras would engage, making it harder to remain undetected. He wondered why the meeting had been scheduled so late. It was risky. But he was at the whim of others. His job was to show up when and where he was told to.

He grabbed his jacket; thankful it was a dark navy blue. It would help him blend into the shadows. He was reaching for the doorknob when his mother came into the room.

"Going out?"

"Only for a bit."

"Where—? Never mind. I'd rather not know. Please be careful. The patrols are increasing."

Carson turned and walked to where his mother was standing. He gave her a quick hug.

"I'll be careful. Be back in a couple hours."

She hugged him back and watched in silence as he slipped out the door.

It took Carson longer than expected to reach his destination. His contact was clearly annoyed.

"What took you so long?"

"I had to make a couple detours. The squads are patrolling this area more often than usual. You know why?"

At the man's head shake, Carson continued. "They've added an extra camera at the main intersection. Coming this direction is getting more difficult. Perhaps a different meeting place could be entertained?"

"I'll consider it. What did you learn from your friend?"

Carson updated his contact on the conversation he'd had with Troy. He was careful not to mention his request about Jimmy. While his contact seemed concerned about almost everything, Carson instinctively knew that Jimmy and those like him were not a priority for the man.

"The reproductive studies are interesting. I've heard there have been requests for volunteers to join some ongoing medical investigation concerning the topic. Male volunteers only, of course."

Carson didn't comment. He was getting royally sick of this general lack of acknowledgement for the female population. It seemed like those who thought they ruled, or were on the side of those who ruled, simply wanted to put women in a contained space and never let them out. They were a necessary evil of nature. To be tolerated. That's it. Nothing more. Carson thought that viewpoint was insanely stupid.

He truly believed in the concept that all should be equal before the law. He privately acknowledged that equal before the law and equal in societal acceptance were two very different things. And always had been.

But these days, the predominant opinion was only white males were worth anything. However, not all white males. Just those who were chosen. He smothered a snort. His mind had automatically put quotation marks around the word chosen. He well knew he wasn't one of the chosen. He wondered if his contact was. If so, then he needed to be more careful. No telling when his perceived usefulness would be discarded. And where would that put him? Perhaps in a settlement similar to Jimmy's. His thoughts were interrupted by the realization his contact was still speaking.

"See if you can find out more about the studies. Which doctors and facilities are connected to them. What the ultimate goal is."

"How am I supposed to do that?"

"You'll figure it out."

Then, in a complete shift of subject matter, the man asked Carson if he knew anything about cryptocurrency.

"No. Only what little bit they're saying on the news, and even then, I barely listen. I don't understand the stuff."

"Your friend's father is heavily involved in the matter. We've heard the powers-that-be plan to make it the main, perhaps only, acceptable currency. We want to know if that's true or only rumors."

"And you think I can find that out? How? I have no interaction with Troy's dad. He barely tolerates me. In fact, I don't think he even does that. I'm surprised Troy is still willing to meet with me, because I'm pretty sure his dad wants him to stay away from me."

"I don't care how you do it. Just get us information on the topic."

"But—"

"Do it. Or you might not like the consequences."

"What does that mean?"

"I don't think I need to spell it out. Just be smart and do it."

With that, the man turned and hurried away in the opposite direction. Carson heard the distant closing of a door and knew the man had left the building the same way he had the last time they met.

As Carson carefully made his way home, his anxious mind was racing with thoughts of impossible tasks and undefined consequences.

15

It was dark when Jimmy awoke. He knew that meant he'd slept for several hours. He wondered what the time was. There was no clock in the barracks and the residents weren't allowed watches. They weren't allowed any personal items.

Jimmy sat up and looked around. He was the only one in the room. He assumed the others were at dinner. Perhaps if he hurried, he might still be able to eat. He stood, fighting the slight nausea that swept him. He moved to the door then stopped at the sudden noises he heard.

Yelling. Cries. Gunshots.

In a panic, he ran to the one window that allowed sight to the outside. All others were boarded over. He watched in horror at the chaos unfolding in the main yard. Residents ran in all directions. Uniformed men were trying to restrain and contain them. Some were using their weapons. Jimmy watched as several people he knew fell and didn't get up. He assumed they were dead.

He backed away from the window and looked around the room. He didn't see any place to hide. He could go into the bathroom, but he knew that would be the first place they'd look. He was afraid to go outside.

In desperation he looked at his cot. Not consciously thinking about what he was doing, he puffed up some pillows and threw his blanket over it. His mind vaguely registered that it looked like a person, even as he moved to the end of the room.

Grabbing the blanket that was on the last cot, he opened it and arranged it in a way that it hung to the floor, effectively blocking the view beneath the cot. He wrinkled it up a bit to make it look like it had been tossed down without thought. Then he crawled under the cot and curled up into as small a ball as he could. Closing his eyes, he worked to control his breathing as he prayed to any god that would listen.

His body jerked as the door to the barracks was violently flung open.

"No one is in here," a deep voice called out.

"Check the toilets," another voice responded.

Jimmy maintained a stillness he never thought possible. Every boot-fall echoed in his head as he tracked the person's progress to the door of the bathroom. A tear squeezed out from under one tightly closed lid. He heard laughter. The footsteps stopped.

"What?"

"Looks like they had a runner and didn't even know."

"What do you mean?"

"This cot. See the lumps? They're pillows. Someone was hoping they'd believe whoever slept here was still here."

There was an echoing laughter.

"We gonna look for him?"

"Nah. Likely they'll be rounded up again at some point. Might even be in the crowd outside. Don't really care. Anyone in the toilets?"

"No. Place is empty."

"Let's go then. This whole operation stinks. Let's finish it up and get out of here."

Jimmy heard the footsteps retreat. Ten minutes later he heard several gunshots. Then silence. He remained where he was. At some point he drifted into an uneasy half-sleep.

The sound of birds brought him back to awareness. He stayed still, listening. He heard nothing but the birds. He grunted through his stiffness as he crawled from beneath the cot. Peeking over the top of the bed, he registered that the room was empty. Other than the blanket removed from over the pillows where he'd placed it, nothing was changed in the room. There was no evidence anyone but he had been there all night.

Slowly he stood, stretching his muscles as he did so. His first few steps were unsteady, but he soon gained his balance and stride. He first went to the window. What he saw when he looked out caused him to gasp and step back quickly. He fought his gag reflex, taking deep breaths. When he felt ready, he moved back to the window and stared at the carnage.

Bodies were everywhere. He knew they were all dead. He heard the birds again and looked to the tree branches. Two cardinals were perched, calling out their song. Jimmy's mind couldn't process the happy sound with the devastating sight just beneath them.

He forced himself to move to the door and step through.

"Hello? Anyone here?"

When there was no answer, he tried again. Louder. Still no answer. Not knowing what else to do, he walked in the direction of the clinic building. Careful to step around the bodies, he recognized most on the ground. There were a few he hadn't seen before. He wondered if they were new arrivals or were simply a different population, segregated from his.

The clinic door was closed but not locked. He opened it and stepped in. By now he was more hardened to the sight of dead bodies. He didn't even flinch when he looked at the two on the exam tables, IVs still attached to their arms. He briefly wondered at that. He'd never had an IV administered to him. Injections, yes. Forced consumption of pills, yes. But never an IV. Shrugging, he dismissed it as unimportant considering their current situation. The medical specialist who'd given him his last treatment was in a corner, slumped over. Blood pooled around the body.

"And you thought you were one of the good guys," Jimmy said sadly.

At this point, he was certain he was the only one who'd survived last night. But he still moved cautiously, constantly surveying his environment. Not realizing he was actively seeking it out, his eyes rested on the cabinet that held the settlement's medical supplies. Or treatments, as they were called.

He went to it and pulled on the handle, surprised it opened without protest. He began reading labels, working his way through each shelf. He didn't know what most of the items were. But on the third shelf, he recognized the name of the hormones he'd been taking before arriving at the settlement. His heartbeat quickened.

He took the bottles out, placing them on a nearby table. When he was certain he'd removed the entire stock of the same dosage, he looked for other dosages. By the time he'd finished, he had amassed fifteen bottles. Most were full, totaling several hundred capsules.

Jimmy looked around for something to put them in. The only thing he saw was the plastic bag that lined one of the small trash cans. Not wanting to use that, he looked through the cabinets hoping to find a box of unused ones. After several minutes, he was successful.

He tossed the bottles into the bag, but as he was tying the top, he realized two things. The multiple bottles were bulky, and the capsules were noisy as they rattled inside them. Without hesitation, he quickly emptied the bottles, careful to separate the different dosages into different bags. Being loose, the resulting stash was quieter and easier to carry. Pulling the labels off the appropriate bottles, he tucked them inside the bags to identify the dosages.

While a part of him was screaming at him to hurry and leave the settlement, another part recognized that preparation was the key to surviving whatever came next. He went back to the barracks and found boots that fit and outer wear that would help protect him from the elements. He tucked the bags of pills in various pockets.

Next, he went to the administration building. He'd only been in it once. The day he'd arrived, confused and scared. Now he entered with a purpose. Bypassing all technology represented by phones and computers, he searched for anything that resembled a paper map of the area. He found nothing. Frustrated, he stared at the phones and computers but knew not to access any of them. Instead, he searched for papers that might provide an address. Something that would tell him where he was. Anything.

He finally found a discarded envelope. He hoped that it was addressed to this place and was not some random thing someone brought in from home. If it was addressed to this location, he now knew generally where he was. Not yet convinced how helpful that knowledge was, he knew it was better than nothing. Still hoping for a map but knowing he wouldn't find one, he left the building and hurried to the dining hall.

The odor that hit him when he opened the door was not pleasant. Not gag-worthy yet, but definitely on its way there. He strode into the kitchen and went straight for the large refrigerators against the back wall. Opening one, he pulled out some cheese and immediately began eating it as he reviewed the other contents. He knew that anything he took from here would need to be consumed relatively quickly, before it spoiled. From each refrigerator he gathered a few items that looked promising, then moved to the storage area.

He made his choices, putting them next to his previous selections. When he looked at the items, he realized he had the same problem he'd had with the pills. He had to figure out a way to carry everything.

This time he was able to find some canvas bags. It took a few attempts, but he was finally able to package everything up and create a backpack of sorts. He looked out into the dining room, totally unmoved by the dead bodies he saw. He recognized he was functioning in a survival mode. The shock and trauma would come later. Hopefully he'd be able to navigate through it.

Understanding he could not afford to spend any more time where he was, he left the dining hall and hurried to the main gate of the settlement. He almost cried when he saw the chain and padlock. But even as he was processing the idea that he might be stuck here, his eyes saw the gap between the gate and post. Maybe. Just maybe.

He pushed at the gate and saw that the opening became slightly wider. It would be a tight fit, but he thought he could do it. He pushed the food through first. It took longer than he thought it would, and he knew he'd have a few bruises to show for his efforts, but he finally squeezed through the opening.

Taking a deep breath, he reached down for his pack of food. Surveying his surroundings and noting both the sun's position and its shadows, he chose a direction and began walking.

16

Troy was at his desk when David arrived.

"Aren't you the early bird. What's with that?"

"I had a ride in. Didn't have to walk."

"Wait. You walk here? Every day?"

"Sure. It's not that far. Gives me a chance to wake up and mentally prepare."

David chuckled. "Mentally prepare for what? Another long boring day?"

Troy smiled. "I guess you could say that."

"Aren't you worried you'll be attacked by gangs or something?"

"Nah. Not with all the cameras and enforcement squads."

David grunted. "Cameras are only good for after the fact. To watch what happened. And I wouldn't count on any enforcement squad to help you. More likely they'll join the attackers."

"Why do you say that?"

David didn't respond. Instead, he went to his desk and switched on the computer.

"What say we ditch the reports for a while and try getting into the system again?"

"But don't we have some kind of timeline for these things?" Troy lifted a portion of the stack of papers on his desk.

"Not that anyone said. Besides, I think they just dumped them here to say they were in process." David gestured quotation marks in the air.

Troy didn't comment. He wasn't sure how serious David was. He figured if they'd been asked to read and comment on the reports, someone somewhere thought they were important. He watched David tapping on the keyboard.

"Aren't you ready to give up on that? How long have you been unsuccessfully trying? And aren't you worried someone might see what you're doing?"

"No to the last question. Too long to the second question, and in answer to the first question, on whether I'm ready to give up, I have some new ideas I want to try."

"Why aren't you worried about someone seeing what you're doing? Or attempting to do."

"They have bigger worries. You hear about the attack on one of those settlements?"

Troy frowned. "Settlements?"

"Yeah. You know. The ones where they rounded up and put those people who have gender issues." David again gestured quotes.

Troy felt a jolt. Almost like he'd touched a live electrical wire. With a feeling of dread, he asked the question to which he wasn't sure he wanted an answer.

"What happened?"

David stopped tapping the keyboard and looked at Troy. He didn't say anything for several moments. Troy had the impression he was deciding whether to continue the conversation. Troy waited.

"Yesterday a group of armed men essentially annihilated an entire settlement."

"Armed men? You mean enforcement squad? I didn't hear anything on the news."

"It's being kept very quiet. The bigwigs are doing major damage control, trying to keep it completely out of the media."

"Then how do you know about it?"

"My dad hangs with the justice sector guy. That's how he heard. The guy was at our place last night. They didn't know I could hear them talking."

"So, do they know who it was? Who attacked?"

"My dad asked. The justice guy was a little dodgy on it. But he said something I don't think my dad picked up on." David looked intently at Troy. "This is not for repeating. You understand? There could be serious consequences."

Troy nodded, feeling a slight nausea in the pit of his stomach.

David lowered his voice to a near-whisper. "I think it was government people. But they're going to blame some extremist religious group. Say it couldn't be foreseen. Express sorrow to those who lost loved ones. Then they'll make noises about searching for those responsible, but nothing will be done. Because they were responsible all along."

"That's nonsense! I don't believe you!" Troy tried to keep his voice low, but it came out louder than he'd planned.

"Shhhhhhh. Not so loud."

Troy tried again, lowering his voice close to the whisper David was speaking in.

"Why would our own government do something like that?"

"To them, those people are no better than all the immigrants they deported. I wouldn't be surprised if most of the deported are now dead, too. Either directly by our hand or by the consequences of our action. Face it, Troy. Accept it. If you aren't white. Rich and white. Make that male, rich and white." He paused, then continued. "Or dedicated-to-the-cause white, you're nothing. Mere obstacles to be dealt with as expediently as possible."

David's words appalled Troy. He had questions. He didn't know which to ask first, or even which to ask. Carson's request floated back into his mind. *Can you find out where Jimmy is?*

"Do they have lists of who's in those settlements? How are they going to notify relatives or others?"

"I'm sure somebody somewhere has a list. Why? You know any of those weirdos?"

"Don't call them that. They may be different from us, but so what? What harm does that cause?"

David laughed. "You do know some!"

"One. I know one. Went to school with him. Found out a while back that he'd been swept up and placed in a settlement. Don't know which one. But I'd be curious to know."

David looked at Troy for a long time without speaking. So long that Troy became uncomfortable.

"What?"

David shrugged. "Nothing. I just didn't peg you for having a trans friend."

"We went to school together. That doesn't automatically mean we were, or are, friends."

"But you are. I can see it in your mannerisms."

Before Troy could object, David continued. "Never mind. It doesn't really matter. I also know a few. I'd be curious to know if they were part of what happened, too. Want to see if we can find out?"

"How do we do that?"

"I bet if we could get into this system, we'd be able to find out."

Troy was confused. "I thought you said this system was defunct. Not used. Just a history book."

David smiled. "I may have stretched the truth on that a bit."

"What's that mean?"

"The system is active. Someone is using it in real time. We just weren't given access."

"Must be a reason for that. Security clearance or something?"

David snorted. "Security. The Leader doesn't think that way. Maybe a few of his cronies do, but probably more to hide what they're getting away with than because they're worried about access to sensitive information."

Troy didn't comment. If he were honest with himself, he was having trouble comprehending everything David was saying. In fact, a lot of it sounded close to Carson's outburst the other day. Troy paused his thoughts and looked at David more closely. He kept is voice low, just above a whisper.

"Are you loyal to the Leader? Or are you part of the resistance?"

"Good grief," David dismissed Troy's questions. "You sound like some dystopian movie or novel or something. Get your head together."

David's attention returned to the computer. Without looking at Troy he asked, "Are you in? Today's hacking adventure? Because if you're not, just read your reports and leave me to my continued efforts."

Troy sat silent for a few moments. Then stood and walked to David's desk, pulling a wheeled chair close with his foot. When he positioned it where he wanted it, he sat.

"I'm in."

For the next two hours Troy watched David perform a variety of actions to access the system. Each attempt failed. He was getting bored.

"You're never going to break in," he told David.

"Don't be such a spoilsport."

"Right. You've been at it forever. No success. Admit it. You can't do it. Probably no one can. And my guess is that even if you do ultimately get in, you'll find it simply wasn't worth the effort."

At that precise moment, the screen flickered. Suddenly they were looking at a menu of various options.

"Ha!" David exclaimed. "O ye of little faith. I've done it! I'm in!"

Troy scooted forward to the edge of his chair, stared at the screen and read the options aloud.

"Which do you think we should look at first?" he asked David. "And don't take this the wrong way, but do you remember what you did to get in so you can duplicate it?"

"Of course I remember. But never mind that. Let's see if we can set ourselves up for easier access."

"How?"

David clicked on an option. "I'm going to try the administration section. See if we can add ourselves as authorized users."

David's selection resulted in another list of options.

"Great, Watson. What now?"

"Who?"

"Watson. You know. That guy in—" Troy could see David was clueless. "It doesn't matter. You have any idea what you're doing?"

"Not really, but how hard can it be?"

David clicked one menu selection after another. Each action took him deeper into a system that seemed incomprehensible to Troy. After a few more clicks, David murmured a quiet affirmation.

"What? You find something?"

"I believe so."

David started typing rapidly. Five minutes later he told Troy to grab pencil and paper. When Troy was ready, he recited a series of letters and numbers, followed by a phrase interjected with special characters.

Troy looked at the paper. "What's all this?"

"That's your username and password. Don't lose it. It's your access to treasures unknown."

"If you say so."

"I do. Now get ready to write mine down."

David dictated another string of letters and numbers, followed by a different phrase. Troy dutifully wrote everything down.

"Let's test it. Go try yours on the computer at your desk."

Troy stood. Taking the paper with the information David said pertained to his access, he strode to his desk, sat, pulled the keyboard close and began typing. Within seconds his screen lit up with the original menu he'd seen on David's machine.

"It works!"

David's laugh was almost a giggle. "Poke around. See what you find."

Troy glanced over at David and saw he was already deeply engaged in exploring different screens. He shrugged his shoulders and turned back to his monitor. He wasn't sure what he should be looking at or for. After clicking a few options, he stumbled onto a screen that allowed him to change his password.

Quickly verifying that David's attention was on his own monitor, Troy went through the process of changing the password David set up for him. He wasn't sure why he thought this was important, but some instinct told him it was. Jotting down the new information, he stuffed the paper in his pocket and continued to select different menu items.

Not sure how he found it, or even why it was on this system, he suddenly was looking at what appeared to be a list of settlements. Each was labeled by location and type. Troy wasn't sure what was meant by type, but he understood as soon as he chose one of the file listings. Quickly returning to the main menu, he looked for those listings that included the word gender.

He was on his fourth list when he saw Jimmy's name. His hand shook as he navigated the screens that not only gave him Jimmy's location, but everything that had been done to him since arriving at the settlement.

Troy didn't understand all the technical clinical data but knew enough to realize that the main purpose of the settlements was not to simply contain people like Jimmy, as he thought. No, the stated objectives were to reestablish the biological gender of the residents. He knew this from seeing the administered hormone therapies.

He understood the difference between testosterone and estrogen. He knew Jimmy had been taking testosterone supplements, but based on what he was seeing, it looked like those had been stopped and replaced with estrogen supplements. Before he could contemplate the consequences of such actions, David's voice coming from directly behind him nearly made him jump out of his skin.

"I see you appear to have found someone you know."

Troy didn't know how to respond. His hesitation made David chuckle.

"Don't worry. I won't tell on you. What settlement is your friend in?"

David's comment and question made Troy wonder how long he'd been there, looking over his shoulder. Deciding it easier to answer than try to deflect, he told him.

"Jeez! That's the one that was attacked. Annihilated."

Troy spun slowly around in his chair and stared at David.

"When you say annihilated, you mean there were no survivors? None?"

David's reaction wasn't what Troy expected. He turned and went back to his desk with only a murmured comment of condolence. He said nothing more as he began typing on his keyboard. Troy waited, but when it was clear David wasn't going to speak, he turned back around and stared unseeingly at his monitor. Memories of Jimmy and their shared adventures flew through his mind.

A single tear slid down his cheek and landed on the back of his hand.

17

"He's dead."

"What? Who's dead?" Carson looked at Troy with a confused expression.

"Jimmy."

The two were walking along the river path. The day was sunny, but despite that fact, Carson felt a chill enter his body. He forced himself to keep walking.

"How do you know?"

Troy told him about the successful entry into the system and some of the files he'd seen.

"Poor Jimmy. He must have really suffered through those treatments. If you can call them that. But has there been an official headcount? Maybe some escaped. Maybe Jimmy escaped."

"Highly doubtful. Once David told me about the attack, I looked for more files. He was right. The government is trying to bury all information related to the incident, but I found a few more bits. They're still identifying everyone. Once they've finished that, I'm sure there will be some official statement of remorse, condemnation of events, and a general promise to pursue the aggressors."

Carson slowed his walking. Putting Jimmy aside in his thoughts for a moment, he asked a question that had been bothering him since Troy had described the hack into the system.

"Why would you be able to see files that should be connected to the justice sector? Or if not there, somewhere other than the health sector?"

"Got to admit, I wondered the same. Maybe they were just trying to consolidate stuff. Part of the whole efficiency thing. The hormonal therapies they were giving the settlement people do relate to the health sector. At least from the clinical side of it. And there was a full list of residents. To wrap up the records on them, maybe someone thought it easiest to just toss everything into one place."

Carson frowned. The explanation wasn't the worst thing he'd heard over the last two years. Trying to figure out anything these days was a task. There were so many twists and turns.

About the only thing everyone agreed on was that the billionaires running the government were only out to make more billions. And their idea of building efficiency into the system meant that accumulating more wealth for themselves was easier. Even the hardliners finally had to admit that. But that's about the only thing they admitted. And yet, they still made excuses.

Carson figured they just couldn't completely admit they'd been snookered. To do so would be tantamount to confessing pure ignorance or stupidity, be it intentional or something else. And no one, regardless of what political views they held, wanted to admit such a thing. Human nature.

He mentally grimaced. Human nature. He wasn't even sure what that meant any more. But he needed to think about just what kind of access to official government records Troy had stumbled into. It could be vital to the cause of reining in the extremist viewpoints and returning the country to a more balanced approach. He increased their walking pace again and tried to keep his voice as casual as possible.

"You have a chance to see what else you can get into?"

Troy glanced at Carson. "Not really. Why do you ask? I'm already positive I've overstepped anything close to a line I shouldn't have crossed. David doesn't seem to think there's any risk. I'm not convinced of that. Sooner or later, someone is going to figure out we're reading files we shouldn't be reading. I'm concerned the consequences will be dire. That it won't matter we're the sons of important people."

Carson grunted. He didn't want to go there. The social and economic differences between them. They'd explored that path before, with little gained from the exercise. But a part of him noted Troy's acknowledgement and wondered if Troy was starting to better understand the reality of the current environment. He was quiet so long Troy prompted him.

"Carson? What are you thinking?"

"My brain is kind of spinning. If you have access to a large swath of information, think about how you could use it."

"Use it? What do you mean?"

"Oh, I don't know. These settlements, for instance. Everyone thinks they're designed to segregate people and that's all. But you now know that's not the case. I mean, maybe it is for some of the classification of people those in power don't like, but you can't deny they were doing more than that to people like Jimmy. You've seen it with your own eyes. Maybe someone could release that type of information to better educate the public."

Troy looked at Carson without speaking. Carson wasn't sure what the look meant, but he didn't read pure hostility in it. Only curiosity. Deciding to push his luck, Carson continued.

"OK. Maybe forget that. But think about how the information could be used to better yours or my positions."

"As in?"

"Well, I heard cryptocurrency is the new god to bow down to. Maybe you could find out what's happening there. Give an opportunity for someone like me to better my financial position. I mean, nothing huge. But maybe enough to not have to wonder if I'm going to eat tonight."

"You really worry about that?"

Carson shrugged. "Not the focus, here."

"You brought it up."

Carson refused to be sidetracked. His contact had instructed him to find out as much as he could about the Leader's stated intention of making cryptocurrency the official monetary system. Carson couldn't see a better way being offered to gain information on the topic. He tried a different tactic.

"Do you even understand how cryptocurrency works?"

"Not really. It's something intangible. More so than even the basic concept of cash. But at least with cash, there's something physical to hold. Assigning value to that is a kind of wonky concept, but everyone accepts it and acts accordingly.

However, there's no physicality to cryptocurrency. It's just numbers on a page, far as I can reckon. Actually, numbers in a computer. If the numbers go up and you got in lower than that, you make money. If things go the opposite way, you don't make money. If there is a transfer to it as official currency, I assume at some point, everyone will have their current liquid assets converted to an account set up in their name. To accomplish anything, you just show your account, and it goes up or down as required to obtain what's needed or desired."

"But who monitors that all is working as it should?"

"I don't know."

"You think anyone will monitor it?"

"I don't know."

"So, it could be greatly manipulated to benefit those with the most, and pretty-much completely shut out those without."

"That seems a little exaggerated."

"You think so? It wouldn't be much different than what's happening with everything else right now."

Troy was quiet for a few moments. Then, hesitantly, "You know, my dad is involved with people who are involved with this subject. He told me the other day he's heavily invested in the stuff. Even opened some accounts in my name."

"There you go. It's already started."

"What do you mean?" Troy's tone was aggressive. Challenging. "My dad wouldn't be part of a scheme to manipulate the markets."

Carson bit back his immediate response that that's exactly what Marcus Hubbard would do, knowing Troy would shut down if he spoke it. Instead, he moved the topic in a different direction.

"I don't have much to spare. Mostly what I garner with my side hustles. But I understand anyone can get into the cryptocurrency system. Large initial investments aren't necessary. Do you think you could find out if this whole cryptocurrency thing is real? And if so, when it might be implemented? Maybe I can do a few more hustles and start building a safety net." He smiled. "Or lose it all and be worse off. But my choice, right?"

Troy slowed their pace. "You serious?"

"About trying to make a little extra? Sure. Why wouldn't I be?"

"No. I mean are you serious about wanting me to try and access files on that subject."

"I wouldn't want you to do anything you think is wrong. And I certainly don't want to get you in trouble."

Carson kept his gaze slightly averted, pretending to pay attention to the path so as not to stumble. He wondered what Troy was thinking, since his friend had not spoken for several minutes.

"I'll see what I can find out. I don't know if I can even access those files."

"That'd be cool," Carson said, using phraseology from years past. Troy smiled at it. "But be careful."

"No worries on that."

"Could you do something else?"

Troy looked at him suspiciously. "What?"

"Can you see if you can confirm whether Jimmy died at the settlement? His mom would want to know."

18

Jimmy walked for hours. Exhausted, he finally sat on a large rock and rummaged in his makeshift pack for water and a snack. He drank half the bottle of water he found, then ate some ham he'd taken from the settlement's refrigerator. He knew he had to eat that food first, before it spoiled. The packaged stuff could be used later.

He looked around his surroundings. He realized he had no idea where he was in relation to anything else. He only knew he was in a true wilderness area. That was both good and bad. Good in that it was easier to stay hidden. Bad in that he didn't know what types of hazards he might encounter in terms of animals or other people who might be out here in the vastness.

He rubbed his face and shifted his position on the rock. The unruly pack tipped over at his feet and one of the bags of pills he'd transferred to the pack fell out. He reached down and picked it up, reading the label as he did so. He wanted to immediately restart the testosterone supplements, but he hesitated, remembering when he'd first started his transition. He'd had a few mild side-effects. Sweating, mood changes, general edema. Thankfully nothing worse and all manageable. And he'd had his doctor available to monitor everything.

He was unsure if restarting the supplements after having been off them would increase the intensity of what he'd previously experienced or possibly create additional issues. Also, he'd originally had injections, then transitioned to pills. He didn't know if that made any difference.

He sighed as he pushed the bag back into the pack. He'd give it some more thought before taking any action. His priority right now was to get as much distance between him and the settlement as he could. With that thought, he stood, picked up his pack and began walking again.

It was dusk when he surrendered to his weariness. The last hour had been a mental endurance test to place one foot in front of the other without tripping. He found a small clearing and collapsed to the ground. As he sat, somewhat uncomfortably, he realized he needed a better plan than just walking. His supplies would soon be gone, and he'd need to worry about food and water.

He also knew the chances of finding fresh water were minimal. So much of the country had been polluted with industrial waste runoff, pesticides, and things he didn't want to contemplate. The idea of finding a stream of clean or at least drinkable water was almost laughable.

Only bottled water was considered safe these days, and he often wondered if that was even true. Additionally, recycling efforts were less than they'd been before the new administration had taken over. Thus, trash, including used bottles, was everywhere. A few tried to control the ever-expanding waste centers, but Jimmy thought it a losing battle. Unless something drastic happened, that is.

But nothing would happen. At least not soon. Those in power didn't see recycling as a money-maker, thus there was no incentive to invest. He figured only government intervention would address the issue. In the past, environmental regulations had kept a lot of what was currently happening under some control. Now there were no controls, the regulations all having been removed under the guise of efficiency. The billionaires called it efficiency. Everyone else had other words for it.

His short laugh was tinged with sadness. Recognizing these thoughts would provide no tangible benefit to his current circumstances, he pushed them aside and looked around his clearing. He saw an area where two small trees had fallen over. Their positioning created a natural shelter, and he crawled towards it too tired to stand and walk.

He peered into the dark opening hoping his chosen spot wasn't already occupied. A long stick was conveniently close at hand. He picked it up, pushed it into the opening and moved it around. He sighed in relief when nothing came charging out at him. He dropped the stick and slid into the opening. Then, having second thoughts he reached out and grabbed the stick, pulling it into the shelter with him. As a weapon, it wasn't much. But he figured it was better than nothing.

The space was small, but if he positioned himself carefully, he could settle onto his side. *It'll have to do,* he thought. Just being concealed gave him a sense of safety he hadn't experienced in a long time. As he let his body relax, he had a fleeting thought that a fire would add to his comfort. He was asleep before that thought took hold.

He awoke with a start sometime in the predawn hours, heart beating rapidly. He remained still and listened with his entire being. Had he heard something? He took a mental inventory of his physical body. Sore and stiff was his conclusion. But nothing debilitating. He continued to remain still. Listening. Fighting panic.

"Whoever you are, come out. Slowly."

The voice caused Jimmy's entire body to jerk. He tightened into a small ball. Hoping he'd imagined the words, he stayed where he was.

"Come on, now. I know you're there. You've left tracks and drag marks everywhere. A five-year-old could track you. Come out. We won't hurt you."

We! There were more than just the person speaking! Jimmy's thoughts were in turmoil. And he was scared. Very scared.

The voice gentled to just short of a pleading sound. "Seriously. We won't hurt you. Are you hurt? Are you hungry? Thirsty? We have food and water. We'll share. Just come out slowly. Don't do anything stupid."

Realizing he had no choice, Jimmy pushed his pack out first, then slowly crawled through the opening. He cringed when he saw the group of about twenty uniformed men. He pushed back against the outside of the shelter, staring at them with wide eyes.

"It's OK. We won't hurt you. What's your name. What are you doing out here?"

"J-J-Jimmy. Why do you have guns? Military guns? Who are you?"

"Well, Jimmy. Clever of you to recognize our weapons as military grade. Why are you out here and how did you get here?"

"I walked."

"Walked? From where? There's nothing around here for miles."

One of the men leaned in and whispered something to the man talking. He looked thoughtful then studied Jimmy more intently.

"You from the settlement? That's a long way away. You walked from there?"

When Jimmy didn't respond the man sighed.

"Look, Jimmy. My name is Rowan. These are my men. We're part of the military. We—"

Jimmy interrupted. "There is no military. It was disbanded. Or reorganized. Or whatever you call what happened to turn our proud fighting forces into something called enforcement squads and just general lawless criminals."

The chuckles amongst the men surprised Jimmy. He relaxed slightly.

"You're right about one thing. The military was officially disbanded. But that doesn't mean we just quietly went away. But tell me, Jimmy. Are you from the settlement? If so, how did you escape? We were there. It was a bloodbath."

Jimmy pushed back against his shelter even further, although in truth that was only a few inches. His earlier ease returned to panic and fear.

"You were there? You did that? You murdered everyone?"

"Whoa. Hold up. We didn't murder anyone. I said we were there. We saw the aftermath. We didn't create it. But how did you survive?"

"I hid. They didn't find me. I don't think the ones looking wanted to find anyone. They weren't very thorough."

"You're probably right about that. Did you see it? What happened?"

"No. Only heard it. I didn't see anything or anyone. When I came out of my hiding place, everyone was dead. Residents, staff. Everyone. Do you know who they were? Why they would do that?"

Rowan exchanged looks with his men. Rather than respond to Jimmy's questions, he asked if Jimmy was hungry or thirsty. At Jimmy's hesitant nod, he gestured for him to come closer. One of his men dropped their pack and pulled out some rations and held them toward Jimmy. When Jimmy didn't move, the man waved the food in an invitation to come and get the food.

The standoff lasted only a few moments. Jimmy struggled to his feet and came hesitantly toward the group. He stopped just out of reach and looked into the eyes of everyone. The dawn was well underway, and he could better see all of them. They looked tough. But not particularly mean or menacing. He shuffled forward just close enough to accept what the man was holding out to him. He glanced down at it and saw a military logo. Startled, he looked at Rowan.

"It's OK. You can eat it. Maybe not the best tasting stuff, but it'll keep you alive."

He gestured to his men and six immediately peeled off and disappeared into the woods. He looked at Jimmy.

"Let's all sit. We can exchange more information while you eat."

He motioned to the man who'd pulled out the rations and the man reached back into his pack and brought out a container that held liquid.

Jimmy could hear the slosh as it was held toward him. Jimmy took the container, looked around, spotted a log and, after inspecting it for anything threatening, sat down. The men arranged themselves on the ground in a loose circular pattern. Some facing outward, others facing Jimmy.

"What's your last name, Jimmy?" Rowan asked.

"It's just Jimmy."

Rowan looked at him for a long moment.

"Fair enough. How long were you in the settlement?"

"I'm not sure. A couple of weeks, maybe more."

"How'd you come to be there?"

"I was picked up by a squad when I was on my way to meet some friends. It was like they were waiting for me. I don't know how they knew where I'd be."

Rowan refrained from saying it was probably an informer. He was sure Jimmy knew that but was still in a state of denial over it. He felt bad for the kid.

Rowan thought everyone younger than him a kid. He could see Jimmy was somewhere in his twenties, but being in his mid-forties, and having experienced the things he'd experienced, Rowan viewed others as either kids, contemporaries, or inconsequential. The latter being mostly anyone tied to the Leader and his assembly of supporters, be they within or outside the actual governmental mantle.

"What was your experience there?"

"What do you mean?"

"How were you treated?"

"Do you mean was I treated like a guest at a spa?" Jimmy asked bitterly, then shook his head. "Well, they fed us. Gave us a place to sleep. Regimented our day to a point. But mostly, they tried to remove our identities and turn us into something we aren't."

"Can you be more specific? We've heard some disturbing reports but haven't been able to confirm anything. You're the first person we've met who can give us a firsthand narrative about these places."

Jimmy sat quietly for several minutes, taking the opportunity to consume the food he'd been given. Rowan was right. It lacked a wholesome taste, but he was sure it contained ingredients that would sustain one's life. It had to be better than the packaged stuff he'd taken from the settlement. Rowan and his men waited patiently.

Finally, when Jimmy began speaking, he found he couldn't stop. Just telling what he'd endured acted like a psychic purge. The more he talked, the stronger he felt. Rowan noted it and decided he liked the change he was seeing. *The kid's got stamina. Courage.* He thought to himself. *An inner strength he's probably not even aware he has.*

The silence stretched when Jimmy finished. He wasn't sure what the men were thinking. But he could see various expressions. Some he recognized as disgust. He hoped it wasn't disgust over him and his life choices. He was also sure some looked sad. Others, just stoic. Like they were trying not to think.

After several minutes, Rowan crouched down to Jimmy's height and spoke. His voice expressed both gentleness and kindness.

"I won't lie. There are many who disagree with your life choice. Think it's some kind of sin. I'm not one of them. I'm sorry you've experienced the darker side of humanity. But you survived. Hold onto that victory. I hate to ask. I'm not sure how all this works. If you aren't taking the appropriate therapies, what happens?"

Jimmy answered. Then confessed to having taken all the needed supplements from the clinic before he left the settlement. When asked if he'd restarted his therapies, he explained his fears.

Rowan smiled. "I think we can help with that. We have a doctor in our group. Several, in fact. We can oversee the process."

Jimmy looked at the group in front of him, but Rowan quickly clarified his statement. "Not with us. Back at our main camp."

"Main camp?"

"Yes. You'll see. If you choose to come with us, that is. You don't have to. You can remain on your own if you prefer. We'll give you extra food and water. But it will only last so long. After that—"

Rowan's voice trailed off. He didn't need to state the obvious. Jimmy knew he'd never last long on his own. It had only been a day and he was already feeling desperate. If these men hadn't come along, he wasn't sure what he'd have done.

"I'll come."

Rowan stood. "Great. Then we need to go." He looked at the pack on the ground. "That all you have? Nothing more inside?" He gestured toward the makeshift shelter.

"That's it."

Jimmy stood and walked toward where he'd left his homemade pack. As he reached down to pick it up, he heard a strange whistle and felt, more than saw, the men tense. He straightened up and looked around fearfully. Rowan sent an answering call and soon the six men who had earlier left came into the clearing. One went directly to Rowan and spoke softly to him. Rowan nodded, then looked at his men.

"Let's go. Stay alert. We're not alone out here. Put Jimmy in the middle somewhere."

The men arranged themselves into some predetermined formation. One gestured to Jimmy who moved to where he was directed. The group moved out of the clearing. Jimmy noted their movement couldn't be described as stealthy, but they also weren't what he would call relaxed. Without being consciously aware he was doing it, he matched their pace and mannerisms as the wilderness absorbed them.

It took a while for Jimmy to realize he still knew nothing about Rowan and these men. They'd denied the settlement incident, but that didn't mean they weren't part of that group. Had he willingly surrendered his freedom back to those who would not be concerned about his welfare? He shook his head, letting go those thoughts. They'd given him sustenance. Rowan had been kind. Understanding. But they were obviously military. Their clothes, bearing, weapons all reinforced that conclusion. Yet, Jimmy knew the formal military and been disbanded. So then, who were these men? He was so absorbed in his thoughts he didn't realize the men had stopped as a unit. His next step sent him right into the back of the man in front of him. Luckily for both, neither fell.

"Sorry," Jimmy murmured softly as he stepped back and regained his balance. The man didn't reply.

Jimmy looked around, wondering why they'd stopped. The next thing he knew he was thrown roughly to the ground and gunshots erupted around them. He heard someone grunt as the men shifted positions and returned fire. Jimmy was told to stay put. He didn't need to be told twice. With his arms over his head, he shoved his face into the dirt and said a silent prayer.

The chaos ended as abruptly as it began.

"Status!" Rowan called out.

As the men checked in, Jimmy stayed still and silent. Finally, he heard his name. When he didn't answer, it was repeated with more urgency. Jimmy slowly rolled over onto his back and propped himself up on one elbow.

"I'm here. I'm OK."

He looked around and saw one man attending to another whose pant-leg displayed a lot of blood.

"Is he going to be all right?" Jimmy asked.

"Fine, kid. You sure you're good?"

"Yes. What happened?"

"Just a roaming band of troublemakers. They won't be causing any more trouble."

Jimmy had a good idea what that meant and chose not to look around the area to confirm it. Instead, he looked towards Rowan and realized the man was staring at him. He straightened his shoulders and returned the look without flinching. Rowan acknowledged him with a quick nod then addressed his men.

"Let's go. Not much further. Shouldn't be any more of these around, but don't let your guard down."

Jimmy watched the men regroup. Several had extra weapons strung across their shoulders. Jimmy assumed they once belonged to those who no longer needed them. As they assembled, it seemed like the men ignored their commander's comment. As if they couldn't be bothered responding to an obvious statement. Within seconds they were pulling Jimmy into their midst and continuing their trek. Business as usual was the vibe Jimmy got.

He had no idea of the time, but judging by the position of the sun, Jimmy thought it mid-to-late afternoon. He was trying to guestimate how far they'd traveled when the group slowed and stopped. This time, Jimmy avoided colliding with anyone.

Rowan walked back to Jimmy.

"We're almost at our camp. It's just over that small rise. When we enter, keep your eyes down and your mouth shut. We'll escort you to the med tent where you'll be checked out and assessed for treatment."

"Am I a prisoner?"

Rowan chuckled. "No. Of course not. But until I can relay the situation to everyone, you'll be looked at with suspicion. Don't worry. You'll be safe. No one will harm you."

Jimmy opened his mouth to respond, then closed it and simply nodded his ascent.

"Good."

Rowan walked back to the front and gestured for his men to follow.

Jimmy studiously followed Rowan's instructions as they entered through a checkpoint. Even so, he had the impression of a very large contingent of people. He heard noises that reinforced his impression.

People, equipment, motion all around. He wanted to look but focused on the ground in front of him.

He was soon standing in front of a structure that looked more like a building than a tent.

"Go on. The people inside will assist you. I'll come back after I've seen to my men and checked in."

Jimmy pushed at the door and stepped inside. It surprised him how bright, clean, and welcoming the room was. Four people were inside, all wearing white clinical coats over their standard uniform. Jimmy had a fleeting thought that the coats seemed redundant, then realized they immediately depicted medical staff status.

He next noticed a couple of people on cots with IVs attached to them. It looked very like the settlement environment he'd just escaped. The thought threw him into momentary panic. One of the medics looked up and saw Jimmy. He straightened from what he was doing and came forward, stopping several feet from Jimmy.

"Hi. Can I help you?"

"What is this place?"

"This is our best version of a clinic or hospital. However you prefer to think of it. Either way, the facilities are a little rustic, but," he looked around, "adequate for our immediate needs. What's your name? Why are you here?"

"I'm Jimmy. Rowan left me here. Said he'd come back."

This response had everyone's attention. Four pairs of eyes studied Jimmy. An older man stepped forward.

"I'm Dr. Boise. I guess you could call me the bossman here." He ignored the snorts and quickly smothered laughs behind him. "Are you hurt? Do you need medical attention?"

"I—I—" Jimmy stuttered, not knowing quite what to say. He stepped back closer to the door.

At that precise moment the door opened, almost hitting Jimmy where he stood. Rowan walked in and Jimmy felt the atmosphere in the room immediately change.

"Gentlemen. I see you've met Jimmy. He's going to need some medical supervision. Dr. Boise. May I see you outside for a moment?"

Rowan turned to leave, then stopped and looked at Jimmy. "It's OK. Just have a seat over there and wait. Everything will get sorted."

He gestured vaguely towards some chairs against the wall. By this time the other three in the room had lost interest in the interruption and were focused on their own tasks. Jimmy walked over to the chairs and sat. He watched Rowan and Dr. Boise leave, and the door shut behind them.

The door opened and the man who'd been injured in the skirmish came in, limping slightly. He went straight to the group who immediately began attending to him.

Ten minutes later, Dr. Boise returned alone. He watched the medics and their actions for a few moments, assuring himself all was functioning well. Then he looked at Jimmy.

"Come. Let's take a walk."

19

Troy sat at his desk staring at the blank monitor in front of him. He thought about his conversation with Carson. He was afraid to explore any more of the system than he already had, yet a part of him desired to find out if what Carson had asked of him could be accomplished. Both the cryptocurrency and finding out about Jimmy.

But he didn't know where to start. And despite David's assurances that no one cared what they were doing, he still feared triggering some alarm somewhere that would bring down on him all kinds of unhealthy consequences.

He glanced at the still unfinished reports on his desk. Sighing, he decided he should finish the only assignment they'd been given before initiating anything else. He picked up the top one and flipped it open.

He was three pages in before he realized the title did not correspond to what he was reading. He looked to see if there was any indication that the title page had been misapplied to the report, thinking things might have come apart somewhere along the line and then been carelessly reassembled. But everything looked intact. No signs of tears, second staples, or anything else.

"Weird," he said aloud to the empty room.

"What's weird?" David entered at that moment. Troy looked up and acknowledged his arrival. Then waved his report in the air.

"This. The title of the report says it has something to do with adverse effects of vaccines."

"What's weird about that?"

"The report is talking about designing a drug to increase Y-chromosome counts in male sperm."

David walked over to Troy's desk. "That is kind of weird. No mention of vaccines? You sure the correct cover is on the correct report?"

"No. I'm not sure. But I checked it out. There doesn't appear to be any indication it was newly attached or changed or tampered with."

"Interesting choice of word, tampered. Don't go all conspiracy theory on me. I'm sure there's an easy explanation. But, out of curiosity, is the report at all interesting? Or more of the same stuff we were reading before?"

Troy was quiet for a moment. "I'm only three pages in. Got distracted by the title versus content thing. But this seems tied to the other research project we were reading. The one talking about pesticides affecting male sperm counts. You still have that?"

"Yes. It's on my desk. Why?"

"Just curious to see if these two research reports involve any of the same people."

"Why would that matter?"

"I don't know that it does. But if the larger topic is male sperm, and it's the same people, why not just combine the research and report on everything at once?"

"Maybe different funding streams?"

Troy looked at David. "What do you mean?"

"The government gives out multiple research grants. They don't all come from the same sector."

"I suppose you're right, but with all the emphasis on efficiency, you'd think the process would have been consolidated by now. After all, it's been a couple of years since the Leader took office."

David chuckled. "Haven't you learned anything, yet? If there's no profit motive in it for the billionaires, the urgency to fix it falls way down the list of things to address." David gestured quotation marks in the air when he said the words 'fix it'.

"You're so cynical."

"I'm so realistic. But that aside, let's check out your thoughts."

David went to his desk and retrieved the report in question. Walking back to Troy, he pulled up a chair and sat. For the next twenty minutes they compared authors, named researchers, funding sources, hypotheses, and anything else that made sense for them to look at.

"We must be missing something," Troy murmured.

"Not sure what. Different people, different sectors supporting the work, different topics. Stop looking to slay dragons where none exist to slay."

"Maybe."

"C'mon, Troy. You're really over the top now. What's set you off? Girlfriend won't give you any?"

Troy blushed and muttered a curse. "Don't be crude."

David laughed. "Let it go, Troy. Your imagination is out of control. Finish reading the report and move on to the next one. How many more of these things do we still need to get through?"

"Probably about a dozen. But what happens when we finish with them?"

David shrugged his shoulders. "We send them on to the next schmucks who will waste time reading them. At some point someone will make decisions and none of it will have anything to do with what we think or recommend."

"Yeah, you're probably right. What say we read until lunch, then afterwards, see what mischief we can get into with the system."

Looking down at the report on his desk, Troy missed the look David threw his way.

"Sounds like a plan."

David stood and went back to his desk. For the next two hours both read in silence. As if synchronized, they both looked up at the same time and glanced in the other's direction.

"Lunch?" David asked.

"Lunch." Troy responded.

~

David entered their room and stopped so quickly Troy crashed into him.

"Oomph. Use your signal." Troy muttered as he righted himself. "What's the matter?"

"Someone's been here."

David took a step forward and Troy entered the room proper. He looked over David's shoulder.

"Holy crap!"

Both surveyed the chaos. Desk drawers had been pulled out. Chairs shoved away from desks. Computer monitors tipped over. And this was in the section of the room the two didn't use. Almost as one they looked to their corner. Neither said a word as they saw that their desks had been ransacked. It was immediately clear that the reports they'd been reading were gone. What was surprising was that their computers were untouched.

"Why leave our computers alone, but knock the other ones around?" Troy asked.

"Good question. A better question is why take reports that no one in this universe wants to read anyway?"

"Obviously someone does."

"Or maybe they just don't want us to read them."

"Or maybe both," Troy said.

They walked to their desks and looked at the empty spaces where slightly over an hour ago two dozen or so reports were stacked.

"I don't get it," Troy reached down and tapped his keyboard and saw the monitor light up and display the password screen.

"I don't, either." David also tapped his keyboard and got the same results.

"Should we report it?"

"Report it where, or to who?" He chuckled. "To whom, is the correct grammar."

Troy looked at him without commenting on what he figured was a joke.

"Mr. Darwin?"

"Darwin wouldn't care about this. Doubtful he's even aware of our existence here. Sure, he hired both of us, but only to please our fathers. As for the reports? I can guarantee he doesn't know about them, so he certainly wouldn't care if something he didn't know about no longer exists in a place he isn't aware of."

Troy stared at him. "You're kidding, right?"

"About which part?"

"Well, all of it. But mostly that he doesn't know we exist or that we're here in this department."

"Trust me. He doesn't."

"But he talked to me at a party I went to with my dad. Welcomed me. He seemed very nice."

"An act. He wouldn't know you in a line up. Darwin has one objective and one objective only. To stay on the Leader's good side. He doesn't want to happen to him what happened to others who didn't appear one hundred percent behind the man supposedly running our country."

Troy looked at him, confused. "What do you mean supposedly running our country? He's the Leader."

"In name only. Others control him."

"Control him? How?"

"The man is bought and paid for. He does what he's told when his funding is threatened. Sure, he projects strength. Well, he sort of does. You must admit he's seemed shaky recently. But aside from that, his public-facing side, what happens behind the scenes is very different. He's not calling the shots. No matter what the press and others say."

"How do you know all this? Are you just making things up?"

David was very serious as he spoke quietly. "No. I'm not making things up. Besides what my father tells me, I have other sources who have observed things. Actions and words that don't make it out of closed rooms."

"Well, if you know about it, the stuff must make it out of those rooms. How do you know you can trust what you're told? Maybe you're the one being manipulated. Not the rest of us."

David looked at Troy and just sighed. He opened his mouth to speak, then closed it. Troy waited, but David said nothing more. Instead, he looked back into the room.

"C'mon. Let's clean this mess up, then see if we can get back into the system. Maybe the reports are in there somewhere."

Troy followed David toward their corner. "Why do you care? Not so long ago you were complaining we even had to read them. Now you want to?"

David shrugged. "If someone wanted them bad enough to remove them from here, there must be something in one or more of them that same someone prefers not be seen. By anyone. Even lowlifes like us. I'm curious. Very curious."

"Whatever."

They spent the next twenty minutes straightening up their desks and verifying that all the reports were gone, not just some of them. They didn't bother with the part of the room they didn't use. They ignored the chaos and mess, focusing only on their small piece of the universe.

"Any of your personal items missing?" David asked.

"No. Well, I didn't have any personal items here to be taken." He looked up. "Did you?"

"Just a picture of my dad and me on a fishing trip we did when I was very young. I always liked it."

"And it's gone?"

"Yes."

"Not just tipped over or on the floor?"

"It's gone, Troy."

Troy grunted. "Odd. Who'd want it, other than you?"

"I don't know."

Something in David's tone made Troy look at him, but David was bent over going through a lower file drawer and didn't see the look. Troy watched him for a few moments, then went back to his own tasks. David's voice interrupted him.

"Ready to attack the system?"

"Attack seems a bit extreme, but yes, let's try."

Troy walked to David's desk. It seemed more efficient to him to work together off one computer. He watched as David typed in the password he'd set up for himself. Nothing happened. David tried again with the same result.

"Huh." David muttered.

"You sure you're typing it in correctly?"

David didn't respond, other than to throw an exasperated look Troy's way. He tried again.

"Let's try yours." David began typing what he'd given Troy the other day.

"Stop. I changed it."

"Changed it? Why'd you do that?"

"Seemed the smart thing to do."

"What's your new one?"

Troy hesitated. Without speaking, David pushed away from his desk and gestured toward his keyboard.

"Try it."

Troy scooted up to the desk and quickly typed in his password. Both were surprised when the screen accepted it and the menu they were used to seeing popped up. Troy tossed a triumphant look at David who childishly stuck his tongue out.

Troy started to get up, but David told him to stay. Since he was able to get in, he should do the honors.

"Where do you want to start?" Troy asked.

David thought for a moment, then pointed to one of the menu options.

"Really?" Troy asked.

"Why not? It's the sector that funded the last report you had. If we can't find anything there, we'll look in the health and environmental sectors."

Troy shrugged and clicked on the link. The screen that came up was unlike any of the others they'd explored. They exchanged a puzzled look. Together they read their new options. After a brief discussion, Troy clicked their choice.

Neither were prepared for what happened next.

20

Carson waited impatiently for his contact to show. The meeting was in a place different from the warehouse they'd been using. This one was more difficult to get to, which made it both safer and more dangerous. Safer because it was farther from populated areas. Dangerous, because if they'd been tracked or followed, there'd be no witnesses to whatever might happen. Carson pushed those thoughts out of his head. Whatever happened, happened. Today's world was so topsy-turvy, the definitions of right and wrong changing almost hourly, that one could literally go insane if they dwelled too deeply on the topic.

He shifted positions. It was chillier today than the last few days and, although he'd pulled on a jacket, he realized he should have chosen a heavier one. He heard footsteps and stilled. Carefully he slid further into the shadows and waited.

"Are you here?"

The voice was a loud whisper, but what caught Carson's attention the most was that it didn't belong to his contact. He was sure this person was female. He stayed silent.

"Carson! Are you here? Please, show yourself if you are."

The voice was insistent, and Carson now thought he recognized it. He moved slightly to confirm his guess.

"Shannon! What are you doing here? Quick, move over here, out of sight."

Carson looked Shannon up and down, not sure what he was looking for, but somehow convinced he'd know it if he saw it.

"Why are you here?" he whispered fiercely.

"I was sent."

Not a response Carson remotely expected, he stepped back in surprise. "What do you mean?"

"I was told to meet you here and get whatever information you had to share."

"Who told you?"

"No names. But you know who I mean." Shannon gave a brief description which matched Carson's usual contact.

"You're working with him? For how long?"

"Carson, we don't have time for this now. The person in question is involved in something bigger than us. But he still needs whatever information you have."

Her words distracted Carson. "Bigger? What's he involved in? Do you know, or are you just repeating something he said to you?"

"Carson," Shannon drew a breath, but Carson cut her off before she could continue.

"No. Tell me what you know. I'm not sharing anything until you do." He folded his arms across his chest and stood resolute.

They stood in silence staring each other down. Finally, Shannon dropped her shoulders and began speaking.

"I've been involved since shortly after the election. There's—"

"So you've known about me all along?"

"No. Really, I haven't. I only found out a few days ago. I didn't know that day we talked on your steps. I swear."

As he tried to pull that memory from his head, and not completely sure he believed her, Carson gestured for her to go on.

"I'm not sure how much you know, or how much I can share. The whole operation is kept safer by compartmentalizing information. You know that."

While he personally didn't believe that was the smartest approach, at Carson's nod, Shannon continued.

"I'm tied into the women's rights piece of it." She smiled. "Makes sense, correct? But while most people focus on the obvious," she gave a quick shake of her head, "abortion, healthcare, and even keeping our ability to independently vote, I work with those being marginalized because of race, social status, and," she hesitated, "other life decisions."

"Why separate issues? Women in general are being marginalized. Pushed into the background as if they're not even considered part of humanity. Just property to be used and discarded when the owner becomes bored. Their primary function to remain quiet and be breeders."

"That's harsh, but I agree with you. However, it's almost impossible to address everything at once. Maybe years ago, or even a couple of years ago, the bigger picture could be pushed as the agenda. But not since the new Leader. Society has fractured into so many little cult-like groups and beliefs that choosing specifics and tailoring the approaches works better. Shannon shrugged. "Or at least it seems to."

Carson didn't speak. Just waited. Shannon sighed.

"Look, right now, all this isn't the point. What our mutual friend is involved in is more important."

"And what is that?"

Shannon looked defeated. "I honestly don't know." At Carson's look, she repeated herself. "No really, I don't know."

"He asked me to find out about cryptocurrency. You think it has something to do with that?"

Shannon shrugged. "But tell me what you know, and I'll pass it along."

"I don't know much." Carson updated her with the information he had. When he'd finished, she smiled.

"You're right. You don't know much. But no matter, I'll pass along what you've told me."

She turned to leave, then turned back. "Do you think it will happen? That the Leader and his followers will accomplish a switch to it as our only form of currency?"

"I don't know. And to be honest, I'm not sure what it would all mean if it happened. The Leader wants our country to set the standard for the world. But, based on history, I'm thinking all that's going to do is open the door for international criminals to control more than what they already control, and the billionaires who run this country aren't going to care, provided they make billions more off the transactions."

"That's pretty cynical."

"Have you seen anything in any of their behaviors to disprove it?"

"Unfortunately, not. But those who are already struggling are going to struggle more. There will be lots of unnecessary deaths due to the hardships suffered."

Carson's face hardened. "They don't care. If there are enough to do the menial tasks that need doing, in other words, everything that supports their lifestyle, a few of the excess being sloughed off won't matter to them in the least. A few of them have always said the world is overpopulated. To them, this is an easy way to unpopulate it without getting their hands dirty."

Both were quiet, lost in their own thoughts. Carson broke the silence.

"What exactly do you do on the women's side of things?" He was thinking of her younger sisters and an earlier comment about hoping things would work differently by the time they were grown.

"This and that. Whatever needs doing."

"Not much of an answer."

"Why do you want to know?"

"I thought maybe I could help, if you ever needed it."

Shannon gave him an intent look. "The women I help have often been abused. Usually by the men in their family. Sometimes by others. When we can, we work to provide passage to somewhere safe. Away from their situation. And there are those who need medical services. To correct a situation, if you understand my meaning."

Carson was uncertain he did. "You mean abor—"

"I mean appropriate health care for the situation they're in. Leave it at that. It's a bigger picture than what you're thinking."

Carson knew he was being scolded, as well as slightly insulted. He let it go, because he was curious about something else.

"There have always been women who are, or have been, abused. What makes things so different now?"

Shannon took a deep breath, then let it out. Carson could tell she was unsure about answering him honestly. Then her expression hardened slightly.

"Yes, women found themselves in abusive situations in the past. But back then, it seemed society found such situations worth speaking out about. Doing something about. Sure, there were always those who either didn't care or thought it was the woman's fault or figured it was private between the woman and her mate. Mostly, those attitudes were confined to a certain group of people who stuck together. Now, those same people have political power they never had. Instead of using it for the betterment of all women, they use it to further relegate women to the shadows and to untold miseries. I don't understand it. But I mean to do anything I can to fight it."

"I really do want to help, if I can."

"The work is dangerous. If we're caught transporting someone away from their established residence, the penalties are steep. Just last week one of our couriers was caught. No one has heard from her since. We think she was incarcerated, or at the very least, transported to one of the settlements no one wants to talk about. But we don't know. We're hoping she's still alive."

Her comment caused Carson to think of Jimmy, and a stab of grief hit him hard.

"I'll still help, if I can."

"Think of your family. You'll put them at risk."

"What I'm doing now already puts them at risk."

They shared a long look. Neither said anything. Finally, Shannon nodded. "I'll contact you, if we need you."

She began walking back the way she came. Then she slowed and looked over her shoulder.

"Thanks," she called out softly.

21

Jimmy and Dr. Boise walked along a path that, while not taking them directly through camp, it gave Jimmy a good sense of how large the area was.

"What is this place? Why are you all here?"

"I'll let Rowan explain all that to you. Let's talk about you."

Dr. Boise proceeded to ask several questions. Jimmy felt like he was being interrogated, yet at the same time, there was an obvious caring attitude coming from the man. Caring, but clinical. Jimmy realized he was experiencing the equivalent of an office visit with a new physician. It was just happening as part of a walking tour instead of him sitting on an exam table in a small room.

After fifteen minutes, Dr. Boise stopped walking, forcing Jimmy to also stop. He looked at Jimmy with both kindness and some uncertainty.

"This is not my specialty. And I will happily admit you'd be my first patient. But if you're willing, if you trust me, I will oversee your therapies."

Jimmy hesitantly nodded, and Dr. Boise nodded in return.

"C'mon, then. Let's get back to the med tent. I need to take the usual vitals and create a baseline record, so we have a starting point to work from."

They turned in unison and began walking back the way they came. The atmosphere between them had changed. Jimmy felt it, and with it, experienced his first relief since being taken to the settlement in what seemed years ago.

The tent was empty when they arrived. Even the patients were gone.

"Where is everyone?" Jimmy asked, a trace of fear in his voice.

Dr. Boise smiled. "No need to worry. I'm sure the medics are just getting something to eat. As for those that were being treated earlier, they've been released, subject to necessary monitoring." He gestured to a cot. "Here, have a seat. Let's get started."

The next hour was spent gathering additional history and clinical information. Jimmy was hesitant about turning over his stash of pills, but Dr. Boise assured him they'd be kept safe and in a better-controlled environment than the current bags-in-his-pack scenario. When Jimmy surrendered them, Dr. Boise read the labels. He turned away and shook a few into a small prescription bottle and handed them back to Jimmy with instructions. Just as things were winding down to their natural conclusion, Rowan appeared in the doorway. He exchanged a quick look with the doctor before addressing Jimmy.

"You ready to see where you'll bunk? Also, I expect you're hungry. I'll show you where the dining tent is."

Jimmy stood and started toward the man. He hesitated just long enough to turn back to the doctor and thank him.

"Monitor yourself. Let me know if you're experiencing anything we talked about."

Jimmy nodded and continued to Rowan, who stepped aside and let him exit first. As they walked along a well-worn path, Jimmy looked around with interest. Rowan remained quiet, observing his reactions. Finally, Jimmy spoke.

"When are you going to take over?"

"Excuse me?"

Jimmy hesitated. "Well, you must be amassing all this fire power for a reason. The Leader disbanded the formal military, creating the enforcement squads in its place. I just assumed you were planning to reassert yourselves."

"If you're suggesting we're bent on insurrection and installing martial law, you can forget about that."

"Then why—"

Rowan interrupted. "We remain ready and willing to serve when called upon. We took an oath to the Constitution. And even if much of that document, as we knew it, has been suspended, we honor our oath. We're not here to take over anything. We're here to serve and protect our country."

"But—"

"The legal authority of the enforcement squads is questionable. I'll grant you that. But they're also domestic. The military's mission is not domestic. At least not in the sense of what would be considered police power. Having said that, if we come across a squad who is blatantly abusing the people or what we consider to be just wrong, we deal with it."

Jimmy wanted to ask what dealing with it meant but decided he didn't want confirmation of what he suspected. He had a brief memory flash of the attack in the woods. Instead, he asked a different question.

"Is the current leadership aware of your existence?"

Rowan smiled. "Perhaps. But the billionaires prefer to ignore us since we haven't posed a threat to them, and we purchase things made by them. The Leader is kept distracted by other things."

Again, Jimmy wanted to ask what those other things were but thought he might be better off not knowing.

"So you just sit here? Waiting? And how do you have funds to purchase anything?"

"We train. We patrol. We stay prepared. Should a threat arise that would normally be handled by the military, we'll answer the call. As to the source of our funding, we have friends. Let's leave it at that, okay?"

Jimmy nodded hesitantly, then focused on what caught his attention. "When you say threat, you mean a threat by a foreign power?" When Rowan remained quiet, Jimmy continued, "What if no one calls?"

"There's no predicting the future. But there is an ability to prepare for whatever might happen."

Jimmy looked at him. "You think something's going to happen, don't you? And the military usually has a top commander of some sort, right? If you aren't reporting to the Leader, who are you reporting to?"

"You ask a lot of questions, Jimmy. You may want to curb your curiosity. Some might not be as tolerant of it as I am."

Jimmy wasn't sure if Rowan's words contained a warning or a threat. But he heard the message loud and clear. Before he could comment, Rowan slowed, then stopped.

"Here's where you'll sleep. Sorry we can't give you solo accommodations, but this tent only sleeps four. It's the best we can do. Your tent mates should be accepting. I'll bring you back here after I take you to the dining tent for some food. Come on."

Rowan shifted to a different path, picking up his speed. Part of Jimmy realized he was walking faster to keep conversation to a minimum. Another part of him wondered if Rowan just wanted to be done with him. He felt guilty for all his questions.

They reached their destination five minutes later. Rowan pushed the door open and stepped in to a loud, cheerful environment. Jimmy followed and looked around with a mix of apprehension, confusion, and relief. He didn't know which emotion was the strongest.

"Sir! Over here!" shouted a voice.

Rowan looked in the direction of the shout and smiled. Jimmy also looked and felt his own face relax into a smile. The call had come from one of the men in the group who'd escorted Jimmy to the camp. They walked to the group who shifted around making room for them.

Jimmy felt the stares of others as he crossed the room but kept his attention on his destination. Time enough later to confront the curiosity of others. He clung to the familiarity of the group he already knew. His mind registered that he was the only one not in some sort of military dress. He figured that fact alone would create curiosity.

He sat next to the man who'd been beside him on their trek in. Uncertain of his accuracy, he hesitantly said the man's name.

"Yup, you got it. Winthrop. Pretentious, isn't it? I think there's a third or fourth that's supposed to follow it, but the family dropped that nonsense a while back. That's why I forget which. I suppose if I were curious enough, I could figure it out."

Jimmy smiled, not knowing what to make of the speech. Winthrop didn't notice. He continued, "I understand we're going to be tent mates. You cool with that?"

Jimmy nodded, relieved. "Who else?"

Winthrop pointed out two of the other men in the group, then leaned closer and lowered his voice. "Watch your back on Bruno. Not sure of his views around your situation, if you get my drift."

Jimmy did and felt his relief dissolve. Before he could fully process his reactions, Winthrop's voice broke into his thoughts.

"C'mon, eat up. I'll take you back to our tent when you're finished. Give you a bit of a tour on the way."

As Jimmy picked up his fork to attack the plate of food in front of him, he glanced up to see Rowan watching him. He couldn't interpret the look on the man's face.

22

Troy and David looked at each in panic. David recovered first. He looked at the flashing screen, then pointed to an option and told Troy to click it. Troy did, dreading what might happen.

Surprisingly, the screen stopped flashing and displayed a new set of options.

"What do you think that was all about?" Troy asked.

"No idea. Maybe just a power surge or something."

Troy didn't bother to comment. He knew David didn't believe what he'd said any more than Troy himself did. He read the options, then hovered over one of them. Before he clicked, he looked at David.

"You really think we should keep going? You don't think the flashing screen was some type of alarm system?"

David shrugged. "Probably was. But who's going to notice? The IT staff was cut to one or two bodies."

"That you know of. There may be a completely different sector doing the work. One not obvious to the usual scrutiny."

"You mean like a shadow agency or something? You read too many spy novels."

Both laughed at that, knowing that the ability to read anything these days was severely curbed. One either already owned the books, having kept them from one of the many purges, or the options were limited to what were essentially equivalent to the old *Dick and Jane* series of children's stories.

"Go ahead. Hit the option. Let's see what happens."

Troy did as instructed. The screen changed. They leaned forward and read with interest the list that appeared.

"Wow. This looks like the list of reports. Who'd have ever guessed?" David's voice reflected his surprise.

Troy wasn't listening. He was scanning the list, looking for the last two reports they'd read. When he found them, he looked at David.

"You think we can print them?"

David stood and rushed to the only printer in the room. He checked the paper supply and turned the machine on, hoping it worked, had ink or toner or whatever made the words come out on the paper, and that the thing was magically connected to the computer.

"Try it."

Troy selected an item and entered the command. Both waited. The silence stretched. Just about the time they were giving up on the idea, the printer labored into life and began spewing out pages. David collected them and tapped them into a neat pile.

"Do another one!"

Troy did. The machine continued to spit out pages. As David busied himself with the emerging pages, Troy continued to scan the list. One title caught his eye. He knew he hadn't read the report, and he wasn't sure it had been in his pile or David's. He set it to print and kept scrolling the screen.

"There seems to be a lot more reports here than what we were given."

David was only half-listening. "Anything look interesting?"

"A couple. I've put them to print." A short pause, then, "There used to be a way you could download stuff onto an external device. You remember? With all the advances in technology, it seems like those types of options are limited. Everything goes into the cloud these days."

David left the printer and returned to Troy. "I remember. Flash drives or something like that, I think they were called. Only the really old machines have that ability now. But hey. This doesn't look like the latest and greatest. Let's see if there's something."

They both studied the device. Troy saw it first. An opening on the back.

"There! I think that's the slot."

"Great. Now we just need to find something to put in it."

Troy began opening the desk drawers and ruffling through the contents. David went over to Troy's desk and did the same. Without speaking, they both moved to the other desks in the room. Unsuccessful, they stopped and surveyed the room.

"Let's try those cabinets over there." David pointed.

"You ever look in them?"

"Nah. No reason to."

"Not even out of curiosity?"

David shook his head. They moved as one to the cabinets. Each chose a different one and opened the doors. Inside was a treasure trove of unused office supplies. Pens, pencils, note pads, file folders, and other items considered indispensable when the place had been humming with people. They looked at each other and grinned.

"Bet some of this stuff would command a pretty penny on the black market," David murmured more to himself than Troy. Troy glanced at him but said nothing. He wondered at David's knowledge of black markets, but decided this was not the time to pursue that topic.

Troy spotted a box on the bottom shelf of his cabinet. He reached in and pulled it out. Opening it, he whistled his surprise.

"Check this out. They must have bought in bulk back when."

David looked at Troy's find. It wasn't a large box, and it looked like it had been repurposed from something else. But inside it was a jumble of multi-colored flash drives. Troy reached in and pulled out a handful. He read the writing on the side as he tossed them back into the box.

"It looks like these are all different sizes."

"What do you mean? They all look the same to me. Just different colors."

Troy laughed, almost choking on his amusement. "Not size, size. Dummy. Content size. Each one has a different capacity for storing data." He paused, then continued in a thoughtful voice. "I wonder if there's anything on them or if they're all blank."

"Only one way to find out. You know how to do it? I must admit, I was never much into computers. Didn't take any of the offered classes in school. Thought they all looked boring." He smiled. "Or too hard. I just talked into my phone and let it do the heavy lifting."

Troy smirked. He wasn't surprised at David's lack of interest. He would have been the same way if his father hadn't forced him to take the classes and learn the stuff. Troy couldn't even count the times his father had emphasized that technology was the future and those who didn't conquer it would be left behind. Now he was grateful for that continued push. But he was more grateful that his teachers had thought the history of technology was just as important as the future of it. Not all his classmates had agreed. Today, he felt that training just might be the most important knowledge he could call on.

He picked up the box, tucked it under his arm, and walked back over to the computer, glad to see the screen he'd left still displaying. Settling himself in the chair, he pulled the keyboard close.

"Let's see what we've got. But before I do anything, I want to print a couple more of these reports. Is there enough paper in the printer?"

David nodded. "The drawer was full. You should be good, assuming it isn't hundreds of pages."

Troy chose the reports he wanted, entered the command, then looked into the box of flash drives. He chose one that had a large storage capacity and plugged it into the back of the machine.

Nothing happened.

David grunted. "Rather anticlimactic, don't you think?"

Troy was staring at the screen and didn't bother to answer. He knew he had to find the computer's directory to see if the drive had registered. Finding what he was seeking, he clicked on it and waited. He was happy to note that the other screen minimized, but didn't completely disappear when the new screen displayed.

He saw the external drive listed and chose it. A new screen opened that showed two small-sized files but nothing else.

"This one's empty. Let's see if we can put some of the reports on it."

"How do you know it's empty? Jeez! Were you hiding the fact that you're some kind of computer wizard?"

Troy laughed. "You really don't know anything about computers, do you? How'd you even think you could hack into the system in the first place?" He paused, "Come to think of it, once you did get in, you seemed pretty comfortable moving through administrative screens. Who's the one hiding talents?"

Troy missed the color that momentarily flooded David's face. He was too busy trying to figure out how to download the reports onto the flash drive. As the silence stretched, he cast a quick glance David's way.

"Beginner's luck," murmured David, leaving it at that. "You figure out how to get the reports on the disk?"

Troy was too engaged in what he was doing to fully comprehend David's answer or distracting question.

"Yes. I'm doing it as we speak. But I don't know how helpful it will be. This may be the only computer that will allow us to use the drive. Pretty sure mine at home isn't set up for this. What about yours?"

"Nah." David didn't expand on his answer, leaving Troy to wonder if David meant that his computer wouldn't accept the drive, or that he didn't even have a computer. Troy decided it wasn't worth pursuing. But a part of him registered that David's whole demeanor and reactions had been a little off throughout this process.

It took almost an hour to put everything on the flash drive. Troy was a bit surprised it all fit on the one but then remembered the high capacity designation. When the last report finished, Troy suggested they make a copy of the drive.

"Makes sense," David agreed.

Troy set about taking care of the task and while the files were transferring, he asked David if they should set up new access for him.

"Try it. Use a different name to set up the account."

Troy was going to ask why, but David interrupted him before he could speak the words.

"Just in case my name is flagged or something."

"Why would it be flagged, particularly if mine wasn't?"

David didn't answer. Instead, he gestured with his hands toward the computer as if to emphasize a 'just do it' command. Troy shrugged and began looking for the screens that David had accessed the other day. Once he found them he turned to his companion.

"Any requests?"

"Chase Emerson."

Troy didn't bother commenting or asking why that particular name. He just typed it in where he was supposed to and asked David for additional information to complete the account setup. When it came time to create a password, he pushed aside and motioned for David to type one in.

Without speaking David leaned in and typed something into the appropriate box. When it appeared everything had gone through without a hiccup, they both relaxed.

"We've been in the system for quite a while. Think we should call it a day, or is there something else you want to check out?" Troy asked.

David hesitated. Then indicated for Troy to sign out, which he did. Troy glanced at the clock on the wall, noting their workday was almost finished.

"You want to take some of these reports to read?"

"Nah, you take them. Even if you don't read them all before you come in tomorrow," he smiled, "it might be better to not leave them here in the office considering what happened."

"Agreed. What about these drives? You think we should each take one for safekeeping?"

"Sure."

David held out his hand and Troy dropped one of the flash drives into it. He put the other one in his pocket. Then he walked over to the printer and stacked all the reports into one big pile.

"This is kind of big. I think I need something to put them in. Walking around with a few inches of paperwork probably isn't a thing these days."

David smiled. "I saw a briefcase or something in my cabinet. Hang on. I'll get it."

He hurried over to the cabinets. After a few seconds he pulled out a portfolio-type case. He held it out to Troy.

Troy looked at it with some misgivings. "It looks brand new. You think someone will notice it's missing?"

David gave him a don't-be-stupid look and told him to put the papers in it. Troy half-grinned as he did so, correctly interpreting David's look.

David glanced at the clock and told Troy to go ahead and leave. He would tidy things up and follow him out shortly. Troy was about to protest, then shrugged his shoulders, picked up the filled case, and walked towards the door.

"See you tomorrow," he called over his shoulder as he left the room.

David waited a few seconds, making sure Troy wasn't coming back. Then he quickly hid his flash drive in a corner of Troy's bottom desk drawer, covering it with some miscellaneous papers and folders.

As he left the room, he flicked off the lights.

23

Carson walked through the streets of his neighborhood, more for something to do than for any other purpose. He felt at a loose end. It had been a week since he'd last connected with anyone involved in the uprising of the common people. At least, that's what he called it in his head. He was unsure if there was a formal name for the various groups that labored in the shadows to combat the effects the new leadership created with their policies and so-called efficiency edicts.

Sometimes it was hard to quantify the results of the last election. He didn't question it had been a fair and open process. But he knew the reasoning behind many of the votes was flawed. More hopeful than analytical. And that hopefulness had morphed into a cult-like mindset that fed itself a continual loop of fantasy. The realities that had emerged over these past two years came as a shock to many who'd voted for the new Leader. For others, they were so far into their own wishful thinking world, they simply refused to see or admit to the realities they were experiencing.

Carson didn't understand how someone, now unemployed due to economic shifts, could literally be starving in their own homes, yet think the cause, or blame if you will, should be placed anywhere but at the

Leader's feet. Yet those very same people were some of the most skilled when it came to bartering and manipulating the various alternative markets that had sprung up. Carson wondered if that had always been their world, and that's why they excelled at it, while everyone else was playing catch-up. He only knew that he'd had to learn the ins and out quickly to help feed his family. He was still learning, but felt he'd mastered some, even if minor, aspects.

He kicked a rock out of his path and looked around him to confirm a general normalcy to the neighborhood. Nothing caught his attention as being outside expectations. He let his thoughts continue. It wasn't long before he was thinking of Jimmy. He missed him. He still couldn't understand Troy's seemingly callous dismissal of the whole situation. The three of them had been close friends in high school. While that closeness had lessened somewhat as the years passed, Carson still considered them good friends. He had fully accepted Jimmy's choice and honestly could only think of him as Jimmy.

Carson slowed his pace. Maybe that was part of it. Troy had known Jimmy before he'd become Jimmy. Carson had met him after the fact, making it easier to accept him at face value. He wondered if Troy had even tried to find out what happened to their friend. He wondered if there was any way he could find out something on his own, then immediately rejected the idea. Inquiries such as those would paint a target on him, and he already risked enough with his current activities. The thought depressed him and created a strong sense of guilt.

He turned the corner and saw a disturbance ahead of him. Two members of an enforcement squad were dragging a protesting old man towards a vehicle. Carson stopped, a desire to help warring with a need to remain uninvolved. He watched in horror as the man was struck on the head with a club and went limp. The two squad members shoved the man into the back seat of the vehicle and closed the door. Carson thought he heard laughter as they climbed into the front and with a screeching of tires pulled away from the sidewalk.

Time stood still for Carson as he processed what he'd just witnessed. He didn't know the man personally but recognized him from the neighborhood. Uncertain of the man's ethnicity, he just knew the man wasn't white. And that realization made Carson understand what he'd seen.

His thoughts were interrupted by someone bumping him from behind and a voice saying, "Leave it. Nothing you can do."

He turned to see Shannon staring at him intently.

"You saw what happened?"

"Yes. It happens frequently. Part of the promise to rid the country of illegals."

"But—"

Shannon smiled sadly. "Yes. I know. He's been in the neighborhood for ages. I know his daughter. She's a couple of years younger than me. I've been to their house many times. Have had dinner with the family. I happen to know they immigrated legally. The two youngest were born here."

"How can they just take him? Isn't there some process they have to follow?"

"There's supposed to be, but who's going to challenge them? Good way to also get hauled off."

"What will happen to him? How will his family know?"

Shannon rubbed a hand across her face. Carson wasn't certain whether that was to wipe tears away or something else. Her voice was soft as she spoke.

"I'll go tell the family. Doubtful they'll be able to do anything. They'll be too scared. Which is the whole point, I suppose. But they're going to have to leave the neighborhood. It won't be long before the squad comes back for them."

"But how can they do that? If the family is here legally, how can they just take them? That's got to be against some law!" Carson was outraged and his tone conveyed it.

"Laws have always been a matter of interpretation. More so in today's environment. Even in the past, the laws heavily favored whites over people of color. Why do you think prison populations are such a percentage of non-whites? You think whites don't commit crimes? Of course they do, but often they avoid jail time. Resources for better lawyers, biased system, whatever. It is what it is."

Carson didn't want to debate the topic. A part of him acknowledged the truth of Shannon's statements but he instinctively fought acceptance of such an outlook. His faith in a system based on equality before the law was deeply imbedded in his psychology. He returned to his original question.

"What will happen to him?"

"Presumably he'll be sent to some detention center somewhere and await deportation."

"Deportation to where? And are you talking one of the settlements?"

"Call them what you will. He'll be lucky if he survives. His age. The injury he just sustained. Odds are stacked against him." Shannon looked at him. "Want to come with me to tell the family? Maybe help them prepare?"

"Prepare?"

"To go into hiding. It's their only choice at this point."

Carson stood, indecisive. He was still trying to wrap his mind around everything Shannon had said. Without giving him a choice, Shannon grabbed his forearm and tugged.

"C'mon. Let's go."

Her tug was enough to move him forward and Carson found himself walking beside her back the way he'd come. It wasn't long before they arrived at the man's house and Shannon knocked at the door, calling softly to the occupants inside.

The door opened a crack, and dark eyes peered out. When they recognized Shannon, the door was opened wider, and they were welcomed inside. Shannon introduced Carson as they were ushered to a well-used table near the kitchen. Carson looked around with interest, noting items of cultural art on the wall. But other than that, the place didn't look much different from his own home.

Shannon quickly explained the circumstances, but when she reached the part about the family going into hiding, she hit a wall. The wife refused and the oldest, the one Shannon's age, reinforced her mother's decision.

"But it isn't safe for you to stay. They'll be back. They'll take you all. Think of the little ones."

"The little ones are citizens by birth. We are citizens," the woman pointed to her daughter and herself, "because we fulfilled all the requirements and were sworn in three years ago, along with my husband."

"Things have changed since then," Shannon said. "and you know the new Leader has been trying to void the birth citizenship status."

"I know he is trying. But he hasn't succeeded. Too many fight him on this. We are not fleeing. We will search for my husband and bring him home."

"That could not turn out well for you. You must reconsider." Shannon's voice had an urgency that couldn't be ignored.

But the family did ignore it. "No. We are free citizens. We belong here. This is our country. What they have done is wrong. We will fight them on this."

As Shannon started to object, Carson touched her arm. When she glanced at him, he shook his head and said softly. "You won't change their minds." He looked at the woman. "I'm afraid I agree with Shannon. You should leave and remain safe. I doubt there's much we can really do, but if we can help, we will." Looking again at Shannon, "C'mon. Let's go and let them figure out their next moves."

He pulled her towards the door. She didn't want to just leave and was going to make one last attempt to convince the woman when the daughter spoke.

"Shannon. Thank you for coming and telling us. It's good we know what happened to Father. We will be okay. We will figure out what to do. Perhaps you shouldn't come here anymore. It might put you in danger." She glanced at Carson. "Thank you, also, for coming. And for your offer to help."

As she spoke, she'd hurried ahead of them to the door and carefully opened it, looking outside before pulling it wider for Carson and Shannon to leave. Carson wasn't quite sure, but he thought she'd gently pushed them out before closing the door firmly behind them. They walked down the steps and turned in the direction of Carson's home.

"I don't like it. They're not acting rationally," Shannon said angrily.

"They've made their decision."

"But they don't fully understand the consequences of it."

"I believe they do. As much as you'd like to, you can't save everyone. What happens next, happens. I was sincere. If I can help, I will. I'm sure you will, too. But right now, there's nothing more either of us can do. Let it go."

They continued down the sidewalk in silence.

24

Jimmy followed Winthrop out of the dining tent and along a path that was new to him. It led a little further away from the main encampment. At the end of it were two tents. Jimmy could easily tell these were the hygiene facilities. He slowed and stared at them.

"Maybe not the most luxurious accommodations, but they get the job done." Winthrop gestured to one. "Do your business there." Then the other. "Showers in that one."

"Showers? How?"

Winthrop chuckled. "Quite ingenious, actually. Not up to spa-like offerings, but they work. C'mon. I'll show you."

Winthrop led Jimmy to the tent, called out a singsong 'hoo-eee', and pulled the flap aside. "No actual door on this one. Not sure why. But you might want to call out a warning before entering. Give anyone inside notice."

Before Jimmy could ask why, his attention was diverted to three walled stations, all empty. Offering minimal privacy by way of a rigged curtain one could pull across the space, Jimmy could see a standard shower head and controls. The floor was a slatted wood square over a basin with a drain that directed water outside the tent.

"How do they work?"

Winthrop grinned. "Like any other shower. Hot and cold controls, although the hot really isn't hot. But it's warmer than the cold, at least."

"No. I mean where does the water come from."

"That's the ingenious part. We have a rather elaborate water catchment system. You'd have to ask the engineers for the specifics. Just know that they work. It's a godsend to even have them. But I must warn you. They have timers on them. Another one of those engineer things. The allotted time is short. Couple of minutes. Gotta be efficient."

"Good to know," Jimmy murmured, wondering how he was ever going to take a shower in this environment. "Are there specific times assigned? Or can anyone use them at any time?"

Winthrop looked at Jimmy questioningly. Then comprehension dawned in his expression. "Ah. I see. I'll talk to the Major about it."

"Major?"

"Rowan."

Momentarily distracted, Jimmy asked, "Should I be calling him Major? He introduced himself as Rowan."

"That's because you're a civilian. You should ask him what he prefers. But between you and me, I don't think he'd object to you addressing him as Major. Keeps the discipline consistent, and that's important in a place like this."

Jimmy absorbed that information, then came back to his more pressing issue. "The showers?"

"Something will get worked out. C'mon, let's get out of here." He stopped and looked at Jimmy. "You need to use the other tent?"

At Jimmy's head shake, they made their way back to their sleeping quarters.

"You've got the big stuff now. Med-tent, dining tent, facilities, sleep. I'd suggest you stay within that circle of boundaries. I wouldn't go wandering around. You understand?"

Jimmy didn't. Not completely. But he nodded as he knew Winthrop expected it.

Bruno and another man were in the tent when they entered. Jimmy recognized him as the one Winthrop had pointed out in the dining tent, but couldn't recall his name, or even if he'd ever been told it. The man stepped forward and held out his hand.

"Mike. Welcome."

Jimmy acknowledged the introduction, and Mike went back to his tasks. He looked at Bruno and nodded his head. Bruno returned the nod, but didn't speak. He sat on his cot with his back to Jimmy. Jimmy exchanged a quick glance with Winthrop, who shrugged his shoulders.

"We're off duty the rest of the night. Want to play cards or something? There's a couple of books over there, if you'd rather read." Winthrop gestured to a corner. Jimmy followed the movement with his eyes and saw a stack of books piled in the corner.

"If you don't mind, I'd rather read a bit?"

It was then that Jimmy realized there was a small bedside lamp on a nightstand by each cot. He glanced at Winthrop who grinned.

"Generators, and solar."

Jimmy wondered why he hadn't seen any of that on his walks. He decided not to ask. Just accept. He walked over to the corner and studied the available books. He'd read most of them. But he saw one he hadn't. It looked like a thriller or mystery. He didn't really care. He grabbed it and went back to his cot. Settling in, he opened it and began reading. Less than twenty minutes later he was fast asleep.

Something woke him. He stayed still with his eyes closed, listening. He realized harsh whispers was what had penetrated his sleep. Bruno was talking to Mike.

"Why do we have to share our tent with this insult?"

"Jimmy's all right. Give him a chance."

"That's just it. Jimmy's not a him. A name doesn't change things. Why pretend?"

"He's been through a lot. You heard his story on the trail. Leave him alone. His choice doesn't affect you."

"It does if I have to share my tent. As for what happened. Too bad they didn't finish the job."

Mike sat up on his cot. "You can't mean that."

"I do mean it. This I-can-choose-what-I-am nonsense is just that. Nonsense. God made two genders. Male and female. You're one or the other. That's it."

Jimmy felt the familiar anxiety begin. He forced himself to maintain normal breathing. He didn't want the men to know he was awake.

Mike stared at Bruno through the darkness. "You got a problem with women serving in the military?"

"Not now, since they no longer can. But yes, I did."

"Didn't realize you were such a bigot."

"I'm not. I just see reality for what it is."

Mike hesitated. When he replied, there was no mistaking his tone even in its whispered state.

"Jimmy is off limits. You hear? You do something? Anything happens to him, anything. I'll make it my business to ensure you regret it."

Silence followed Mike's speech. After what seemed like hours that stretched Jimmy's control to the maximum, Mike spoke again.

"You understand me, Bruno?"

Bruno acknowledged Mike with several soft curses, then abruptly stood and left the tent. Winthrop stirred. He called softly across the tent to Mike.

"Think we can trust him?"

"You heard all that?"

"Yes."

"So did I," Jimmy entered the conversation.

Mike swore. "I'm sorry Jimmy."

"It's OK. I'd rather know."

"Unfortunately, his views aren't isolated. There are others who think the same. Some more strongly. But they're in the minority. And the camp discipline will keep you safe."

"You're sure?" Jimmy didn't think Mike would deliberately lie to him, but he also thought that Bruno's attitude may be more prevalent amongst the troops than Mike believed. Having lived with it for so long, he knew the extent of the prejudice that existed.

Winthrop spoke, his voice no longer a whisper. "Perhaps we should ask the Major to make some adjustments to the tent assignments."

"Won't that just make it worse?" Jimmy asked.

"We'll figure it out in the morning. Go back to sleep. Sorry we woke you." Mike turned over in his cot and a few seconds later Winthrop did the same. Soon after, Jimmy heard their deep steady breathing.

Sleep didn't come to Jimmy quite as quickly.

Three weeks had passed since the whispered nighttime conversation. Bruno had voluntarily transferred to other sleeping quarters and his cot remained empty. The three remaining tent mates soon formed an alliance others recognized and respected. Jimmy was feeling more a part of the everyday operations.

His therapies were going well. Thankful to not experience any meaningful side-effects, he nonetheless was impatient to see the physical changes he'd hoped would come faster. Dr. Boise assured him that time would be his friend. Jimmy hoped he'd get that time.

He'd exchanged his clothing for a more generic military dress that allowed him to blend better with those around him. The result reinforced his more positive outlook. He was on his way to the dining tent when Rowan fell into step beside him.

"Jimmy."

"Major."

Jimmy had fallen into the practice of addressing the man by his military rank and often included 'sir' in his responses.

"You seem to have adapted well to your new environment."

"Yes sir."

"Any issues?"

Jimmy knew Rowan was asking whether he was experiencing harassment. He shook his head, then clarified. "I'm treated with respect, if not always full acceptance."

"You good with that?"

"It's often the best I can hope for. Many times, it's more than I've received in the past."

Rowan nodded thoughtfully.

"You've chosen a tough path. Takes courage to do that."

"Takes courage to be yourself no matter the circumstances."

Rowan agreed with that, but didn't express it. Instead, he went in a different direction.

"I've seen you working out."

Jimmy smiled. "Trying to rebuild muscle mass. Anticipating the therapies will help with that. But in the meantime, strength training is strength training."

"How would you feel about joining the new recruits in their bootcamp training?"

"There's new recruits?"

Rowan smiled. "We always have new recruits. We may not be in our old formal bases, but we try to operate as if we were. That means recruiting, training, and absorbing more into our ranks."

"Won't that cause an issue? An outsider training with the troops?"

"What if you weren't an outsider?"

Jimmy stopped and stared at Rowan.

"Are you saying what I think you're saying?"

"That you could be a formal recruit, if you wanted to be? Yes. That's what I'm saying."

"But the military kicked out folks like me." Jimmy began walking again.

"The recent attitudes aren't always observed by this military. The last two years have seen many changes, not the least of which is the fact that there is no official, formal military. Therefore, policies that once were, can be modified to suit current situations." He paused. "Within reason, of course."

They were almost at the dining tent. "Can I think about it?"

Rowan smiled. "Yes. But don't take too long." He turned and began walking back the way he came.

Jimmy watched him. Without being consciously aware he spoke the words out loud, he said, "I won't."

25

Troy and David were playing catch with a scrunched-up paper ball, after David's late arrival. Neither had referred to their computer explorations from three weeks ago. David never asked if Troy had read the reports, and Troy never volunteered information on them one way or the other. It was as if, by some unspoken accord, that day hadn't existed for them.

After twenty minutes, both became bored with their game.

"You got anything on the to-do list?" Troy asked David.

"Nope. You?"

Troy grinned. "Nope. I don't get it. Why put us here and then forget about us? How efficient is that?"

"We're nothing to them. My dad says they're all focused on one thing these days."

"Something other than making money?"

"Oh, it's all about making money. But apparently things aren't going as they'd planned or hoped."

"What do you mean?"

David looked at Troy with exasperation. "Don't you ever watch the news?"

"What's the point? It really isn't news, anyway. Just propaganda."

"The markets are plunging. Even cryptocurrency has dropped thousands of dollars. To those with large holdings, that multiplies into millions."

Troy thought about the changes he'd noticed in his dad recently and wondered if David had just given him an explanation for them.

"What's causing it?"

"Pretty much everything the Leader has instituted since taking office. It's all catching up. That's the problem with economic upswings and downswings. They never happen immediately. People constantly forget that. Blame or praise is given to people for things they may or may not have anything to do with. And by the time someone figures it out and reports on it, no one believes it anyway. But most of what's going on right now is clearly a result of actions taken by the Leader early in his term."

"I know about the high unemployment. Seemed kind of an obvious result of all the cuts from the so-called efficiency edicts. But I thought everything else was rolling along just fine."

"Not really. Those who aren't working are really struggling. More so than past times of high unemployment. These folks don't get the support that used to be in place. Again, spending cuts. They're victims twice over. First, they lose their job, then they lose the benefits that kept them somewhat afloat while they got re-situated. They can no longer participate in the economy.

Now, you'd think the lack of buying power from such a large segment of the population would cause prices to lower. You know, that old supply-demand situation?"

At Troy's confused look, David sighed. "Less demand creates more supply, usually causing prices to go down," he smiled, "generating more demand, often creating shortages, at least short-term, that allow for prices to be raised again. It's the usual give and take of a capitalist economy. But now add to that this whole cryptocurrency should be our only form of currency thought process. The markets plunge as people rapidly sell their holdings, looking for other places to plant their funds."

"How do you know all this?"

David smiled but didn't answer. Instead, he continued his current rant. "Of course, there are always those who buy when the market goes down because they see it as a fantastic opportunity. But to do that, you've got to already have money. Lots of money."

"Which is exactly what these billionaires have!"

"Yes and no."

"What do you mean?"

"Many are billionaires only on paper. It's not like they have all that wealth in a bank account. Their funds are highly leveraged and tied up in things that often can't be easily liquidated. When the valuation of those things drop, their debt ratios rise and they become almost as much a credit risk as the average schmuck walking the streets. I say almost, because after all, it's a club. They look out for each other."

"If all that's true, then I don't see the problem. The average schmuck, as you call them, are probably no worse off since they had virtually nothing to begin with, and the billionaires simply play games with numbers on pages. Everything churns along as usual."

David chuckled. "I suppose you could sum it up that simply." He sobered. "On the other hand, the hit to the cryptocurrency market could make some reassess the idea of turning that into the official currency. The original nay-sayers may gain more leverage."

"And how does that help or hurt people like you and me?"

Troy was tiring of the conversation. It involved far more thought process than he was willing to invest. But he was curious how David would answer.

"People like you and me could turn into one of the average schmucks on the street if our fathers lose everything in the topsy-turvy market. You might think otherwise, but we're simply not prepared to survive in such a scenario." David's intense look made Troy uncomfortable.

Troy thought of his friend Carson. He realized David was correct. He, Troy, would never survive the way Carson would. He was ill-equipped to navigate a system that didn't pander to his every desire. He figured Jimmy would have even better skills, considering the obstacles he had to overcome every day of his life.

Jimmy. That thought brought him up short. He allowed himself a moment of grief. And guilt. He'd never followed up on trying to figure out what happened to him. While he hadn't definitively told Carson he would, he knew Carson assumed he would.

He glanced at David. "Want to see if we can get any info off the system about all this? And if we get in, there's something else I want to try and check on."

David hesitated. They hadn't pursued access into the system since the day they didn't talk about. The day of the invasion and disruption of their space. The day Troy copied the reports. David thought about the flash drive he'd hidden in Troy's desk. He knew Troy hadn't found it. He'd have said something if he had. David wasn't sure he wanted to tempt fate yet again. They'd apprehensively waited for dire consequences to befall them from the last time. When none did, they'd settled into long days of boring inactivity.

He realized Troy was waiting for an answer. Smothering his feeling of dread, he nodded. Troy swung his chair around and faced his monitor. David was relieved Troy hadn't suggested they use his station. He stood and walked over to Troy's desk.

"Your password or mine?" Troy asked.

"Yours."

Troy glanced at him, his fingers hovering over the keys. "Sure you don't want to see if the access we gave you last time works?"

"Just use yours. We can check mine later."

"Righto."

Troy typed his credentials into the machine. They both waited. Time seemed to slow. An icon indicated that something was supposedly happening, but nothing came up on the screen.

"Is it just me, or does it seem like this is taking a lot longer than the last couple of times?" Troy almost whispered the words.

"It is. Think we should cancel and try again?"

Troy thought about it. Before he could do anything, the familiar menu screen appeared.

"There we go," he murmured.

David stared at the screen. "I don't see anything that might give us economic information."

"Let's poke around a bit. Remember, we didn't expect to see those reports last time we chose an option."

David took a breath, then dove in. "You ever read them?"

"Yup."

David waited, but when Troy didn't elaborate, he sighed. "And?"

"Nothing much to write home about. Besides, you yourself said someone else would make the real decisions on them. Not us. So what's the point of even talking about them?"

Troy didn't want to share that not only had he read them all, he'd read them multiple times and compared authors and funding sources and objectives. He'd even gone so far as to create a large chart which organized the information. He still wasn't sure if he'd uncovered anything particularly important, but he had seen a pattern in the research. And he thought one of the reports was in some type of code, or at least written in a way that disguised what he thought was really going on. And that was experimentation on humans. Unauthorized, nonconsensual experimentation. And it all seemed to tie back to decreases in sperm counts as well as the degradation of the Y chromosome. He didn't understand all the biological and medical technicalities, but he understood the basic concern and objective underlying all the research. He just couldn't wrap his head around the idea that humanity may be heading toward extinction. And before that big event occurred, males would be the first to succumb.

Then there was that last report he'd read. It didn't seem to relate to any of the others. It wasn't even a research paper so much as a report on certain events. It too seemed in code. It used names to describe activities instead of just saying what those activities were. Troy had realized that to understand the thing, one needed to understand what the various names meant. What the hell was *Twinboy*, or *Rangebelt*, or *Goldnug*? There'd been other names, too. When read within the text of the report, they all seemed silly and irrelevant. Almost as if someone was playing games by randomly inserting the names. Yet Troy knew there was a deeper meaning. He'd made notes and promised himself he'd find a way to decode the writing. He just hadn't figured out how, yet.

His thoughts were interrupted when David pointed to the screen and indicated an option that looked interesting.

Troy chose it and they waited for the new screen to appear. Again, it seemed to take forever, and both wondered what could be causing the system to run so slowly when the last two times it had seemed almost immediate in its responses.

Finally, the screen displayed their choice. Both leaned in to study the results.

"What the—" Troy began.

"Holy shit!" David spoke over him.

They looked at each other. Without really understanding why he did it, Troy pulled out his phone and snapped a picture of the screen.

"This has nothing to do with what we chose. Why do you think it's here?" Troy was confused and wasn't afraid to admit it. "And what do we do next?"

When David didn't answer, but continued reading the screen, Troy prompted him. "David?"

"Page down. Before it goes away."

Troy did as instructed before asking why David thought the information would disappear. Again, he snapped a picture of the new display.

Suddenly the lights in the building flickered followed by the computer screen going dark. A mechanical voice came through a speaker instructing all personnel in the building to exit quickly in an orderly fashion. The message continued to repeat.

"Get your stuff. Let's go." David said as he stood and rushed to his desk to grab his phone he'd left there when coming to Troy's desk. He reached down and picked up the small pack on the floor. Troy watched but didn't immediately register the fact that this was the first time he'd seen David with any kind of pack or bag.

"Troy!" David called urgently.

David's voice spurred him to action, and he quickly gathered up his own things, stashing his phone in his back pocket. He was first out the door and walking rapidly down the hall when he realized David wasn't behind him. He slowed and started to turn back when David came through the door waving him on. Shrugging, Troy continued, and David soon caught up with him.

"What kept you?"

"I had to get something I forgot." David didn't tell Troy that what he'd stopped to get was the flash drive he'd shoved in Troy's desk drawer. He wasn't sure why, but something told him it was important to get it out of the building.

They'd just cleared the front doors when they heard a low rumble, and the earth seemed to shake under them. A piece of concrete fell a few feet from their position.

"Quick! Let's get away from here!" David yelled as he started running.

Troy followed fast on his heels, and both were across the street as the building they'd just left started to fold in upon itself. The last thing Troy was aware of was the screams he heard as he slammed into the wall in front of him. It was as if a giant invisible hand had shoved him.

He must have blacked out momentarily from the impact. When he opened his eyes, he took a quick inventory. He was covered in dust. All limbs seemed to be moving properly. His head hurt. And there was a huge pile of rubble in place of the building he'd just exited. He slowly turned his head toward David who was also covered in dust.

"You OK?" his voice cracked.

David didn't immediately answer, yet when he did, his voice seemed much stronger and more controlled than Troy's.

"Yes. Gonna have some bruises, I think, but otherwise all good."

"What happened?"

"Our building collapsed."

"Duh."

David chuckled. Troy pushed into a more upright sitting position.

"Why would it do that? Do you think it was a bomb?"

"Hard to say. Who would have access to be able to place a bomb?"

Troy shrugged, then winced as the movement caused pain somewhere he couldn't yet identify.

"Anybody? I mean, it's not like there's a ton of security. No one ever questions me. Or ever did for that matter. I just walk in like I own the place. I imagine anyone else could, too. The door isn't secured, there's no one stationed there. There're no working cameras. Honestly, anyone could get in."

David knew what Troy said was true. He'd counted on it. But he'd never admit as much.

"What do we do now? Obviously, we can't go back to work."

"Guess we wait to see what happens. But I'm thinking we ought to just go home." David responded.

They both stayed quiet as the first responders began arriving. At first, no one paid them any attention. They watched as people scrambled about the ruins looking for survivors. A few were helping those who hadn't made it far enough away and were on the sidewalk in front of the building. It seemed forever before someone noticed the two propped up against the wall of the building across the street. Troy and David waited for those approaching them to get closer.

"You two all right?" a gruff voice asked. "Were you in the building?"

Before Troy could answer David confirmed they'd been working in the building but had gotten out and far enough away to have suffered minimal injury. Mostly bruises.

"That it?"

"My head hurts a little," Troy confessed. "I think I knocked it on the wall. Felt like someone shoved me hard."

The man smiled. "Let's take a look."

He did a quick field examination and suggested Troy might have a concussion. Troy was given instructions, and then the man turned his attention to David.

"I know you."

"Yes. We've met. You know my father. Head of the environmental sector."

"Of course. Any injuries I need to check?"

"No. I'm fine. A little bruised is all. Didn't hit my head or anything. You don't need to waste your time with me."

The man knelt and looked at David closely for a few seconds, then shrugged and stood. "OK. I'll take your word for it, but if you're not as fine as you declare, let us know."

David nodded, then looked over the man's shoulder in an obvious hint that his attention and concern would be better served across the street than with him. The man took the hint and returned to where the action was. David looked at Troy.

"You have a headache?"

"Not really. More like a specific spot that hurts."

"Probably where you bumped it." David stood and reached his hand down to Troy. "C'mon, let's get you up and get out of here."

"Shouldn't we report to someone?"

"You have anyone in mind? Remember, we essentially don't exist to the upper level."

"But—"

"Don't worry about it. The guy who was just here will let my dad know we're OK. Let's call it a day and leave."

It took David a few steps to get his gait under control, but he was soon guiding Troy away from the scene. As they made it to the end of the block, a media truck rounded the corner and sped towards the ruined building. David picked up his pace and pulled Troy along with him. Once they'd rounded the corner and were out of sight of the activity, he slowed to a steady unhurried walk.

"What about tomorrow?" Troy asked.

"Stay home until someone calls you. Sooner or later, they'll figure out they need to put us somewhere else. Until then, enjoy your unscheduled vacation."

"Just like that?"

"Just like that."

They reached the next corner and slowed only enough to exchange glances. Then David turned in a different direction and Troy continued straight.

26

Carson watched the news video with horror. He recognized the area around the collapsed building. In fact, he was pretty sure the building that no longer stood was the one Troy worked in. He worried about his friend. He'd tried calling Troy, but the call went straight to voicemail. Carson left a brief message asking for a check in. He said nothing else.

He still worried that all calls were monitored as part of the security protocols initiated two years ago. He'd trained himself to use his phone as little as possible and when he did, to express himself in as few words as possible. He thought he'd mastered the process, even if it was only his opinion.

He wondered if this event signaled something bigger. He'd met with his contact a couple of days ago. His original contact, not Shannon. After refusing to answer any specifics around why Shannon had been sent previously, the man told Carson to be prepared. Things would be happening. Ignoring the obvious questions Carson asked, the man indicated the general population was more disenchanted than ever with the Leader and his billionaires. That message would be conveyed in ways that couldn't be ignored.

Carson wondered if this attack on the health sector building was part of the message. He couldn't think of it as anything other than an attack. Buildings didn't just collapse on their own, did they? He wasn't an architect, but he didn't think so.

He flipped through the remaining stations on the television to see if the others offered updates. He sighed when he realized they were all showing the same scenes repeatedly. No speculation was given. He knew that, in and of itself, was significant. Such events always encouraged speculations. The lack thereof spoke to the unified message the government wished to send. He understood that whatever was behind this attack, the public would never know the truth. They would only know what the government wished them to know. And watching the footage, it was clear the government wanted the public to believe the collapse was due to some random fluke of a flawed building component. He shut the television off in disgust.

He stood and paced his small living room. He was the only one home. His dad was working, his mom shopping, and he had no idea where his younger sibling was. He felt as if the walls were closing in on him. He strode to the door and escaped outside.

Not wanting to wander the streets, yet realizing he wasn't mentally equipped to stay inside, he sat on his steps and watched the neighborhood activities. Not that there was much going on. A couple kids he'd seen before, but didn't know, were playing down the street. It made him long for the days when there was nothing bigger in his world than what next bit of childhood mischief he and his friends could get into.

He saw Shannon walking towards him. He waved her up onto the steps beside him. He noted her somber expression as she sat.

"You see the news?" he asked.

"Yes. It's concerning to say the least."

"Troy. You remember him? He works there. I can't reach him. Phone goes straight to voicemail."

"I'm sure he's fine."

"I'm not. Not until I hear from him. What makes you so confident he's fine?"

Shannon looked at him. "They haven't reported any deaths or injuries."

"That doesn't mean anything, and you know it. They'll only report what they want us to know. And I can't believe something that catastrophic hasn't caused deaths. I would think it's a given there are injuries. Even if not to anyone in the actual building, anyone near that collapse would likely have suffered some injury, if only minor. Troy works in the building. What if he didn't get out in time? Do they even have some kind of warning system in those places? How would he have known to get out? You can't just sit here and calmly say you're sure he's fine when you don't know!"

"You're right. I don't know. I was only trying to ease your mind." Shannon's tone grated on Carson's nerves. He thought it patronizing. He took a deep breath and forced down the words he was about to speak. He knew they'd only make things worse. He changed the subject.

"How's the family down the street doing? Have you checked on them? Have they found out anything about the father?"

"No, they haven't. What's worse is I've heard that others have been swept up. Squads have been going into companies and taking people, not giving them any opportunity to prove they're a citizen. Seems the companies aren't doing anything. Just letting it happen."

"Probably afraid to protest. They'll lose whatever protections they have, assuming they have any. If they don't, I'm sure they don't want to get on some list."

"Still. To just take people without any kind of due process."

"Why are you surprised? That's what the Leader promised would happen." Carson half-laughed. The sound that resulted seemed painful. "One of the few kept promises."

"Yeah. And one of the many promises not kept concerns the women. Their healthcare, their freedoms, their independence. It's getting worse."

Carson looked at her curiously. "How so?"

"They're trying to pass new legislation that says women can't even go to the doctor without a man's permission. All women. Married, unmarried. Doesn't matter. Girls, too. Can you even imagine?"

"No. I can't. Why would they do that?"

"So far, they haven't been successful in passing a national abortion ban. Surprising, considering the current culture. But this is another way around that."

"Do you think it will pass?"

Shannon shrugged her shoulders indicating she didn't know.

"How can men who really love their wives buy into such nonsense?"

"Peer pressure. Cult thinking. Lack of thinking. I don't know. But it's pathetic."

"Anything being done to counter it?"

"Some are trying. But who knows if they'll be successful. It does give me hope, however, that there are at least some men out there willing to work for the benefit of women rather than against it."

"Maybe the women should arm themselves and make their concerns known more forcefully? That could get interesting. They could take over. Doubtful they'd do worse than what's currently happening."

Carson smiled. "Unless, of course, they locked up all the men and treated us like animals in a zoo. Fed daily but confined to a designated pen. To be pointed at and observed. Little placards explaining our usefulness or lack thereof. Maybe an area for adoptions, like they used to do with stray cats and dogs. And since we wouldn't generally be let out into the real world, they'd have to come up with some process to continue the species. Set up some kind of harvesting program. Use us and abuse us. Maybe even—"

Carson was getting into his fantasy world with gusto. Until he noticed Shannon's thoughtful expression. He stopped his ongoing litany.

"You know I'm kidding, right?" he said hesitantly.

Shannon smiled, but didn't answer. Instead, she stood and looked down at him. "Look, I've got to go. It was good seeing you. I'm sure Troy is fine." At Carson's look, she amended, "At least I hope he's fine. Let me know what you find out."

She skipped lightly down the steps and walked briskly away. Carson watched her, both confused and thoughtful.

27

Troy was lounging on the couch in the living room, watching the news. It seemed the collapsed building event was on a never-ending loop. No updates were given. The video from the scene was simply shown nonstop. He still marveled that he and David escaped with minimal consequences. He hadn't been completely truthful. He'd had a slight headache, but it cleared later that same day, and other than some painful bruising, he felt fine.

His dad questioned him repeatedly, but Troy couldn't tell him anything other than what he'd experienced. He kept his narrative to running from the building and being pushed into the wall across the street. He professed no other knowledge. He didn't mention they'd been in the computer system when the warnings had gone off. He didn't think his dad needed to know that. It could generate uncomfortable questions. Questions he couldn't answer anyway, so why start the process?

He'd taken David's advice and stayed home waiting for someone to call. It'd been two days and so far, no call or even an inquiry regarding his safety. If nothing else, it reinforced David's declaration that they were nothing to anyone. At least regarding their employer. But maybe his dad had let folks in his circle know he was okay. And David's dad, as head of the environmental sector, would surely have reported to someone that they'd made it out. At least, Troy thought that might be the case.

He stood and stretched. He could still feel the soreness from hitting the wall. But he'd steadily improved. He was alone in the house again. Beth, the cook, had come and gone. His dad had left early. It was times like these when he missed his mother. Although it had been years since she'd walked away from her husband and child, Troy had never gotten the full story. All he knew was, one day she was hugging him and feeding him breakfast, the next she wasn't. He'd asked his dad numerous times but never got a straight answer. Anything referencing her was gone from the house. Except the one small picture he had of the two of them when he was nine or ten. He'd squirreled it away when the big purge was taking place. He currently carried it in his wallet, carefully protected in an envelope of plain paper he'd made for it. Never once did he let his dad know he had it. Now an adult, something told him he'd still be forced to discard it if his dad knew he had the picture. Therefore, he kept the memory close.

Deciding against continual monitoring of the news, he went into his room and pulled out the chart of reports he'd been working on. For what seemed like the hundredth time, he read through the information he'd organized. Still frustrated that no new insight had come to him, he picked up the one that he'd labeled in his mind as the coded mystery report. As he read through it again, the word 'Twinboy' jumped out at him. Suddenly his body stiffened. He'd seen this someplace else! But try as he might, he couldn't recall.

Before he could give it further thought, he heard his phone buzz across the room. He went to it and saw he'd missed a text and had a voicemail. He picked up the device, swiped the screen, and entered the code to gain access. He read the text first. It was from David, telling him not to worry about coming in. His dad had verified they would be placed somewhere new eventually, but everyone's attention was directed elsewhere. Troy acknowledged it, then accessed the voicemail.

He felt guilty hearing Carson's voice asking for a check in. He tapped the displayed number, but the call went to voicemail. He wasn't surprised. Carson hated using the device, convinced the government monitored everything the people did.

Troy used to think that attitude was sheer nonsense, but since reading the coded mystery report, and his conversations with David, he had to admit he'd been rather trusting. Naïve, really. He now acknowledged there was more going on under the surface of which he, or most, were unaware. He left a quick message stating he was fine, and they should get together soon.

Troy was about to put the phone down, when he remembered the screenshots he'd taken just before evacuating the building. As he walked back to his reports, he scrolled through his apps to find them.

He read the information three times before the significance hit him. This was where he'd seen Twinboy. Only not in that form. It had been broken up. Almost as if someone had deliberately obscured the use of the actual word, or name, or whatever it was supposed to be.

He read the screenshot again. Taken by itself, it seemed innocent enough. He and David hadn't been able delve further into it because of the evacuation. But he remembered David's reaction to the displayed information. While his had been confused, David's had been surprised. Almost horrified. Troy thought about that. Had David understood what they'd been looking at? And if so, what did his reaction mean?

Troy reread the report and the screenshots but could only infer that the two were connected somehow. He wondered if David would share his thoughts or knowledge. He was about to call when he experienced some of Carson's paranoia. He smiled as he recognized the reason for his reluctance to call. But he honored the feeling and decided to wait until he could talk to David in person. However, the need to talk to someone was strong.

He decided to see if Carson was home. He gathered up the reports and tucked them back were he'd kept them hidden. At the last minute, he tapped his phone and printed the screenshots. He added them to the stack of reports.

Grabbing his jacket as he walked to his door, he glanced over his shoulder to verify everything looked as it should. He closed his door and headed down the stairs. He glanced at the television as he passed through the living room. Same news reels. He quickly opened the front door and exited the house.

The fresh air felt good. Well, fresh was a relative term. He could smell far-off factory smoke along with some unknown chemical odor. But these were normal in today's world. He felt lucky that was all he could smell. He understood the odors were less here, in his neighborhood, than in others. Carson had told him that in some places, everything was covered in a black soot-like substance. It even floated on the water sitting in the toilets. If left to settle, you could see it in the tap water. On top of that, garbage lined the streets as services to dispose of it were sporadic in the extreme. With that came pestilence and increased cases of disease and death. No one seemed to care. At least no one outside those neighborhoods. Troy had always thought Carson was exaggerating. Now, he wasn't as certain.

He looked around his streets with renewed awareness. Everything seemed clean and well-maintained. No litter, yards mowed, hedges trimmed, cars put away. He realized he hadn't been in Carson's neighborhood almost since the last election. They'd always met somewhere between their two residences. As he walked along, he wondered what he'd find when he got there.

He turned down Carson's street. At first glance, it didn't look much different from his own. The houses were less grand, of course, but the streets were free of garbage. He noticed the general odor was stronger, though.

He climbed the steps to Carson's door and knocked on it. As he waited, he looked around him and began to notice things he hadn't seen at first. Both the street and sidewalks were in disrepair. He could barely see the sports court down the street, but he knew it was there. He'd played basketball on it with Carson and Jimmy and others. He wondered if it looked anything like the street, with bits of broken pavement and potholes developing into dangerous hazards.

He realized no answer had come from his knock and he turned back to knock again.

"If you're looking for Carson, he's not home."

The voice caused him to turn around. He saw a young woman who looked vaguely familiar. He waited for clarification.

"I know you. Tim, Ted. No. Troy, that's it. Troy."

Shannon smiled as she said it. Something in her demeanor made Troy think she knew his name all along and was just messing with him. He decided not to play along.

"You know where he is?"

"Do I look like his keeper?"

Troy was getting frustrated. His tone was aggressive as he asked, "I know you, don't I? At least, you look very familiar."

Shannon laughed outright.

"High School. Shannon."

Troy snapped his fingers. "That's right. You ran for some office. Carson said he voted for you."

"Did you?"

"No. I voted for the other one. The guy."

"Figures," Shannon murmured. She looked Troy straight in the eye. "I bet you don't even remember the other guy's name, do you?"

Troy had the grace to look momentarily embarrassed. Then he smiled, "Can't say as I do."

He descended the steps and stood next to Shannon. "You live around here?"

She waved vaguely behind her. "Down the street." She shifted her stance. "Carson was very worried about you. The collapsed building? I told him you'd be fine. Guess I was right. What happened, anyway?"

"I don't know. One minute we were doing our thing, the next we were running for our lives."

"What's doing your thing, mean? What do you do, anyway? I know you're in the health sector. I thought they'd decimated that sector with all the cuts."

"They did. Not much going on. But we manage to keep busy." Troy had no intention of telling her their main form of keeping busy was getting into a computer system they weren't supposed to be in.

Shannon looked at him intently, then shrugged. "Where are you working now?"

Troy shifted his weight from one foot to the other. "I'm not. Been told to sit tight until someone contacts us to come in."

"Still getting paid?"

Troy hesitated. "I think so. No one ever clarified. Why? What's it to you?"

"Oh, I don't know. Just the rich get richer, and the poor get poorer thing, I guess."

Troy didn't comment. He knew anything he said would fuel her wrath. Instead, he brought the fight to her. "What do you do? You working? Or living off government support?"

"Typical. You people are so predictable." She emphasized the words 'you people'. "You think everyone else mooches off the government, when it's you who does the mooching. You're just oh so much more clever at it. You disguise it as government contracts, all written to benefit you more than whatever the project is you've been contracted to do. I'd bet some projects don't even get done. Wouldn't be surprised if they were completely made up. But that doesn't stop y'all from taking the money. Oh, no. If it means sticking it to the ordinary people who try to do the right thing and pay their taxes, you go for it. All the while telling us that if it weren't for you employing us, we'd be worse off. How much worse off can we be, earning a pittance and having to use all of it just to eat and keep sheltered? And that's assuming we even get to work. Yet we still go further into debt just to maintain. I'm not talking luxury. I'm talking survival."

Troy looked at her. "That's harsh."

"It's the truth."

Troy was trying to formulate some type of response as he worked to not show how her attitude and speech intimidated him. He was rescued by a call from a familiar voice.

"Troy! You're safe!" Carson hurried up the street toward them. When he reached them, he placed on hand on Troy's shoulder and gave it a squeeze. "Why didn't you return my message?"

"I did. But only just today. I hadn't looked at my phone. I'm sorry."

Carson seemed to pick up on the tenseness in Shannon and the relief in Troy's voice. He looked between the two.

"What's going on?"

"Nothing," they both answered together.

Carson laughed. "Right. You both look like a big fat nothing is going on. What gives?"

Shannon shrugged. "I'll leave you two to it."

She turned and walked away without further comment. Carson looked at Troy. When Troy said nothing, Carson sighed and said, "Never mind her. She can come across rather strong at times. She's got a lot on her plate." He shifted context. "What are you doing here?"

Troy was having second thoughts about confiding his concerns to Carson. "Just needed to get out of the house. You up for anything?"

"Sure. Let's take a walk."

They started down the sidewalk towards the sports court, which reminded Troy of his earlier observations.

"How come this neighborhood isn't drowning in garbage? I hear all the time that that's the state of the world now. Can't say as I've seen much evidence of it."

"It's a concerted effort of everyone here. We keep it as clean as we can. But often there's no pick up services for the trash."

"So what do you do?"

"You'll see." Carson answered cryptically.

Troy was confused, but as they got closer to the court, his nose picked up a much heavier smell than before. He wasn't ready to believe what he thought was happening, but within the next ten steps, his eyes and nose confirmed his suspicions.

"You use the sports court as a garbage dump?"

"No other place. At least this has a fence around it to keep it somewhat contained. But as you have probably figured out, it doesn't contain the smell."

By this time Troy had put his arm across his face, sheltering his nose.

"How do you stand it?" His voice was muffled through the material of his sleeve.

"You get used to it after a while. Sort of."

Troy was thankful Carson said no more. He didn't want a repeat of Shannon's tirade. He'd had a lot thrown at him in a short amount of time. He wasn't sure he could take any more. Especially from Carson. His thoughts were interrupted by Carson's question.

"The news doesn't say much about your building. You know anything more than what they're reporting?"

"No." Troy summarized his experience, but this time he included the fact that he and David had been accessing the system when the alarms went off.

Carson didn't speak for a moment. Then, "You think you might have triggered the event?"

Troy stopped and stared at Carson. It took Carson a couple of steps to realize the situation and also stop. He turned back to Troy.

"Why would you think our being in the system would trigger that disaster? How could you think that?"

Carson gestured with his head for Troy to catch up and they both continued their walk. When he didn't answer Troy's questions, Troy asked them again.

"I'm not sure I do think that. I just asked. Wouldn't be the most bizarre thing I've seen or heard these last two years. What were you looking at in the system?"

Troy hesitated. This was the very reason why he'd wanted to talk to Carson, but now the opportunity presented itself, he wasn't sure he could do it. Afraid he'd sound like an idiot spouting coded reports and whatnot. He put off the topic by addressing the issue of Jimmy.

"I haven't been able to find out anything about Jimmy. I know you wanted me to look into it, but I just haven't been able to."

Carson glanced at him in his peripheral. "Doesn't much matter now, does it? I'm assuming he was killed with everyone else in that settlement attack. I've talked to his mother. Neither of us hold out hope he escaped. We're trying to reconcile ourselves to his death."

Troy experienced a stab of guilt. Not only had he put off looking for information, he hadn't wanted to do it in the first place. While Jimmy had been part of their crowd, Troy never fully accepted his choices or lifestyle. He felt only a vague sadness around the whole situation. But he'd never admit that to Carson. He somehow understood Carson would look at him very differently if he knew that's how Troy really felt.

"I'm sorry."

Carson nodded acknowledgement, but pursued his other question. Troy sighed. He motioned to a bench further ahead and suggested they sit and talk.

"No. Not there."

Troy looked at him questioningly.

"That bench has a camera pointed directly at it. Have no idea if there's audio ability, but I'd prefer to not sit there and talk."

Troy's eyes widened. It never occurred to him they'd be under surveillance. Carson correctly interpreted Troy's look.

"Surely you realize there are cameras everywhere? But then again, maybe you don't. Doubtful they'd be in your neighborhood."

Troy heard the soft accusing tone, but didn't comment. He glanced around trying to see if he could spot the offending objects.

Carson chuckled. "Don't bother. They're well concealed, for the most part. But those of us who live here? We know where they're at and try to avoid them as much as possible."

"If they're well concealed, how did you find out about them?"

Carson just gave him one of those don't-be-stupid looks. His eyes narrowed. "You've avoided my question multiple times. Why? What were you looking at in the system?"

Troy's shoulders drooped. "It's a long story with a few twists and turns. It will take a while to give you the whole perspective. Or at least, my perspective. Is there any place we can go where we won't be seen or heard?" He hesitated. "Maybe we should go to my place. Then I can show you the things I can only describe if we just talk."

Carson raised an eyebrow. "You're inviting me to your home? What about your dad?"

"He's gone for the day. And lately, he's been coming home late at night."

Carson smiled and avoided saying the obvious. Instead, he merely said, "Let's go."

28

Jimmy's beard was starting to come back. He knew it would still take time before it looked the way it had before his settlement experience. But the new growth was encouraging. If only to help him blend with the others better.

He had yet to notify the Major of his decision regarding enlistment, realizing he hadn't fully made the decision. He often loitered near the training fields. A few of the new recruits noticed him and gestured for him to join them, but he always smiled and shook his head. He preferred to watch. And he was observing behavior. Trying to make a final decision. His experience with Bruno was still on his mind.

He knew dealing with such attitudes was a part of the life he'd chosen. As a civilian, he could choose his friends and colleagues. In the military, he'd have less freedom around that topic. He wasn't completely convinced he wanted to subject himself to the potential hostility for an extended time period. And regardless of what the Major said about rules or no rules, Jimmy knew that things were always changing. If the military was officially reinstated, would he be accepted or discharged? The uncertainty kept him from fully committing.

The tent flap opened, and Winthrop stepped in.

"Still being a lazy ass?" The words were said with a smile. "The least you could do is clean up around here."

Jimmy laughed. The only person who seemed to leave a perpetual mess behind was Winthrop.

"Not your housekeeper."

"Pity."

Winthrop stuffed some clothes into a convenient hiding place. They both knew his actions didn't address the real problem but on the surface, at least, there was less clutter.

"The Major wants to know if you've decided to join up."

"I can't."

"Can't decide, or can't join up?"

Jimmy was silent. Winthrop looked at him.

"Jimmy?"

"Decide. Or join." Jimmy sighed. "Both."

"What's the issue?"

Jimmy shared his concerns. To Winthrop's credit, he didn't immediately regard them as frivolous. Instead, he asked if Jimmy had considered any alternatives.

"Alternatives?"

"Canada, for one."

"You think I should leave the country?"

"Didn't say that. Simply said it might be an alternative to consider. I've heard others have made the move and are glad for it."

"When you say others. You mean others like me? Or others more generically."

"Meant the word generically, but I get your point. Anyway, something to think about. The current political environment seems to be getting worse. We're not supposed to communicate with the outside world very much. Mostly just with family, to assure them we're okay. But I heard from one of my friends that the sweeps are getting more aggressive. Seems like the enforcement squads don't care one way or the other if they're targeting the correct people. And by correct, I mean those on the official lists.

People in general are simply disappearing. With no explanations. Surveillance is increasing. And not just by cameras and drones. You know electronic transmissions have been monitored for quite a while, right? Well, I guess they've figured out how to make that even more intrusive. Not sure how, but my friend says the ability to shut someone out of society is a simple flick of a switch now."

Jimmy dropped his head into his hands.

"How'd we ever get to this? I feel like I've fallen into a time warp and am reliving history I read about in school."

"You are. Or, at least, the direction we're going will put us there more quickly than most realize. Then again, since they stopped teaching history in schools, most won't recognize the similar behaviors and actions of times past. I can't decide if we're the lucky ones, who have a point of reference, or if we're cursed because we do."

"Both." Jimmy said the word with a finality that Winthrop recognized. He circled back to the original point of discussion.

"Anyway, the Major is waiting for your decision. A new bunch of recruits are set to arrive next week. You need to decide if you're going to be one of them. I'd say you have a couple more days at most before the Major comes knocking on the door." Winthrop smiled. "So to speak."

Jimmy stared at the tent flap for a long time after Winthrop left. The conversation hadn't helped his mood. He felt more restless and insecure now than he'd felt earlier. One thing was clear, though. He needed to make a decision. The problem was, he didn't know what it would be, or how he'd make it.

29

Carson followed Troy into the large house, reminded again of the differences in their circumstances. He wouldn't admit to Troy he was a little nervous being here. What if Marcus came home and threw him out? Carson wouldn't put it past the man. He mentally shrugged. Nothing he could do about it, so he decided not to dwell on it. In any event, he was more curious about what Troy wanted to tell and show him.

He sat at Troy's desk and watched as his friend pulled a large stack of papers from what was obviously meant to act as a place of concealment. He remained silent as Troy placed them on the desk and pulled up a small stool next to Carson.

As Troy sorted the papers into three different stacks, he explained what they were to Carson. Momentarily distracted by the research around the Y chromosome, Carson asked several questions.

"I'll let you read it yourself. I found all the statistics tough to get through. Maybe you'll do better with it. But this is what I really wanted to show you."

Troy pulled out the report that he considered to be in code and set it in front of Carson.

"Go ahead. Read some of it. Tell me your first impressions."

Carson picked it up and looked at the title. Not commenting, he flipped to the first page and started reading. He was five pages in before he looked up at Troy. Troy waited.

"This seems," Carson's voice drifted into silence. He cleared his throat. "This doesn't make sense. Or rather, it makes sense in a science fiction movie way."

"Explain."

Carson did. When he finished, the two just stared at each other.

"Maybe you should read a bit more," Troy suggested.

Carson nodded and focused on the page in front of him. After another four pages, he asked hesitantly, "Do you think I could get a copy of this? I'd like to study it a bit more than just this quick read. It seems to be saying something in addition to the obvious. Know what I mean? Like, if you read between the lines, there's a different meaning being presented."

"Like it's written in code?"

Carson thought about it. "Yes. Like that. Is that weird?"

"If it is, we have the same definition of weird. Because I thought the same thing. But there's more. I need you to look at something else."

Troy pulled out the report that had the various names sprinkled through it. "Read some of this."

Carson glanced at the title, but didn't dwell on it. He immediately started reading the report. This time he stopped after three pages.

"What's with all these stupid names? Twinboy? Rangebelt? Goldnug? Is this for real?"

Troy chuckled. "Yeah. My initial thoughts, too. But now look at this."

Troy pulled out the screenshot photos he'd taken and pushed them in front of Carson. Carson read the two pages, then looked back to the report.

"Not sure how, but these two things are related. What were you looking at when you took these screenshots?"

Troy explained.

Carson grunted. "David seemed like he understood the context? And at that particular point in time the building alarm system went off? Seems a bit more than a coincidence, don't you think?"

"I don't know what to think."

"Did you ask David?"

"No. We were literally running for our lives, and I haven't seen him since."

"And what was the menu option you chose to see this?"

Troy told him.

"Curious. Do you think I could get a copy of this report, too? And these screenshots?"

Troy glanced at his small printer. "It'll take a while to do it here. But my dad has a bigger machine in his office. Won't take near as long."

Troy stood, grabbed the relevant papers, and was out his door before Carson could ask him how wise this course of action was. His earlier nervousness came back with a vengeance. He hoped Troy's dad wouldn't return unexpectedly.

Not knowing what to do while he waited, Carson picked up one of the other reports and started skimming it. He was quickly bored and put it down. As he reached for another, he saw the chart Troy had created. He picked it up and studied it.

Even without having read all the reports, he saw a pattern in the chart information. He studied it. Debating whether to turn his phone on and take a picture, he decided it was worth what he considered a risk of location verification to have the information. He'd just finished his task and put his phone back in his pocket when Troy reentered the room carrying a larger stack of paper than what he'd left with.

Troy thrust the reports at Carson. "Here. I trust you'll keep these safe?"

Carson took the papers and, without saying anything, unbuttoned his shirt and put the reports inside, shoving them around so they rested against his back. His tucked-in shirt kept them in place. He re-buttoned his shirt.

"That should get them home safely. I'll figure out where to hide them when I get there."

Troy nodded. Satisfied. Then he noticed his chart. He gestured toward it.

"Notice anything?"

"Yes. There's a definite pattern. But the meaning is unclear."

Troy told him his theory of nonconsensual human experimentation. Carson said nothing. He'd heard rumors and often wondered about the truth of them. This was the first time he'd come anywhere close to possibly having confirming evidence. The problem was, the evidence didn't make a whole lot of sense and could easily be explained away as something else. He had a flash of premonition.

"Do you think having this information puts you, puts us, in danger?"

Troy swallowed nervously. "Not sure. Maybe. I think that's why I haven't told David any of my thoughts. I know it's stupid. Couldn't possibly be connected. But seeing that screen and then the alarm going off. Well, makes me wonder. And David's reaction. The more I think about it, I'm almost certain he knew what it all meant." Troy hesitated, then continued. "It just occurred to me. David had a small pack the day the building collapsed. I'd never seen him carry anything like that before."

Carson stared at Troy intently. "You think David had something to do with the building collapsing?"

"No. Maybe. I don't know!" Troy's frustration with the whole situation was evident. "Why would he want to destroy the building he worked in? Possibly killing both of us in the process!"

"Good question. But if he did have something to do with it, perhaps he also knew there was some sort of delay involved. Then he wouldn't have been risking either of your lives."

Troy thought about that. Then shook his head. "I just don't know."

At that moment, they both heard the front door open. Carson's eyes widened in fear.

"Hello? Troy? You home?" A woman's voice called up the stairs.

Looking relieved, Troy told Carson it was Beth, their cook. But he wasn't sure why she was here. She'd already prepared the meals and left earlier.

"I'm in my room," Troy called out. Motioning for Carson to remain where he was, he stood and went to his door and opened it. "Is there something wrong? Why did you come back?"

"I forgot something in the kitchen. Is your father home?"

"No. He said he wouldn't be back until later. You good with getting what you need, or should I come down?"

"I'm fine, I'm fine," Beth's voice faded as she walked toward the kitchen. Troy stood waiting a moment, but when she didn't immediately re-emerge, he shrugged his shoulders and stepped back into his room, closing the door.

"Maybe I should leave?" Carson kept his voice low.

"Probably. But wait until Beth's gone."

Carson nodded as he reached for another report. "This the one about the Y chromosome?"

Troy glanced at it. "Yeah."

"Can I take it with me? Or do you want to make another copy of it."

Troy hesitated, then reached out. "Let me make a copy here. It's not that long. My machine should handle it."

Carson watched Troy feed the pages through his printer's copy mode. About five minutes later, Troy tapped the pages into order, stapled them together and handed them to Carson. Carson repeated his earlier shirt actions, expressing his thanks to Troy.

Tilting his head to one side, he asked, "Did you hear your cook leave?"

Surprised, Troy muttered, "I didn't. I'll go down and check. Stay here."

Troy got up and left the room. What seemed like only seconds later, Carson heard Troy frantically yell his name. He stood and ran to the bedroom door and opened it.

"What's wrong?"

"Come here! Quick! Something's wrong with Beth!"

Carson hurried down the stairs and into the kitchen. Beth was on the floor. She wasn't moving. Carson saw foam coming from her mouth. He moved toward her and knelt. Putting his fingers on her neck, he moved them around, trying to find a pulse but was unable to.

"I think she's dead!"

"She can't be! How could she be?" Troy shouted the words hysterically.

Carson stood and looked around the kitchen. He noted a package of open cookies on the counter.

"You open those?"

Troy looked around. "No. And I don't remember seeing them before. But I haven't been in the kitchen since earlier today. They may have been here. I don't know. We went straight to my room when we got here, but I certainly never opened them."

Carson looked at the package, then back at Beth. He saw a half-eaten cookie in her hand. He slowly backed toward the kitchen door, careful not to touch anything.

"I think she opened them. See the one in her hand? I think it killed her."

"Someone left poisoned cookies in our house?!"

"Troy. You need to call the emergency people. And I need to get out of here. Fast. Please. Don't mention to anyone I was here."

"You can't leave me here with her!"

"I must. Make the call. I've got to go. Do you want me to put those reports back where you pulled them from?"

Troy just stood staring at Beth. Frozen in place, not responding.

"Troy!" Carson shouted his name.

Troy flinched. Then stared at Carson as if he was unsure who Carson was.

Carson turned and ran out of the kitchen. He took the stairs to Troy's room two at a time. When he got there, he gathered all the papers and shoved them back in the place he'd seen Troy take them from. Stepping back, he made sure everything looked undisturbed, then ran back down the stairs to the kitchen. Troy was just pulling his phone out of his pocket.

"I'm going now. Don't tell anyone I was here."

"But what do I say?"

"Exactly what happened. You were upstairs in your room, she came to the house, said she forgot something. You never heard her leave. Came down and found her. The only thing you leave out is that I was here and that we were looking at those reports. Got it?"

Troy was staring at Carson.

"Troy! You got it?"

Troy's whole body flinched. "Yes. I've got it. Go. Go now."

Troy tapped the appropriate numbers on his phone as Carson turned and ran for the front door. Stopping himself just before he grabbed the handle, he pulled his coat sleeve down and opened the door, careful to not touch anything. Quickly looking both ways and seeing no one on the street, he stepped out and let the door swing shut behind him. Forcing himself to walk at a pace just slightly faster than a stroll, he kept his head down and as he reached the end of the street, took a right. He slowly increased his pace until he was jogging. That soon morphed into a full-out run, which he maintained until he opened the door of his own home.

30

Glad the house was empty, Carson went straight to his room, shut his door and quickly unbuttoned his shirt. The papers he'd pushed to his back were damp with his sweat. He removed them and set them on his bed, noting their crumpled condition. Checking to make sure they were still readable, he tapped them into an organized pile and looked around his room for a place to stash them.

Finally choosing his spot, he put the papers away and sat on the edge of his bed. His heartbeat still hadn't returned to normal. He took a few deep breaths and let them out slowly. He hoped Troy remembered to not mention him being at the house. He knew that could cause all sorts of issues. Not only with Troy's dad, but the authorities would be sure to come here wanting to talk to him. The less he was noticed by authorities, for any reason, the better.

His mind went back to the scene in the kitchen. Beth on the floor, the open package of cookies. He was convinced that something had intentionally been done to the snack. The question was, who had been the target? Certainly not the cook. Troy? Unlikely, but possible. His father? Very likely. But why?

He heard knocking on the front door and reluctantly stood. His feet felt as if each were four hundred pounds. The knocking continued. He forced himself to go answer the door.

He barely contained his sigh of relief when he opened the door to find Shannon standing there. But something about him alerted her to his state of high tension.

"What's up? You look like you've seen ten ghosts. None of them friendly."

Carson forced a smile, stepped back and motioned her in.

"Is there such a thing as friendly ghosts?"

"Sure. Remember Casper?"

At Carson's confused look, she laughed. "Never mind. But seriously, I can tell something's wrong."

Carson hesitated, not sure whether to tell Shannon anything, knowing that to do so meant another person knew he'd been at Troy's. As he searched for something to say, she interrupted his thoughts.

"You hear the news?"

"What news?"

"Where've you been? It's on every station."

"You mean the building collapse?"

"No. That's old news. I mean the deaths."

A cold tension run up and down Carson's back, then settled somewhere in his abdomen. He felt slightly sick to his stomach.

"Deaths?"

"Several very high-ranking people have died within the last couple of hours. Killed is what they're saying. Poisoned."

Carson paled. "Poisoned? Who? Where? When?"

Shannon looked disgusted with his ignorance. "Almost every sector leader and several of the billionaires and their purchased politicians who have been manipulating the economy and country to their benefit. And get this. The Leader and his replacement idiot are both apparently at death's door. Not dead, yet. Of course, they get the best of the best when it comes to medical treatment. But rumor says it's very uncertain whether they'll make it."

Carson stared at her. "All those people? How many in total?"

"Not sure. Twelve or fourteen. Maybe more. Does it matter the number? The point is, the entire leadership as we know it has almost been decimated within minutes of each other. That requires a well-coordinated attack. The question is, was it domestic or foreign?"

"Does that matter? The chaos is the same."

"Of course it matters! If domestic, then some home-grown group has tired of our current situation and figured out how to, in their minds, fix it. What comes next is still within our own legal framework." She smiled. "Or lack of it." She took a deep breath. "If foreign, then does that mean we're under attack? If so, by whom? And who's going to stop it? The military no longer exists, and these enforcement squads will be useless against a concerted attack by a foreign government."

"Why would another government want to attack us?"

"Oh, I don't know. Maybe because the Leader has insulted and abused them from the moment he took office? Before that, actually."

Carson half-smiled. He knew Shannon was right in that respect. The havoc the Leader had created with what used to be the country's allies was likely irreparable. Maybe years from now things could be salvaged. But no time soon. However, all these deaths changed things.

He walked over to the television, turned it on and sifted through the channels. As Shannon said, every talking head was speculating about the who, why, where and when of the recent events. As they watched and listened, it was clear even more had been affected than Shannon's first summary. And news of the Leader and second in command was dire.

The latest predictions were that they wouldn't survive the day. He thought of Troy's cook and without really thinking about it, immediately knew it was Marcus Hubbard who'd been the intended victim. But somewhere in the back of his mind, he realized the execution of the attack had been extremely sloppy. Anyone could have eaten those cookies. And did. Beth was just collateral damage.

He looked at Shannon. "They're obviously focusing on the bigwigs. Do you think others got caught in the crossfire?"

She looked confused. "What do you mean?"

"Well, poison is rather an imprecise way to do away with someone. Unless you know exactly where and what your target will be doing at any given moment. There are all kinds of opportunities for an unintended person to get in the way."

Shannon looked at him intently. "Why do you say that? You know something you're not sharing?"

Carson silently cursed his carelessness.

"No. I mean. I'm just thinking out loud. Who's to say you poison some specific food or drink, but someone other than your target eats or drinks it? It could happen, right?"

"I suppose."

Carson switched through different channels, but all reports involved the important people who'd died. There was no mention of others. Nor was there any indication that anyone knew where the attacks originated from. Speculation. But nothing evidence based. There was also no confirmation of whether the situation was ongoing, or the attacks had been completed.

"What do you think this means for our immediate future?"

Shannon looked thoughtful. "More security and surveillance. I'm thinking we'll want to avoid being out and about for a while."

Carson chuckled. "Hard to believe there could be even more

surveillance. But you're probably right. However, even the least of us must eat. We must go out."

"True. But it might be best to keep it to a minimum. And stay on well-established paths. No deviations." She looked at Carson meaningfully. He simply nodded.

"By the way, although it seems inconsequential in light of current events, but the reason I came over was to tell you that our family is missing."

Carson wrinkled his brow. "Our family?" Then he understood. "You mean the wife and kids of the old man that was taken?"

"Yes. They're gone. I went over to their place earlier and the house was empty."

"Maybe they just went out somewhere."

"No. There were signs of a struggle. Someone hastily tried to erase them, but if you really looked, and you knew how the family lived, you could see it. I think they were also taken."

"The whole family? How could they do that without someone seeing. Making some kind of commotion?"

"Like they always do. Middle of the night, overwhelming numbers. It's the way they operate."

"You talk to any of the neighbors?"

"Yes. No one saw or heard anything. Or at least, that's what they're saying."

Carson thought of the old man being dragged off the street. He thought of his friend Jimmy, snatched up without warning or presumably any ability to struggle.

"But they're citizens!"

"That may or may not get sorted at some point. In the meantime, it's anyone's guess where they were taken or what will happen to them."

Their attention was drawn back to the television. It was obvious something momentous had happened. Carson turned up the volume. The reporter was practically screaming his news.

"The Leader is dead! I repeat, the Leader passed just ten minutes ago in his hospital bed! We're still waiting to hear what's happening with the Vice-Leader. No one will share news on his condition. But we know from earlier reports his condition was critical. We'll update you as soon as we learn more. Reporting live from in front of the hospital, this is...."

Carson turned the volume down. He and Shannon looked at each other. Neither said a word.

31

The general alarm woke Jimmy. He sat up and looked toward Winthrop and Mike. Both were hastily gearing up.

"What's going on?"

"You need to get up. Get dressed. Be ready." Winthrop grabbed his pack and stuffed a couple items into it.

"Ready for what? What's going on? What's with the non-stop siren?"

"Jimmy! Get up! Get your gear together. Be ready to move out."

Jimmy swung his legs over the edge of his cot and reached for his pants. As he pushed one leg in, he asked again what was going on.

"The Leader is dead. Along with several sector heads and billionaires." Mike was also stuffing items into his pack.

Jimmy focused only on the first part of Mike's statement. "The Leader is dead? How? When?"

"Jimmy!" Both Winthrop and Mike spoke at once. They exchanged a quick glance over Jimmy's head then continued with their tasks.

"Okaaaaay! I'm up. Jeez." Jimmy shoved his other leg in his pants and stood to pull them up. After securing them, he reached for a clean t-shirt, then grabbed a fleece sweater-jacket.

Mike and Winthrop grabbed their packs and moved toward the exit. As they left, Winthrop tossed a quick instruction over his shoulder.

"Stay here for now. Someone will tell you where to go and what to take."

Jimmy watched them leave. Unable to decide if he was more annoyed or confused, he started randomly stuffing things in his pack. After a couple minutes, he stopped and pulled everything out. Looking at the mess on his cot, he sighed. He half-laughed as he spoke to the empty tent.

"Get it together, guy. Something big is about to happen. The last thing you need is a pack full of dirty underwear."

He began systematically organizing his things. Not that he had a lot, but what he had he wanted to keep with him. He sat and pulled his boots on, efficiently lacing them tight. Grabbing his jacket off a hook next to his cot, he put it next to his pack. He grabbed a camouflaged hat and set it on top of the jacket.

He wondered how long he should stay in the tent. What if no one came for him like Winthrop said? He had a momentary flashback of the empty settlement. Empty except for all the dead bodies, that is. That thought made him realize that if he had to leave in a hurry, he'd need his therapies. All the excess inventory was in the med-tent.

He stood. He felt a mild panic beginning somewhere in his stomach. At that moment Rowan stuck his head in.

"Jimmy? I see you've got your stuff together. Good. We're moving out. Grab your gear. Let's go."

"I need to go to the med-tent first!" Jimmy's tone was urgent.

"It's taken care of. The doc has everything you'll need. C'mon. Let's go."

"Yessir!" Jimmy automatically followed what was clearly, by tone, the Major's order. He shouldered his pack, grabbed his jacket and hat, and fell into step behind the man who'd once saved him. He hoped with all his heart that whatever was ahead of him, he could trust the man to keep him safe. He ventured a question.

"Where are we going?"

The Major picked up his pace. Almost as an afterthought he responded. "We're waiting for our orders."

Jimmy slowed his pace. *Waiting for orders? From whom?* Realizing the distance between him and the Major was fast increasing, he broke into a jog to keep up.

Less than two minutes later they arrived at the main training field. It was the first time Jimmy had seen the entire camp in one place. He knew it was big with lots of people, but until this very moment, he'd had no idea just how many people there were. And vehicles. He stared both in admiration and with just a small bit of apprehension. The Major directed him towards a group standing off to the side.

As he got closer, he recognized the doctor, along with several support staff, including medics, cooks, and others. While the doctor had a handgun fastened to his right side, all the others were either carrying rifles or had them slung over a shoulder or across their back.

Dr. Boise gestured him over. "Jimmy. Stay close."

"Where are we going? And, could I have—"

Dr. Boise interrupted him, correctly guessing Jimmy's concern. He held out a small canvas pack.

"This should hold you for several months."

"Months? But there wasn't even that much in the beginning."

Dr. Boise smiled. "I took it upon myself to order additional supplies."

"But how? From where?"

"Probably best you not have the details." He shook the pack. "Here. Take it. Keep it safe. I have more in my pack. If anything happens to me, be sure you get them."

"Happen to you? What would happen to you?"

"Jimmy. Times are uncertain right now. Stay close. Do as you're told. Do you want a weapon? Have you trained with one?"

Jimmy was hesitant. He felt naked without a weapon when everyone else had one. At the same time, carrying one was a responsibility he wasn't sure he was ready for. "A little. I know how to load, aim, and shoot. At a paper target. Not sure I could do anything else."

Dr. Boise smiled. "I understand. But you might find yourself in need of something more than prayers to keep you safe."

Jimmy didn't bother mentioning he seldom prayed. Nor did he ask from whom he'd need to protect himself. He simply nodded assent. Dr. Boise raised his hand. Within seconds someone was at his side with a rifle and additional ammunition. Jimmy found himself having to rearrange things to accommodate his new possessions. Quickly tucking the hormone treatments into his pack, he secured the extra magazines on his person and, after shouldering his pack, picked up the rifle and held it close. Dr. Boise nodded, then motioned him to fall in with the others.

The atmosphere was solemn. A few men whispered to each other, but for the most part, all simply waited. After what seemed like hours to Jimmy, but in fact was only about ten minutes, the call came to move out. Immediately jeeps, tanks, cargo trucks, and other vehicles began to move. Without enough vehicles to transport everyone, those like Jimmy's group, were left to make their way on foot.

Still not fully understanding just what was happening, Jimmy fell into step next to one of the medics he'd met that first day in camp.

<h1 style="text-align:center">32</h1>

Troy waited for the authorities to come. It seemed like they were taking forever. He wondered why. In this neighborhood, you barely disconnected your call and someone was already knocking on your door.

He heard the front door open, and his dad's voice call out. He answered that he was in the kitchen. Marcus Hubbard stepped into the kitchen. He started to tell Troy about the deaths when he stopped and stared horrified at the cook on the floor. He knew immediately she was dead.

"What the hell?"

"I found her like this. I think she ate one of the cookies."

Marcus looked at the opened package of cookies on the counter, vaguely noting they were his favorite brand.

"Did you call the authorities?"

"Yes. Some time ago. But no one has come."

"That's because much bigger things are happening."

Troy looked at his father intently. "What do you mean?"

"Come into the living room and see for yourself on the television."

Troy looked at Beth. His father was dismissive.

"She's not going anywhere."

While Troy knew that was true, he also thought the comment heartless. He felt a brief flash of anger towards his father who'd seemingly never even bothered to remember Beth's name, always just calling her 'Cook'. But he followed Marcus out of the kitchen, throwing one last regretful look towards Beth.

Marcus turned on the television and upped the volume. Troy stared at the screen, trying to process what he was hearing.

"The Leader is dead? Along with several of the billionaires and sector heads?" He thought of David's dad and wondered if he was one of the casualties. "Do you know who?"

"Most of them. It's a long list. Darwin, your sector head, is one of those who died."

"And everyone was poisoned? How could that happen?" His mind flashed to the cookies, recognizing that his dad loved them. "Those cookies! You were targeted! But how did they get here? I've been home for a while. No one delivered anything while I was here."

"Then it happened while no one was here."

"But how? Who could get into the house?"

"Troy. That's not important right now. It happened. Accept it. I'm glad I didn't have the chance to eat them. I'm sorry about the cook, but certainly not sorry I wasn't here to indulge my weakness."

Troy stared at his dad. "Her name was Beth. Do you really not remember? Or do you just not care?"

Marcus made a noise of exasperation. "Yes. I knew her name was Beth. Are you satisfied? Now tell me what you did today. When you were here, when you weren't. I need to narrow down when the cookies were possibly placed in the house. Whoever did it obviously knew they are my favorite. That narrows down the suspect list somewhat. But the question remains, did the same person or group of persons target everyone? Or was it coincidence?"

Now it was Troy's turn to look exasperated. "You can't possibly think you were just a random target amongst many. This is obviously a well-organized effort. All these people at once? That takes a lot of planning. I'm curious why you'd be targeted. What are you involved in? I mean really. What do you do all day and every day?"

Marcus waved him off, not answering. He was focused on the television. Troy was about to repeat his questions but then thought about the small pack David had with him on the day of the building collapse. Could David be involved in this? Surely not! He's the son of a sector head.

"Do you know if David's dad died?"

"Who?"

"The head of the environmental sector."

"I'd have to check. But considering who else is on the list, very likely."

Troy breathed a quiet sigh of relief. Not that he was glad to hear that David's dad might be dead, but he figured it unlikely David would be involved in his own father's death. So whatever might have been in that pack, it couldn't possibly have been anything connected to all this.

"It's complete."

Troy roused himself from his musings. "Sorry? What's complete?"

"The Vice-Leader just died."

Troy looked at his dad. He was sure he imagined it, but the look that crossed his father's face for just a moment seemed as if the man was pleased. *Get a grip,* Troy told himself.

"What does this all mean? Who's going to run the country? What happens to us in the immediate future?"

Marcus looked at his son without speaking. The moment stretched so long Troy shifted on his feet.

"Dad?"

"Things will get sorted out. Don't worry about it." Marcus glanced at his watch. "It's getting late. You should probably turn in. Have you eaten?"

"I'm not hungry."

"Then go on up to your room."

"But what about Beth?"

"I'll handle it."

"But—"

"Troy. Just go to your room and stay there. I'll call the authorities again. I'll see this through."

Troy opened his mouth to protest again, but his father's expression made him close it and turn towards the stairs. Without saying anything, he slowly ascended the steps. Once in his room, he sat on his bed and stared into space. His mind a confused mess.

33

"How can this happen?" Carson asked. "All these people dead? How could someone pull that off?"

Shannon just shrugged. "A good question. Obviously, this was well-planned. But is the next phase as well-planned? That's the question."

"What do you mean?"

"You know what I mean. Who's going to run things?"

"The Constitution sorts that all out."

"Except that everyone in the succession line is also dead. Except the Vice-Leader. But he's in no state to lead anything right now."

Carson glanced at the television, then groaned. "The Vice-Leader just died. I think we're screwed."

"Maybe. Try to look on the bright side. How much worse off can we get?"

Carson laughed. "There's some truth to that. But right now, it seems the country is leaderless. How long before the vacuum is filled, do you think?"

"Hard to say. Look." Shannon pointed back to the television. "Condolences from the other world leaders are coming in. Wonder if they'll let things work themselves out, or if they'll try to stir the pot a bit more."

"You think they'll attack us?"

"Maybe not go that far, but I'm sure they're already trying to figure out how to influence what comes next. These last two years have not been easy for them, either."

Carson didn't comment. He was focused on the headlines streaming below the talking head.

"That's weird," he said.

"What's weird?"

"I just read that our military is on the move. We don't have a military anymore, do we? So how could it be on the move?"

Shannon was quiet. Thinking. She'd heard rumors but had discounted them. Apparently, the rumors were true. Or, at least, held some truth.

"Usually the military reports to the current Leader. They used to use a different term, but no matter. If both the Leader and Vice-Leader are dead, along with those named to succeed them, who's directing the military?"

Carson stared at Shannon. "Wait. There is a military? But how? And where have they been all this time?"

"I'd heard rumors the military had retreated but not disbanded. Thought they were just that. Rumors. Guess not. But I'm with you. Where have they been, and who's running the show?"

"I don't like this. I don't like this one bit. Do you think they'll take over? Declare martial law? Can they even do that?"

Shannon laughed. "Who's to stop them if they do? Who knows. It may be the better alternative."

"Alternative?"

"To what else might happen. Someone is going to step up and try to take over. If it's a fanatic follower of the Leader, that could be worse than what we've just gone through."

"What makes you think military rule would be better?"

"Think, Carson. They were disbanded because they refused to follow what they thought were the Leader's unconstitutional orders. That's got to count for something. At least I hope it does."

"I guess that depends on who's calling the shots."

Shannon sighed. "Indeed."

Both were quiet for several minutes. Finally, Shannon roused herself from her thoughts to declare she needed to get home.

"Want me to walk you there?"

Shannon shook her head. "I'll be fine." She looked around. "Where's the rest of your family? Shouldn't they be here by now, regardless of what took them away from home?"

Carson glanced at the clock, noting the time. "You're right. Mom just went out shopping. She should be back. Dad's not due for another hour or so. I have no idea where my brother is."

"Hopefully they'll turn up soon." Shannon walked to the door and opened it. "I'll see you around."

Carson stared at the closed door. He felt a growing unease. He grabbed his jacket and quickly exited the house. He knew the route his mother usually took to the grocery store. He assumed if he followed it, he'd intercept her return. At worse, he'd find her still at the store. Maybe all the news had caused crowds to form and slowed her return. He set off at a brisk pace.

Carson noted that more people were on the streets than usual. They seemed to be milling around in a daze. He assumed the recent news was the cause. He ignored them as he wove his way through them, looking for his mother and/or brother.

About halfway to the neighborhood store, he spotted a canvas bag on the ground, groceries spilling out of it. People were ignoring it. A couple of kids sent an onion rolling down the street with a kick, giggling as they did so. He felt his heart rate increase as he realized the bag was one his mother used to carry groceries in.

He stopped and looked around.

"Mom?" Then louder, "Mom? You here?"

He bent and grabbed the bag, pushing the spilled items back into it. As he straightened, he looked around again. No one paid any attention to him as he stepped first one way, then another, frantically looking for signs of his mother. He hurried to the store.

As he entered, he was relieved to see that the check-out person was someone he knew.

"You know this bag? The woman carrying it? You remember?"

"Hey, Carson. Yeah, your mom and little brother were in here earlier today. You hear the news? What do you think of it?"

"Never mind that! What time were they here?"

The clerk picked up on Carson's urgency. "Who? Oh, your mom? About an hour ago? Why?" Then he focused on the bag. "Why do you have her bag full of groceries, anyway? Something wrong with them?"

"Neither are home. Found this on the street about halfway here. Did anything weird happen while they were here?"

"No. Business as usual. You think something happened to them?"

Carson snorted, thinking the clerk was a little slow on the uptake. Why else would he be here asking questions unless he thought something had happened to them.

"You didn't see anything?"

"No." Right then, someone approached to pay for their items. The clerk sent a quick smile Carson's way, wished him luck, then focused on serving the customer.

Frustrated, Carson ran from the store and back the way he came. He was almost home when someone stepped in front of him forcing him to stop. The man was big. Carson recognized him instantly as the one who'd warned him at the café to be careful.

"You're in a hurry. Lose something?" his smile was taunting.

"Where are my mother and brother?"

"Have no idea what you're talking about. No one has any idea. You understand? No one."

The man stepped around Carson and walked away without looking back. Carson watched him go. He understood. His mom and brother were gone. His mind drifted to the old man on the street. The man's family. Jimmy. All gone.

He slowly finished his journey. The house was empty when he entered, his dad still not home. Operating completely in auto-mode, he put the groceries away, then sat on the couch staring blankly at the television broadcasting updates upon updates, none of which answered Carson's most pressing question.

34

Jimmy was exhausted. He'd been walking for hours. Only two vehicles remained with those on foot, the rest all having gone on to whatever their destination was. Jimmy wondered if some might later come back to pick them up. He hoped so. He felt a blister forming on his heel.

A call came down the ranks and the men slowed, then stopped. Several took the opportunity to rehydrate, while others simply moved to the side of the road and sat.

"What's happening?" Jimmy asked the man next to him.

"Rest break."

"Do you know where we're going?"

"No. But some say we're going back to our base."

"We're turning around?" Jimmy's voice squeaked on the last word. He couldn't fathom retracing his steps to the camp they'd left miles behind.

The man laughed. "Not the camp. Our official base. Where we belong."

Jimmy looked at him in confusion. Before he could ask another question, Dr. Boise was at his side.

"Jimmy. Come with me. I need to speak to you." As he indicated for Jimmy to follow him, Dr. Boise asked, "You doing OK?"

Jimmy hurried to catch up. "Think I'm getting a blister on my heel. Is what that guy said true?"

Dr. Boise smiled. "I didn't hear what he said, so I can't answer that. Did you remember to take your pill?"

"Yes, a few miles back. What's going on, Dr. Boise?"

By this time, they were several yards away from the main contingent of men. Dr. Boise stopped and turned to Jimmy.

"We're waiting here. Perhaps moving on a bit more. That hasn't been decided, yet. Trucks should arrive soon to transport us to base." He smiled. "No more walking."

"Base? That's what that guy said. That we're going to the base. What's that mean?"

"The military is reclaiming its status."

"But—"

Dr. Boise continued as if Jimmy hadn't spoken.

"A lot of things have happened in a short space of time, the most important of which is the Leader, the Vice-Leader, and everyone in the immediate line of succession are dead." He raised his hand to forestall Jimmy's interruption. "It will take some time to sort things out. But in the meantime, the military is returning to its bases. Everywhere."

"Everywhere? You mean there were more camps than ours?"

"Of course. Several."

"But," Jimmy stopped. He had so many questions he didn't know which to ask first. Finally, he voiced those most pressing to him. "Who's running the country? Will the military take over?"

"Things will get sorted out," Dr. Boise repeated, not offering any additional information. "I need to ask if you've decided your future. Are you joining us? Or will you go your own way when we get to base?"

The way Dr. Boise phrased the question made it clear to Jimmy that he wouldn't be welcome to stay on the base. At least, not as a civilian. He remained quiet. Dr. Boise put a hand on Jimmy's shoulder.

"You'll need to decide by the time we get there. Go back and rest. Keep what I told you about the Leader to yourself. The men will be told when we reach the base."

Jimmy nodded and turned to go.

"Wait."

Jimmy turned back. Dr. Boise was holding out a small pack toward him.

"Take this. It's the rest of the inventory of your therapies. If you decide to join us, we'll sort it back out. If not, it will keep you going until you can make alternative arrangements."

Jimmy accepted the pack without comment, then walked back to the group of men.

35

Troy was surprised when he came downstairs and found his father in the kitchen cooking breakfast. Before he could comment, he was told to take a seat. Troy did so at the small table tucked into the corner. He wasn't sure, but he thought Beth had been the only one to ever use the table for its intended purpose. His father brought him a plate of bacon and scrambled eggs.

"Didn't know you could cook," Troy mumbled as he picked up his fork.

Marcus didn't comment, simply bringing his own plate and sitting across from Troy. Troy glance around just enough to verify everything was cleaned up.

"When did the authorities get here? And why no police tapes or other crime-scene things?"

"You watch too much television," Marcus said before taking a bite of his food.

Troy looked up, and stared at his dad until Marcus could no longer ignore him.

"They came very late. Long after I assume you were asleep. They did what needed doing."

"But—"

"It's done, Troy. Leave it. She had no family. There will be no formal services."

Recognizing his father wasn't going to provide any additional information, he closed his eyes briefly and silently wished Beth a happy afterlife.

"Can I ask you a question about the government?"

At Marcus's nod, Troy continued.

"Will there be new elections?"

If Marcus was surprised at the question, he didn't show it. "Yes. At some point, I assume there will be."

"What happens in the meantime?"

"The powers-that-be will choose someone to be the interim Leader."

"Who are the powers-that-be?"

Marcus smiled briefly. "Not everyone in the government died. There's still some semblance of a legislative branch, as well as the court system. They'll sort things out."

Troy wasn't done. "Are the remaining people as corrupt as the Leader was? Have they been bought like he was?"

Marcus stared at his son. "What are you talking about?"

"C'mon, Dad. You know as well as I do, maybe better since you hung with them, that the billionaires were the ones actually running the country. The Leader was a figurehead. Same with the Vice-Leader. I'm thinking their deaths are insignificant in the larger picture. It's the billionaires who died, and perhaps some of the sector heads, since most of them were billionaires, that's really the disruptive factor here. So, what happens now? Are you in line for anything, or were you just a hanger-on?"

"Troy! You're bordering on being disrespectful. Scratch that. You've crossed the line. Apologize at once!"

Troy put his fork down and pushed his plate away. "I won't. Tell me, Dad. Have you something to gain from all this? And if so, where does that put me?"

Anger turned Marcus's face red. He also put his fork down and pushed aside his plate. He struggled to get his breathing under control. When he was sure his breath and tone were normal, he answered.

"I'm not sure where your head is right now. I understand that Beth's death was a shock, and that could have something to do with this. But these questions and accusations aren't like you. Who's filling your head with conspiracy nonsense? Is it Carson? You know I prefer you stay away from him. Do I have to forbid you to see him?"

"I'm no longer twelve, Dad. I'm an adult. You can't forbid me anything. But for the record, Carson has nothing to do with the questions I asked. I'm curious. You're gone all day and through half the night. Just what is it you do? You mentioned cryptocurrency in the past, but I can't believe that takes up all your time. I'm asking for a real answer. I'm seriously interested."

Troy had moderated his own tone to be non-aggressive. He waited. He was curious if he'd get an answer, and if so, what it would be.

Marcus studied Troy for a few moments, then sighed. "I do spend a lot of time with the cryptocurrency markets. I've been advising on the whole issue of making it our national currency."

Troy interrupted, "Do you want it to be?"

"What I want or don't want will not influence the final decision. I'm simply offering thoughts on how it could be implemented if that's the decision that's made. Aside from that, there's a group of us who offer funding for various research projects."

"Research? What kind of research?" Troy's heartbeat quickened slightly.

"All kinds of things. I couldn't tell you specifically even if I wanted to. Don't understand most of it. But the majority of things we fund are within the health or medical field. It's why you were placed in the health sector, I suppose. Someone thought it paired nicely with my activities."

Troy didn't say anything. His mind went to the reports he'd read.

"If you don't understand it, how do you decide whether to fund or not? And what do you get out of it? There has to be some kind of return on investment. You folks don't just give away money for the sake of giving it away."

Marcus smiled. "I'm surprised you even grasp that concept."

Troy refrained from commenting. He knew whatever he said would just set his dad off. Instead, he pushed for an answer.

"So, what's the return? Do you get a piece of whatever is created from the research, be it a pill, device, or something else? Or do you get control?"

"Control?"

"Yes. As in, something is figured out or created, and you and your group take control of it to use as you wish."

"An interesting question. As it stands now, nothing has panned out enough to provide an answer. Look, I need to go. Can you clean up? I'll call the agency today and see if they can send someone to replace Co—" Marcus hesitated a fraction of a second, "Beth."

Troy just nodded as he watched his dad stand and leave the kitchen without even saying goodbye. He sat for a long time after that, thinking. Surprised his father had said as much as he had, he also realized that when analyzed further, there was little substance in the answers provided.

Finally, with little else to occupy his time for the day, he stood, gathered the dishes and began cleaning up the kitchen.

36

Carson was awakened by the sound of his dad coming through the door. He glanced at the television. It had cycled into a sleep mode and the screen was dark. He glanced at the wall clock and was shocked to see the time.

"You're so late!"

Carson's dad, Frank, looked tired and defeated. "Yes, I'm sorry. A lot happened today."

"All the deaths? Yes, I've been watching the television."

"No, not that. Well, yes, that too. But I meant other things."

"You mean Mom? And Eddy? Have you found out anything?"

Frank's body jerked. He looked at Carson intently. "What do you mean? Found out what?"

Carson hesitated. He could clearly see his father knew nothing about his wife and son being taken. Even as he wondered what else could be the cause of his father's tiredness, he tried to figure out how to tell him what happened. He decided direct was best. Like ripping a band-aid off a wound. Painful but fast.

"They're gone. They've been taken."

"When did this happen? Where?"

Carson motioned for his father to join him on the couch. Once seated, Carson described his afternoon.

"When you didn't come home at your usual time, I hoped you'd found out and were trying to get information."

Frank leaned forward. Elbows on his knees, he dropped his head into his hands and quietly wept. Carson was at a loss. He didn't know whether to put his arm around his father or just wait for the storm to pass. They weren't an overly demonstrative family, although they did exchange the occasional hug. As the minutes passed, Carson shifted uncomfortably.

"Dad?"

Frank sat up and wiped his face and nose on his sleeve.

"I'm sorry, son. It's just this on top of—." He drew a breath. "Well, I guess you need to know. I lost my job today. Was told I'm redundant. Unneeded. Unwanted. Tossed out like a piece of garbage. After all the years I've given them."

Carson felt an immediate stab of guilt. It went deep into his psyche. He knew these events were not a coincidence. He had to be the cause. His activities had garnered the wrong person's attention. But why not punish him? Why everyone but him?

He knew why. This was the most painful way. Destroying his family as opposed to simply doing away with him. The realization drove his guilt even deeper. Without giving it any thought, he reached out and put his arms around his father. Frank turned into it and the two held the embrace for a long time, drawing comfort from each other. Carson pulled back first.

"Is it immediate? Your job?"

"Yes. Today was my last day. The reason I'm so late is they made me wait for my final pay. I stopped and put it in the bank on the way home."

A part of Carson was relieved that at least they had that. But he knew the funds would last barely two weeks, and his side hustles and bartering would not make up the difference from the lost income.

"What are we going to do? Will we be able to stay here? And how are we going to find Mom and Eddy?"

Frank addressed Carson's second question first. "We'll be OK with the house. At least for a few months. But if I'm unable to find something soon, we may have few options available."

Before Carson could respond, Frank continued. "As to your mother and brother, I'm at a loss. I suppose I can go to the Enforcement Station and ask questions, but I doubt they'll give us any information."

Carson knew they wouldn't. In fact, if either, or both, of them went, they'd be lucky to be allowed to leave. He told his dad as much. Privately, he wondered if his contact could help. He decided he'd reach out. But he wouldn't say anything to his dad until or unless he had anything to offer.

Frank finally roused himself from his thoughts. "Have you eaten?"

"Not really hungry."

"Neither am I, but we should eat. C'mon, let's see what we can put together."

Frank stood and began walking toward the small kitchen. When he realized Carson wasn't following, he stopped and turned to look at his son. "C'mon Carson, the activity will help us."

Carson reluctantly got to his feet and followed his dad into the kitchen.

"Do you think they're all right?"

"I hope so, son. I hope so. But I've heard stories. They aren't pleasant." Frank shook his head sadly. "We mustn't dwell on negative thoughts. It won't help us get through this."

"I'm sorry, Dad. This is all my fault." Carson's words came out in a rush.

Frank studied his son. "If you're referring to your activities with the resistance, or whatever they're calling it, it's not th—"

"Wait," Carson interrupted, "you know about that? How?"

Frank pulled a chair away from a small table and sat. "I've known almost since the beginning. It wasn't hard to figure out. I don't think your mother knew, though. Nor Eddy."

Carson sat across from him. "Why didn't you say something?"

"It was your decision. And honestly, I hoped whatever you were doing could make a difference."

"But I'd been warned. I knew I'd been targeted. I should have stopped. I didn't. I put everyone at risk, and now they've taken our family members and pushed you out of your job."

"It was bound to happen sooner or later, even had you quit."

"Why do you say that?"

"Because I, too, pushed the boundaries. Maybe not as much as you, but I'm no innocent in this."

"You? You're involved in the resistance? How? When?"

"That's not important now. What's important is we eat, plan, and figure out how to get your mom and brother back."

37

"We've had a breakthrough of sorts," the voice on the phone was cautious.

"Tell me," Marcus Hubbard demanded.

"Not on the phone. But we need to meet. This afternoon, perhaps?"

Marcus thought for a moment. He could easily arrange his schedule to accommodate the meeting and asked for a time and location. He was about to disconnect when another thought occurred to him.

"Which study?"

"Not on the phone," the voice said again, but added, "however, I heard one of your hobbies is to collect identical gold nuggets. Twins, if you will."

The caller disconnected before Marcus could respond. As he stared at his phone, Marcus quickly understood the message, his mind going to the codewords in the most recent report he'd received. Suddenly he was looking forward to the meeting.

38

As the men moved out, Jimmy began to limp slightly. The suspected blister on his heel no longer suspected, but reality. As he trudged along, he wondered how much longer he could continue. Maybe he should quit now and not wait to get to their destination. Self-pity washed through him, and he was in no mood to fight it.

So distracted by his thoughts, he didn't hear the noise of the trucks until they were almost upon the group. In fact, if the men hadn't raised their voices in a cheer, he realized he could easily have been run over had he been alone.

The trucks stopped and the men hurried toward them, helping each other up into the covered beds and quickly seating themselves.

"C'mon, Jimmy! Hurry up!" One of the medics called out.

Jimmy saw the man waving at him and hurried to the truck. Two men reached out and pulled him into the truck, as those inside shifted to make room for the extra body.

"Thanks," Jimmy muttered.

While subdued, the atmosphere inside the truck bed was almost celebratory in nature.

"About time they came back for us," one man commented.

"If you got your lazy ass up in the morning and ran with us, you wouldn't be whining," another responded.

As the men took turns insulting each other, Jimmy listened with a heavy heart. He was going to miss being part of the camaraderie of the group. Even with the few who were not as accepting, he'd still felt more connected to this community than any he'd ever been in. He was going to miss Major Rowan in particular, along with Winthrop and Mike. They'd all been so supportive of him. As he thought this, he realized he'd made his decision. He would not be joining the military.

Part of him worried about his next steps. Where would he go? How would he survive? Should he just go home? Would that be safe? Or should he consider migrating north? Leave the country?

The other part was trying to analyze the bigger picture. Dr. Boise's news of the demise of the Leader and all those in the immediate line of succession was almost more than he could comprehend. But he understood one thing. A huge vacuum had been created, and nature abhorred a vacuum. Even as confusion reigned, which he knew it would, there would be those maneuvering to fill the vacuum. The question was, would they bring more of the same, or would there finally be an end to the enforcement squads, settlements, and all the economic and cultural inequities the country had endured. Things had gotten so bad that most of those who'd earlier supported the Leader had rethought that support. At least, some of it. That which personally affected them, such as unemployment, lack of resources, the high cost of those resources still available. Those kinds of things. But not everything. There was still a hardcore group who would just as soon see him, and others like him, burned at the stake. Not that they hadn't always existed, but the last two years had empowered them to create the scenario Jimmy had endured when he'd been taken.

Jimmy's lips twisted into a half-smile. It would take a long time to get back to the point they were at before the Leader, let alone progress from there. He wondered if progress was even possible. He guessed that would depend on how one defined progress. He supposed time would tell. But the passage of time could be extremely slow for those who suffered.

The truck lurched violently, causing several men, Jimmy included, to slide off their bench seat and land in a heap. As they sorted out their tangled limbs, the truck slowed to a stop. Gunfire erupted; bullets tore through the sides of their tented enclosure. Jimmy was stepped on numerous times as men leaped out of the truck bed, instantly in combat mode even though the full measure of the threat had yet to be determined.

For his part, Jimmy stayed where he was, nursing his bruised hand caused by a boot treading on it. He looked at the man next to him, who also hadn't moved. It took Jimmy a few seconds to realize the immobile man was dead. Panic fought with horror as Jimmy registered that whatever was happening outside the truck was intensifying. Not knowing what to do, but knowing he'd be useless trying to assist in the gunfight waging around him, he squirmed and wiggled his way under the dead soldier. Squeezing his eyes shut, he alternately hoped he'd live through this or prayed his death would be as quick and painless as possible.

It seemed like hours before everything quieted. Jimmy knew it hadn't been that long, but his sense of time was completely disrupted. He stayed where he was, not knowing the victor, hoping it wasn't whoever attacked them.

He heard voices approaching.

"Hello?"

The voice was strong, but Jimmy didn't recognize it. He waited. He heard the flap move. He tried to make himself smaller.

"Status update? Injuries?"

Still not sure whether to show himself, Jimmy stayed quiet.

"No answer, sir!" the voice called. "I think all casualties in this one."

"Pull them out. Let's identify them. The Doc will deal with it."

Jimmy recognized that voice, but he was confused. Major Rowan hadn't been with their group. What was he doing here now? He shifted his position. Apparently, the movement caused enough noise such that the man standing there picked up on it. Jimmy felt rather than heard or saw the rifle point at him.

"Who's there? Show yourself. Now!"

"It's me," Jimmy's voice came out in a squeak. He cleared his throat and tried again. "It's Jimmy. Please don't shoot me."

"Come out. Slowly, now."

Jimmy crawled out from beneath the man he'd been hiding under. By the time he'd freed himself enough to reach the edge of the opening, Major Rowan had joined the soldier whose rifle was still trained on its target. Namely, Jimmy.

"It seems you live a charmed life," the Major commented, a smile on his face. He reached out and pushed the soldier's rifle barrel down. "Is that your blood? Are you injured?"

Jimmy, unaware his face and clothes were smeared with the blood of the man he'd crawled under, just looked at Major Rowan.

"Jimmy. Are you hurt?"

"N-No." Jimmy quickly added, "Sir."

"Good. Good. Come out of there."

Jimmy slid out, his legs collapsing slightly, causing him to grab the truck for support. "What are you doing here, Major?"

"Came back with the transport to pick up the rest of the team. Good thing I did, too. The attack was unexpected."

"Who was it?"

"One of the enforcement squads. Apparently, they think they're running things since the recent events took place."

The way the Major phrased it, Jimmy knew he was still keeping a lid on the news until these troops got to the base. He was staring at the ground, so didn't realize Rowan was watching him.

"Jimmy?" the voice was gentle.

Jimmy looked up, a small tear escaping his left eye. "Sir. I can't. I can't enlist. I just can't. I feel so guilty. Particularly after all you've done for me, but—"

Rowan interrupted him. "It's okay, Jimmy. I think I knew your answer would be this. When you asked to think about it, I knew you were conflicted. Then, when you didn't come forward one way or the other, I surmised this would be your answer. Don't feel guilty. There's no need. You must do what you think best for yourself."

He reached out and put a hand on Jimmy's shoulder. "When we get to the base, I'll see what I can do to assist you making the transition away from us, but things will be busy, and with the current leadership crisis, I'm not sure how much I'll be able to do."

Jimmy nodded, and reached up to roughly wipe away his tears. Rowan squeezed his shoulder, then told him to go get in one of the forward trucks. They'd be leaving shortly. A small contingent would be staying to finish what needed to be done here.

"Are you coming?"

"I'll be close behind."

39

Troy read the reports for what seemed like the hundredth time. He was no closer to cracking the code he was sure was saying something beyond the mere words on the page. Pushing the papers aside, he leaned back and let his mind replay his earlier conversation with his dad. Something was not right. But he couldn't figure out why he was convinced his father was hiding things from him. Important things.

He sighed and checked the time. He wondered how David was doing, and if he should contact him. If only to offer condolences. The news had listed those killed, and David's dad was among them. He pulled out his phone and scrolled through the texts, finding the one David had sent him several days ago.

It took four attempts, but he finally crafted a message that seemed appropriate. He sent it. Twenty seconds later he got a reply.

Thanks. Could we meet? Later today?

Troy was surprised. He hadn't expected a reply, let alone an invitation to meet. But he was curious, too. Why would David want to meet? Neither had been called back to work after the building collapse, and with the current situation, Troy doubted they'd ever be called back. He just assumed he was out of a job. Not that it had been a real job in any sense of the word. But if he were honest with himself, he missed the excuse to get out of the house and the daily interaction with David. He texted back.

Sure. Where and when?

Receiving the information, Troy tucked his phone away and looked at the reports again. He couldn't see how reading them one more time would solve any mysteries, so he put them back in their hiding place. Even as he did it, he realized 'hiding place' barely described the area. He looked around for other options. He even considered putting them someplace else in the house. The residence was large. There should be an abundance of possibilities. But the more he thought about it, the more he felt uncomfortable having them anywhere but here, close to him. He finally settled on a new place and moved the reports and his chart.

He was half-way down the stairs when the loud knock on the door startled him. He moved to it and looked out the small peephole. Surprised, he opened the door.

"Shannon! What are you doing here?"

"The agency sent me. I'm your new cook. First time I've been to your house. Fancy."

Troy stepped back and Shannon entered as if she owned the place. She glanced around as she maneuvered past Troy enough for him to close the door. She smiled as she realized he was somewhat in shock.

"What's the matter? Don't think I can cook? I'm quite good at it, you know."

"No. I'm just surprised it's you. I didn't know you worked for the agency."

"I don't. I work for you. Well, your father if we're striving for accuracy. Surprised they sent a young woman? A few of us are still able to escape the societal expectation of being doormats or breeders. I could use a few other words, but I'll leave it at that. Where's the kitchen? This way?"

Shannon stepped forward towards the hallway she assumed led to the kitchen. Troy just muttered an affirmative and followed her, still processing the coincidence of having someone he knew be their new servant. He shook his head to clear his thoughts. He'd never thought of Beth as a servant. More a trusted part of their household. Why had he immediately put Shannon in the servant class?

"Have you much experience with this kind of thing?"

"Oh. So now you want to interview me? I can assure you, I'm more than qualified to fix your meals and clean your kitchen. That's all they told me I had to do. You aren't expecting me to be a maid or housekeeper or anything, are you? I'm not responsible for cleaning the rest of the house, am I? Because I'm not being paid enough for that, let me tell you."

As she spoke, Shannon had removed her jacket and was peering into the refrigerator, assessing its contents. When Troy didn't answer her, she pulled her head back and stared at him.

"Just the cooking part," he hastily assured her.

"I was told to prepare something that could be warmed up for later today. Then tomorrow, I'll be here in the morning for breakfast and fix another meal that can again be warmed up."

"That's fine."

"Great. You want to hang around while I do this?"

"Ah. No. I can't. I've got an appointment." Troy glanced at the time. "In fact, I need to leave now, if I'm going to make it."

He turned and started out the kitchen then stopped and looked back over his shoulder.

"It's good to see you. Write down anything you need by way of groceries. Dad will see that it gets delivered."

Shannon acknowledged his comment with a quick head nod while she busied herself with her tasks. Troy watched her for a few more seconds, then left the kitchen.

He was late meeting David, who was quick to express the fact. As they started walking towards a neighborhood playground, Troy explained his tardiness.

"Had to get the new cook settled in."

"Ah, yes. I'd heard your other one, Beth, wasn't it? I'd heard she'd died in the great purge. I'm sorry about that."

"Great purge?"

"Good name, isn't it? That's what they're calling it."

"Who's they?"

David shrugged. "Just a phrase. I presume your father was the target. You're lucky they failed."

Troy immediately felt guilty, knowing David's dad hadn't survived. He expressed his condolences again. David shrugged it off. They'd arrived at the playground and were sitting on a bench.

"Unfortunate. But at least we still have our family wealth. We'll be okay."

If Troy thought David's words were callous, he didn't show it. But that's only because he'd been looking down. He was sure his face mirrored his shocked thoughts, so he was slow in looking up.

"I'm glad to hear that. What are you going to do now?"

"Lay low. The investigators have already finished with us. So, our life goes on. At least for now. It's the bigger picture I'm worried about. What's going to happen next? With almost all the current leadership gone, I'm wondering if the common people will rise-up and rebel."

"Common people?" Troy couldn't decide if he was amused or offended by the words.

"You know what I mean. Those whose lives have been miserable the last two years."

"That's just about everyone. Other than those like us."

"Exactly. And there's more of them than us."

Troy looked intently at David. He seemed very different than when they'd worked together. He'd always been somewhat flippant and cynical, but this new attitude seemed more focused. More serious. Troy felt an uncomfortable sense of unease. He tried to lighten the mood.

"For the sake of argument, let's say there is an uprising amongst the common people, as you refer to them. What does that even mean? What could they possibly accomplish? Have group protests? Paint and display some signs? Chant slogans? The enforcement squads would quickly get things under control."

"Maybe. Maybe not."

"What, you think the squads would join them?" Troy laughed as he formed a mental picture.

"Remember. The squads consist of those who were ultra-loyal to the Leader. He's gone. As is everyone in the immediate line of succession. Who are they loyal to now? The new government? The people? Themselves? They have weapons. By the time it gets sorted out as to who's left that should take over, a lot could happen." David paused. "A lot."

Troy thought about that. The gap in a formal governance did offer all kinds of threats or opportunities, depending on which way you looked at it. From the perspective of people on the wealth side, people like David and him, the threat loomed large. For the people who'd suffered greatly and felt oppressed, the opportunities might seem endless.

He suppressed a shudder. He thought he better understood David's comments.

"Which way do you think it will go?"

"That I think, or that I would like?" David half smiled as he responded.

"Aren't those the same?"

"Not necessarily."

Troy was about to ask him to explain when a loud siren sounded. He recognized the sound. It was used to warn of danger. Usually weather-related, but not always. Both waited for the recorded message that would be broadcast in the few seconds before the siren sounded again.

Attention. Attention. All residents must return home or remain at their businesses if necessary. Shelter in place. Repeat. Shelter in place. Do not be on the streets. Stay sheltered until the all-clear has been given.

A short pause followed the spoken words, then the siren blasted from the speakers again. The message was repeated approximately thirty seconds later. The cycle continuously looped through the process of noise and words.

"What do you think is going on?" Troy asked, the alarm apparent in his expression.

"You should go home. I'd suggest you hurry. Stay there."

"But what about—"

David stood and turned in the direction he needed to go. "Troy! Go now!"

Even as he yelled the words to be heard over the siren, David started walking away. His pace soon quickened to a jog. Troy watched him for a few seconds before jumping off the bench and running towards home.

Breathless and with heart racing, he slammed the door behind him as he entered his home. He turned to lock the door.

"Shannon? Shannon! Are you here?"

Silence answered him and he realized he was alone. He could still hear the sirens and announcements through the protective enclosure of his house.

As he fought to control his panic, he had a flash memory of David's face as the sirens sounded. He realized David hadn't looked surprised. Or particularly alarmed.

40

Shannon was almost home when the sirens sounded. She hurried the last few blocks and ran up her steps. As she entered the house, she called out to those she assumed would be inside.

Her mother came from the kitchen. "Shannon, thank goodness you're here!"

"Are my sisters home?"

"Yes. With you here, we're all together."

Shannon knew what she was going to say next would not be popular.

"I think we should pack some stuff and go to the Jacobs. Safety in numbers and all. The two families will be better off together."

Her mother immediately rejected the idea, but Shannon worked to persuade her using both logic and emotions. Finally, her mother consented, realizing having men around might be safer than just the four women on their own. She called to her daughters to pack some essentials and come into the living room. While both girls did as they were told, they complained throughout the entire process.

Shannon suggested to her mother that she pack for the two of them.

"Whatever you're cooking smells great. You should finish it and package it up to bring with us. Once I finish gathering our clothes and essentials, I'll help you pack up the rest of the food we have. We should bring it all."

Her mother agreed and quickly returned to the kitchen. Shannon hurried into her room to grab what she thought she might need, then went to her mother's room to repeat the process. By the time she finished, her two sisters were in the living room, still loudly complaining.

"Be quiet! All this protesting is not helping. We don't know what's going on, but it doesn't sound good. We need to be a team. Take care of each other. Stay here while I help Mom in the kitchen."

The no-nonsense tone of her voice silenced the two girls. They looked at each other, then Shannon. Shannon saw the beginning of fear on their faces. She uttered some comforting words as she moved to the kitchen to assist her mother.

Twenty minutes later they were knocking on Carson's door.

"Carson? It's me Shannon. With my mom and sisters. Please! Can we come in? We've brought food."

Mercifully, the noise of the sirens and announcements had stopped, but Shannon knew they'd start up again soon. Part of the cycle, every half hour they silenced for five minutes, almost as if whoever had originally programmed them knew that people simply needed a break to gather their thoughts.

The door opened a crack and Carson peered out. He quickly opened the door wider, motioning for them to enter. When all had, he closed and locked the door.

"What are you doing here?" he asked in a fierce whisper.

"Strength in numbers," Shannon responded in her normal voice. She looked around, realizing the layout of the house was almost identical to hers. *Not surprising,* she thought, *the whole neighborhood was probably built by the same person or company.*

Frank entered the room. He didn't seem overly surprised to see the group standing there.

"Hello. Who have we here?"

Shannon introduced everyone and repeated what she'd said to Carson.

"I agree. You're welcome to stay with us until we figure out what's going on. Gotta admit, the sirens and announcements are rather scary," he looked at Shannon's ten-year-old sister. "Aren't they?"

"I'm not afraid!"

Frank nodded. "Good for you!" He looked at the girls. "Come. I'll show you where you can put your things. If you don't mind sharing, and it will be a little tight, you can have your own room." He looked at Shannon's mother. "You can also have your own room, or share with your oldest if the girls find their accommodations too tight."

Carson looked to say something, but his father's look kept him silent. Shannon was confused. If the layout was like her house, that meant there were three bedrooms. If she and her sisters had one, and her mother had one, did that mean the entire Jacobs family would share a room? That didn't seem fair. Realizing her mother was still slightly shellshocked from the recent events, she spoke up.

"I don't understand. It doesn't seem right for us to take over two rooms."

"Carson and I will share. It will be fine."

"But—"

Frank smiled sadly. "Later," he said gently. "Let's get you settled, then if you're willing to share whatever smells so good, we'll explain."

The sirens and announcements started up again. Frank led the newcomers to their respective rooms, as Carson took the cooked food and put it on the table. When he'd finished, he noticed the sacks of groceries Shannon had left in the living room. He gathered them up and took them into the kitchen.

Later as they ate the food Shannon's mother had prepared, Frank updated them on their situation.

"Grace and Eddy were taken? Where are they?" Shannon's mother asked, appalled.

"Yes. They were taken earlier today. We don't know where."

"But how are you going to find them?"

"We don't know that, either."

Frank pushed his plate aside. The food had been delicious, and he was thankful for the hot meal. Shannon and Carson exchanged glances. Frank saw it, but didn't comment. He had a feeling he knew what it meant but would wait until later to address it. He stood.

"Shall we see if the television can offer any new information?"

Everyone moved into the living room and found a place to sit, be it on the couch, floor, or a kitchen chair hastily brought in. Frank increased the volume which had been turned down when Shannon and her family arrived.

....Everyone is instructed to remain sheltered. Do not go out into the streets. You will be arrested if you do so. This is a complete lockdown. More instructions will follow. Again, stay inside. That's all we can share. We'll bring you more information as we get it. Reporting live, this is—

Frank turned the volume back down.

"Well, that was totally unhelpful. And I hope we don't have to listen these sirens all night."

"Agreed," Carson murmured. He stood from the chair he was sitting on. "Anyone want to play a board game? It might help pass the time."

There was half-hearted agreement. Carson went to the hall closet and pulled out one of the popular board games from several years ago. They all moved to the table to begin setting it up.

<h1 style="text-align:center">41</h1>

Marcus Hubbard hurried to the appointed meeting place, glad it was in a building and not somewhere in the open. The sirens and announcements were giving him a headache. He wished they'd stop. He was frustrated to be out of the information loop. He had no idea what had triggered the emergency broadcast system. But he was glad the empty streets allowed him to reach his destination quicker.

"Close the door."

Marcus did as told. "Why? It's not as if anyone is around to hear us."

The man ignored the comment and motioned for Marcus to sit at the table. They were in a small office complex. Marcus thought it had been a retail mall at some point but converted to offices a few years ago. The room they were in was in the back of a storefront setting. The large front-facing windows offered a full view of the inside space to anyone passing by. If anyone bothered to look, they'd see empty desks sitting in a rundown-looking room. Just another abandoned space, like most in the complex.

The two looked at each other in silence, almost daring the other to speak first. Finally, Marcus had had enough.

"Tell me what's so important to bring me here."

"We think we've isolated the problem we were working on. The one affecting the degrading of the Y chromosome. But there's an issue."

"Which is?"

"We need a bigger sample size. Or study group, if you prefer that language."

"I thought that situation had been remedied through the sweeping raids being conducted."

"Only to a point. Not all who are swept up in the raids are viable candidates for the program. Wrong gender, wrong age, wrong ethnicity. Whatever. Only a fraction are useable for our experiments."

Marcus was quiet as he thought about this.

"What exactly do you need? I've already significantly invested in this project. I'm not sure I can do much more."

"Preferably, we need young healthy males. Late teens into their twenties. A few older ones, just for comparison purposes. Most importantly, we need those whose exposure to the environmental toxins have been minimal. We're finding the specimens we currently have, to be a bit too contaminated, if you understand me?"

Marcus did. He wondered what the man expected of him. There was almost no escaping the poisons in the air, water, and soil. Things had gone too far. The deregulation everyone first heralded now proved that no controls meant just that. No controls. No restraints. No accountability. Companies had been free to dump whatever they wanted whenever and however they wished. Sure, those in his societal class were shielded to a certain extent, but even that was becoming less certain.

"It will be difficult to find anyone who hasn't been excessively exposed," Marcus said quietly.

"You need to figure it out. The payout for a successful outcome is almost unable to be calculated. We can't let a few pesky details slow us down. This project is top priority."

Marcus knew that was true, but it didn't solve his problem. The recent shake up didn't help. There still was no designated Leader, and people were getting restless. Those thoughts reminded him of the sirens.

"What's with the sirens and announcements, anyway? What's going on?"

"I'm sure we'll all find out soon enough. You should probably head home. Be careful on the streets."

Something about the man's body language and voice made Marcus wonder if he knew more than he was revealing. If he did, Marcus knew he wouldn't share, so there was no point in even asking.

"You're right. I should get home. My son will be wondering where I'm at."

Marcus walked to the door but stopped when the man spoke.

"Your son. How old is he?"

"He's in his early twenties, why?"

"No reason. Just wondering. You should hurry."

Marcus didn't respond. Opening the door, he stepped through and quickly shut it behind him. He wasn't sure why, but he felt the need to almost run to his car. As he drove the empty streets towards his home, he couldn't explain the feeling of dread that seemed to be growing in him. He blamed the sirens. It was easier than analyzing his thoughts and feelings.

42

Winthrop met Jimmy as he climbed out of the truck. After Jimmy hoisted his pack on a shoulder, he quickly ushered him toward an administrative building.

"I heard you'd made your decision not to join. Pity. I was looking forward having you in our division."

Jimmy felt like he needed to run to keep up with Winthrop's pace.

"How'd you hear that? I just told the Major a little while ago."

"He phoned ahead. Said I should meet you when you arrived and take you to the offices."

"What's the rush?" Jimmy was now breathing heavily.

Winthrop slowed and smiled. "Sorry. Just a lot on my mind. Didn't realize I was double-timing it."

"Someone said there's a lockdown. Apparently, sirens have been blasting forever. They just stopped a bit ago."

"They'll start again. They regularly stop for five minutes on some schedule. The quiet is to be worshipped."

Jimmy frowned. "But what's going on?"

"Don't know. I assume it has something to do with all the deaths and disruption. But who's to say? In any event, you don't need to worry about it for tonight. The Major said you can stay on base, just not directly with the troops. That's why I'm bringing you over here. A space has been set up for you."

"But—"

"Sorry, Jimmy. Orders. Tomorrow you'll be escorted off the base. Do you know where you will go?"

"Home. I guess. If I still have a home."

"And after that?"

"I don't know. First things, first. Assuming she's at home, assuming we still have a home, my mom probably thinks I'm dead. It will be a shock for me to turn up on the doorstep."

Jimmy didn't see Winthrop wince. He was too focused on what he would do if his mom wasn't at home. What if she'd been forced out? What if she was out on the streets somewhere?

They'd reached the door of the building and Winthrop opened it, turned back to Jimmy, and stepped aside. He motioned for Jimmy to go in first.

Jimmy's first impression was that the hastily created space was utilitarian in the extreme. Two desks were pushed to one side. A cot with blankets was in the corner next to a hallway he assumed led to a bathroom. There was nothing else.

"Sorry about this." Winthrop murmured. "But at least it's out of the weather and you won't have to hear all the activity going on outside."

"Activity?"

Just then the sirens started up again. Both men flinched.

"Us getting settled in," Winthrop said hastily, hoping Jimmy wouldn't ask any more questions along this line. "And hopefully these dreadful sirens will stop soon."

He breathed a quiet sigh of relief when Jimmy just nodded and moved toward the cot. He watched as Jimmy dumped his pack on the floor, shoved the blankets aside, and sat on the cot.

"You're to stay here. Don't leave. OK? If I can, I'll bring you a meal a bit later. But if it's not me, someone will deliver you food and drink. And then again in the morning. I don't know what time you'll actually have to leave, and I may not get to see you before you go." He hesitated a moment, then added, "Do you have other clothes? You look a bit of a mess."

Jimmy just nodded again as he stared at the floor. Winthrop felt a twinge of guilt watching his despondent friend.

"Jimmy. I'm sorry. I really am. Maybe we can get together after all this madness has passed? I'd like to think we've become friends. It'd be good to stay in touch."

Again, Jimmy just nodded.

Winthrop turned toward the door. As he reached for the handle, Jimmy's questions stopped him.

"What is the military planning to do? Will the country go under martial law?"

Winthrop turned back. "I don't know. Truly. I don't. Maybe the higher-ups have a plan, but I'm just a grunt. I do what I'm told." He took a deep breath and let it out slowly.

"Take care of yourself, Jimmy." He said softly as he walked to the door and quickly exited.

Jimmy stared at the empty space left by Winthrop. In his heart he knew that was the last time he'd see his friend. A single tear slid down his cheek. He wiped it away slowly.

The next morning a young private came to escort Jimmy to the front gate of the base. Neither spoke as they approached the guard shack.

Jimmy had hoped he'd see Major Rowan one more time, but realized the man was probably too busy to worry about the likes of him. He shuffled toward the small building. His heart lifted when he heard the voice that called out his name.

"Jimmy! A beautiful morning, isn't it? Quiet. Peaceful."

Major Rowan stood just inside the door of the guard shack, smiling. Jimmy returned the smile automatically, as he realized it was quiet. The sirens had stopped.

"Major! Thank you for taking the time to see me."

"I couldn't let you just walk away without any kind of acknowledgement. We've shared too much together. Look, I have a small departing gift for you. It's from Winthrop, Mike, and a few others. Me, too."

The Major held out a canvas pack. Jimmy thought it looked rather heavy and wondered what it contained.

"Take it with you. Open it when you get to your destination. What is your destination, anyway?"

"I'm going to go home. At least I hope I am. I don't know if it's still there, or even ours."

"I'm sure it is. Do you need a lift? I can ask someone from the motor pool to drive you."

Jimmy thought about that. It would be a long walk to get where he needed to go. And if he were honest, he was afraid to walk by himself, thinking of the enforcement squads that patrolled the streets. It would be beyond ironic if he was picked up again just before reaching home. A very unpleasant déjà vu experience he didn't want to repeat.

"Would it be too much trouble?" he asked the Major hesitantly.

Rowan studied Jimmy. He had an idea what the lad was thinking. He didn't blame him. If he could ease the boy's fears, he'd do it. On top of that, he'd heard riots were forming on the streets. He couldn't, in good conscious, let the boy fend for himself.

"Not at all. Give me a second. I'll make the call." He stepped inside the guard shack. Moments later he emerged, assuring Jimmy his ride would be there shortly.

He stepped toward Jimmy and placed a hand on Jimmy's shoulder. "Look. I need to go. But I wanted to personally wish you the best. Take care of yourself. Okay? And watch after your mother, too."

"I will, sir. Thank you again for all your kindness."

Major Rowan looked up as he heard a jeep approaching. When he saw who was driving, he smiled. He glanced at Jimmy once more, patted his shoulder, then walked away without further comment.

Jimmy turned to look at the approaching jeep. When he recognized Winthrop at the wheel, he felt a huge relief. His grin was infectious. He happily climbed in when the vehicle stopped next to him.

"Didn't think I'd see you again."

Winthrop laughed. "Code of the day. Never say never. Where to?"

Jimmy gave Winthrop directions as they drove off the base. It took almost forty-five minutes to get to the house Jimmy used to live in. Jimmy had seen a couple of groupings of people, but Winthrop had quickly changed their route to avoid them. He looked at the house with some misgivings as they pulled up in front of it.

"It looks like no one lives there."

Winthrop silently agreed but hastily reassured his friend. "Why don't I go knock and see what's what."

Before Jimmy could respond, Winthrop hopped out of the jeep and hurried up the walk. He knocked with authority and waited. When no one answered, he knocked again.

The door opened a crack, and eyes peered at him. A woman's voice asked who he was. Winthrop identified himself and asked her identity. When the name she gave confirmed she was Jimmy's mother, he told her he had news of her son.

"My son is dead. What do you really want?"

Her aggressiveness took Winthrop by surprise until he realized the trauma she'd probably suffered when Jimmy disappeared. News of the settlement attack had likely affirmed her belief that her son had been killed. And the sirens yesterday and last night certainly couldn't have helped her mental state.

He used his most soothing voice to assure her that not only was her son not dead, he'd brought him home. Winthrop stepped aside and gestured toward the jeep. The door opened slightly wider as the woman looked to where Winthrop pointed. Her eyes widened as she recognized her Jimmy sitting in the jeep.

She flung the door open and screamed his name as she ran towards him. Jimmy slid out of the jeep and ran to meet her. She collapsed in his arms, sobbing, saying his name again and again.

Jimmy held her close, comforting her, his own tears freely falling. He noticed Winthrop gesturing for them to come into the house and realized it would be safer to continue the welcoming behind closed doors versus on the street where they could attract unwanted attention. He gently guided his mother back to the house and inside.

Winthrop watched the two for a few seconds, then waved slightly as he turned to leave. Jimmy mouthed a silent thank you to him as he quietly closed the door behind him.

43

The morning brought relief from the never-ending sirens, but Carson thought that situation was almost as frightening as the constant noise.

He wandered into the living room. Shannon was sitting on the couch. The television was on, the volume low. Carson sat beside her.

"Anything interesting?" He nodded toward the television.

"No. They've offered no updates. Just keep telling us to shelter in place."

"Do you think we should reach out to our contact?"

Shannon hesitated. "I've thought about that, but I'm worried it could bring unwanted attention on us and him. We're supposed to stay off the streets. You know they've upgraded the surveillance systems. It's harder and harder to get around them."

Carson nodded. After a few moments of quiet, Shannon asked, "Do you think you'll be able to find your mother and brother?"

Carson grimaced. "Has anything happened that's allowed you to find out what happened to your father?"

"Good point," Shannon murmured. "So, what? We just give up. Our loved ones disappear into the ether?"

"I don't know. How do we continue to fight when all the odds are stacked against us?"

"Not fighting is just another form of death. A very prolonged, painful death."

Carson smirked. "That's cheerful."

At that moment Frank walked into the room. "What's cheerful? I could use some cheerful news right now."

Carson and Shannon looked at him. He seemed to have aged greatly overnight.

"I was being sarcastic," Carson said. "Shannon is giving me nothing but gloom and doom."

"Speaking of which, anything new?" Frank gestured towards the television.

As one, Carson and Shannon shook their heads.

"At least the sirens have stopped." Frank turned toward the kitchen. "Breakfast? Although I'm not sure what there is to offer."

The young people exchanged a glance, then stood. "We'll help," they said together.

There was enough bread and eggs to cook up a sizable batch of French toast, and Frank was just piling the last two pieces on a plate when the others wandered out from their respective rooms.

"Something smells good," Shannon's mother exclaimed.

Frank smiled. "Hot off the griddle. C'mon, let's dive in."

Silence ensued while everyone satisfied their initial hunger. Frank was the first to break it.

"We need a plan. How to get food. Basically, how to continue to survive. It's hard to believe the lockdown will be enforced. People need to eat.

Get to work. Not that I have to worry about that anymore," he said the last with both a tinge of anger and sadness.

"Shannon and I can test the theory of lockdown enforcement," Carson said. Shannon nodded her agreement.

"No!" both parents forcefully objected.

"They may not pay as much attention to a younger person. We might be able to bypass their processes."

"But what if you get caught? I can't lose another family member." Shannon's mother pled her case.

"We need to eat. We don't know what's going on or how long this situation will last. Soon, there won't be any food left on the shelves. We need to go soon." Carson responded.

"He has a point," Frank interjected. "We can't just sit here doing nothing. I fear we may be headed toward total anarchy. Not only do we need to secure basic food and water, we need to fortify this place as best we can. No telling how low people will go. The survival instinct changes people. They'll do things they'd never have imagined doing in a different time or circumstance."

"Frank, don't scare the children, please."

Frank looked at the two younger girls. "I don't mean to. But they need to understand. Things are very different now, than they were even two days ago. There's a vacuum at the highest level of power. Until we know how and who will fill that vacuum, we must prepare for the worst."

"Dad. Shannon and I will go. We have the best chance of avoiding the squads and other dangers. You know that."

Frank looked at his son. He understood what the boy was saying, and he knew it was correct. But having just lost his wife and younger son to who knows where, he couldn't face the thought of losing Carson, too.

"We'll be careful. But we need to go now."

Reluctantly, Frank nodded his ascent. Carson and Shannon stood. Shannon went to her mother and gave her a hug.

"Don't worry. We'll be careful."

Her mother nodded and tried to hide the tears that came to her eyes.

Frank stood and went to his son. As he hugged him, he murmured words of caution. Then stepped back.

"You'll need some cash. I don't have much."

"Give us half of what you have," Carson said. "We'll figure out the rest." He glanced quickly at the younger girls. Frank understood the message and quietly repeated his words of caution.

They grabbed their jackets, both thankful the garments were dark in color. As Carson opened the door and looked in both directions down the street, Shannon tossed over her shoulder assurances of a hasty return. They stepped out and closed the door behind them.

"Stay together or spit up?" Shannon asked.

Carson thought a moment. "Stay together. No telling what we'll come up against. C'mon, let's go."

They hurried down the street toward the only market in the neighborhood. Carson hoped with all his being that they'd be able to secure enough food to hold the two families over for however long it might be necessary.

Less than ten minutes later they arrived at the market. All was quiet. The lights were out and the door to the building was locked.

"What now?" Shannon asked.

Carson put his face to the window and cupped his hands around his eyes to better see in.

"There're still items on the shelves. Let's go around back."

They made their way around the building. The back door was locked also. Carson yanked and kicked at it to no avail.

"You know, sooner or later someone is going to break the front windows and enter. It will be a free-for-all then. Better that we beat that scenario."

Carson looked at Shannon. "Are you saying we should break in?"

"I'm saying we need to do what we need to do."

"They'll have us on camera."

"Realistically? I think a lot is going to happen in a short time. Whatever law enforcement that exists, in whatever form it takes, is going to be overwhelmed. I think we can take our chances."

Carson wasn't convinced, but he acknowledged the probable accuracy of Shannon's prediction.

"All right. But there's got to be a way to do what we need to do without causing a lot of damage. Broken windows will draw a crowd like bears to honey. We don't need that. We need to get in, get what we need, and get out with the least amount of fanfare."

"Agreed." Shannon reached into an inside pocket of her coat and drew out a small case.

"What's that?"

"Just a few handy tools." Shannon selected an object and began working on the door lock.

"How do you know how to do that?"

"Don't ask questions you might not want to know the answers to. Just let me focus."

Carson remained quiet. It took several minutes, but finally Shannon turned the knob, and the door opened silently. They quickly stepped inside and closed the door behind them.

"Let's get this done. Grab mostly non-perishables. But also get fresh stuff. That will have to be used first, but it will help supplement." Carson whispered his instructions.

"How do we carry it?"

"Damn! Should have brought backpacks."

"There will be those reusable bags up front. We'll have to make do with those. Just pack them carefully."

Carson grunted. He knew those bags would be more difficult to carry and harder to appear innocent. But they were stuck.

"Stay low. Try to position yourself so anyone from the outside can't see you."

Shannon snorted. "Not stupid here. Let's get to work. You might want to grab a couple of those flashlights and batteries, too."

They quickly packed four bags each. Two for each arm. Neither thought they could handle more than that, and the canned goods were heavy. They'd just finished and were opening the back door when they heard a crash followed by loud shouts.

"It's started. Let's go! We'll have to stay off the main street." Shannon's voice trembled.

Carson opened the door a crack and peeked out. "It's clear. C'mon. We don't have much time."

They hurried toward an opening in a fence behind the store. As they were pushing their way through, the noise from the front became louder and more violent. Carson thought he heard a gunshot as they ran as fast as they could from the area.

Even running, it took them much longer to get back to the house than they expected. They piled through the door in a tangle of arms, legs, and groceries. As they sorted themselves out, Carson noted how dark it was inside and looked around. There were boards over the windows, with only small holes drilled in to allow a view of the street. Shannon's mother was busy covering those with dark pieces of cloth.

"How'd you manage this so fast?" Carson asked his father.

"We combined resources from both houses. Used some furniture as necessary. It's the best we can do. Let's hope it will be enough."

Carson described the scene at the market, as everyone worked to put the supplies away. Frank decided it would be better to spread things around, rather than put everything in the cupboards.

"Less obvious."

"Makes sense," Carson agreed. "What do we do if they shut off water and electricity?"

"Already thought of that. We filled as many containers as we could with water. We'll still need to ration, but at least we have something. And as unpleasant as it sounds, we may have to use buckets for waste, if you get my meaning."

Carson did. His nose scrunched up. But he didn't comment. They were going full survival mode now. Niceties such as flushing toilets were a luxury. He hoped they'd have that luxury for a while longer.

He moved closer to his dad and whispered, "Hate to ask, but how do we defend ourselves? For real? A wooden spoon or frying pan isn't going to cut it."

"Ahead of you there. It isn't much, but I have my hunting rifle. Haven't used it in years. But it's cleaned and oiled. And I have ammo. Not a lot. But sometimes, you only need to make a statement, not a speech."

Carson looked at his father with new respect. He looked over his shoulder and saw that the others were still busy with the groceries.

"I have a small handgun in my room. It was given to me a while back. I refused to carry it as suggested and hid it away. I only have two boxes of ammunition. But I guess it adds to our arsenal."

"Good man. Keep it hidden but get it ready. We may need to access it in a hurry."

"Dad, I—"

Carson's words were interrupted by the power going off. The younger girls quickly suppressed their shrieks of surprise. The sudden stillness was disconcerting to say the least. Quite frightening, if everyone were honest with themselves.

Frank took charge. He quickly set up the flashlights and gave one each to Carson and Shannon. They turned them on to allow a quick assessment of the progress made on the supplies.

"Everyone, finish your tasks then come into the center of the room."

"Mom?" Shannon's ten-year-old sister's voice wavered in fear.

"It's okay, hon. Finish up and do as Frank says."

As they all sat together in the living room, a small voice asked, "what now?"

Frank answered. "We wait. We watch out for each other, and we wait."

Outside, on the streets, large noisy crowds began to form.

44

Troy awoke at his usual time. Stretching, he crawled out from under his covers. He wondered what seemed different, then realized the sirens had stopped. He wasn't sure if that was good or bad. He flipped his light switch, but when the fixture didn't respond, he realized the power was out. He wondered why the generator hadn't kicked in like it usually did.

The house was quiet as he descended the stairs to the main level. Wandering into the darkened kitchen, he saw his dad whipping eggs in a bowl.

"Where's Shannon?"

"Who?"

"Shannon. The cook the agency sent yesterday. She said she'd be here this morning to fix breakfast."

"Probably afraid to venture out. After all, everyone's been told to stay off the streets, not that anyone is listening."

Troy sat at the table. "What do you mean? And why hasn't the generator engaged?"

"There's been riots. It's dangerous to go out. And I don't know about the generator. Perhaps it's out of fuel."

"How do you know about the riots? If the power's out, it's not like you can see it on the news."

Marcus ignored his son, concentrating on pouring his mixture into a frying pan. Grateful they had gas appliances that still worked, he wondered if it was worth dealing with the generator. If something other than lack of fuel was the problem, he'd be unable to fix it anyway. And he wasn't even sure they had extra fuel on hand.

The eggs cooked quickly, and Marcus divided them onto two plates. He set one in front of Troy and sat across from his son with his own plate. He began eating.

Troy took a couple bites, then asked, "Dad? What's happening?"

"I'm not completely certain. I've had a couple of texts this morning, but even they've stopped. Apparently, the lack of leadership is causing unrest. People are taking to the streets to demonstrate their unhappiness. And I'm sure that it's more than just recent events that's fueling the violence that's occurring. You need to stay inside with the doors locked. Hopefully, they won't come into this neighborhood, but they seem to be quite brazen in their actions."

Privately, Troy thought this was the very type of neighborhood that would be attacked. The people knew of the wealth contained within the houses on their street. What better target? Even if they were only looking for food and other essentials, as opposed to objects, everyone knew there would be more to find within these walls than those of their own communities. He wasn't sure staying inside with the doors locked offered all that much security.

"Aren't the enforcement squads keeping things under control?"

Marcus laughed. "It seems many of them have joined in the riots."

"But they have weapons!"

"Indeed."

Both were silent as they processed their individual thoughts.

"Are you staying home today?" Troy asked.

"I can't. I have things I must attend to."

"But you just said it was dangerous to be out. Aren't you nervous for your safety?"

Marcus was, but he refused to admit it to his son. "I'll be fine. Just see that you stay inside. You remember how to access the safe room?"

"Yes, but surely you don't think I'll need to use it?"

Troy hated the room. It was small and dark. On top of that, if the generator wasn't working, he wasn't sure the place was even functional. What if he got in but couldn't get out? What if he got in and then found out there was no air? The supplies of food and water would be useless if he couldn't breathe.

"Dad, I'm scared."

"Don't be. Everything will be under control soon. Look, I need to go. Can you clean up around here?" Marcus waved his arm to encompass the kitchen.

Troy nodded as Marcus stood. Marcus placed a hand on his son's shoulder and squeezed it as he walked out of the kitchen and towards the front door. Troy followed him and as his dad opened the door, he saw a car waiting for him at the end of their walk. If he thought it odd that his father was being picked up, considering the unrest, he smothered the thought. He watched his father walk towards the vehicle, then closed the front door. He didn't wait to see his dad driven away.

His actions kept him from seeing the car being stopped at the end of the block and his father being dragged from the back seat by a mob of men. The driver, rather than trying to help, simply drove away from the scene, leaving his charge to the mercies of the mob, which dragged Marcus around the corner and down the street.

45

Jimmy and his mother spent several hours catching up. When each had assured the other for what seemed like the hundredth time that they were fine, both fell into silence. His mother broke it.

"Are you hungry? I can fix something. Need to eat the food before it spoils, anyway. Not sure when the power will come back on. If it ever does."

"Why do you say that?"

Jimmy was confused. While he'd noticed the house was without power, it hadn't fully sunk in that the situation may be permanent. He was so used to not having to worry about such things when he was with the military. He hadn't made the transition to ordinary life.

"There's a lot of unrest going on. People are rioting."

"How do you know about that? Aren't you nervous being here on your own?"

His mother answered his last question first.

"No. Those who've already come by have left me alone. It's obvious I pose no threat, and I have nothing they could possibly want. Their anger isn't directed at people like me. It's directed at those they believe are the cause of their various situations."

Jimmy saw the logic in that but pursued his concern. "Mobs often lose control. And when that happens, they simply attack anything and everything."

"Perhaps. Don't worry about it. Come. I'll fix us something. We can make plans after we eat."

Jimmy wondered what plans she could possibly be referring to, but stood and followed her into the kitchen.

"Anything I can do to help?"

"You can cut up those bananas. We'll add them to the yogurt. There's cereal and milk to go with the yogurt. It'll be a cold breakfast, I'm afraid. Can't cook with the power out."

She gestured to the electric stove. Jimmy shrugged. He thought it was rather late for breakfast, anyway. He'd thought lunch food would be more appropriate, but he didn't know what his mother had on hand. He found a knife and busied himself with cutting the bananas into bite-sized pieces. He'd fold them into the yogurt when he was finished.

They ate in companionable silence. When they'd finished, Jimmy brought up the subject of plans again.

"What did you mean by making plans?"

His mother looked at him intently. "I'm thinking we should consider alternative living arrangements."

"You mean—"

"We've talked about it before. Before you were taken. Now that you're back, I think the idea needs revisiting. Who knows if or when things will ever change around here. We should seriously consider our options."

"Okaaaay,"

Jimmy drew the word out. He was surprised his mother remembered their earlier discussions. He was even more surprised she seemed intent on pursuing them.

46

Marcus briefly struggled against his captors, then realized there was no point. There were too many. Even if he escaped from the two who held his arms and drove him forward, others would take over. He thought he might avoid injury if he just conceded their control.

He realized none had spoken. There was no yelling or threats. Just the constant movement forward. He looked around and recognized his surroundings. Rather than drag him towards the lower-income section of town, they were pushing and pulling him deeper into his own wealthy neighborhood.

He found the courage to speak. "Where are you taking me?"

"Shut up. Keep moving." The voice was gruff. It was accompanied by a stronger push and a tighter hold on his arm and shoulder.

"I have a right to know!"

"You have no rights."

This time rather than another shove, a dark hood was thrown over his head. The instant darkness and cloaking of his senses caused Marcus to stumble. Rather than give him time to recover, the men holding him simply dragged him along; an action that kept him from getting his feet under him. The additional roughness created panic. Marcus instinctively resisted.

It didn't help. In fact, his struggles made it worse. At least, that was his last thought before he lost consciousness from the blow dealt to the back of his head.

When he awoke, he was tied to a chair. The hood had been removed. He looked around the room he was in. The way his chair was positioned, he couldn't see much, but he saw enough to know he was in a well-appointed study. And the lights were on. Obviously wherever he was, the place had an alternative power source. Part of him felt immediate relief. The owner was not some street scum. But then he realized he was still a prisoner. His secured hands and feet made that abundantly clear.

"Ah. You're awake. I hope you don't have a headache from your unfortunate accident."

The voice came from behind him. Marcus recognized it as a young voice. Not someone from his generation. He turned his head back and forth but was unable to locate the speaker.

"I'd hardly call it an accident."

"No matter. Would you like some water? I can have some brought to you."

"Who are you? Why am I here?"

"You're here because we need your assistance. Well, to be precise. We need your money."

"Then you'll be disappointed. I have only a few dollars on me."

"Be serious, Mr. Hubbard. If we only wanted the few dollars in your pocket, we'd just have taken it and left you on the sidewalk."

"How do you know my name? Why are you hiding from me? Show yourself. I'm restrained. You're in no danger."

The laugh surprised him. "It's you who are in danger, Mr. Hubbard. Especially if you don't do as we ask."

"Ask? Interesting word to use. I think demand is more appropriate."

"I don't really care what you think. All I care about is getting what I want."

"You said 'we' before. Who are you working with? But again, more to the point, who are you?"

The silence stretched. Marcus realized he was alone. Whoever had been speaking had left the room. As he swallowed and felt the dryness of his mouth and throat, he hoped they'd gone to get the water they'd offered. The time stretched and soon he dozed off.

He awoke with a start. He heard tapping. Like fingers on a keyboard. Knowing it was useless, he still tried to locate the sound. Whoever had positioned his chair was clever. Between the objects in the room and his limited visual perspective, he might just as well have had the hood over his head. His frustration grew.

"Welcome back." It was the same voice from before. "I hope you enjoyed your nap. There's water positioned so you can have a drink."

Marcus noticed the glass on a table situated such that he only had to lean slightly forward to grasp the straw with his lips. He took a long deep drink. Immediately he felt better.

"Thank you," he said quietly.

"You're welcome."

When his captor didn't speak again, Marcus asked, "How long have I been here?"

"Most of the day. Certainly not long enough for your son to begin worrying about you."

Marcus immediately felt panic.

"What do you know about my son?"

"Oh, I know Troy quite well. He's got a good soul. A little confused about the world, but I blame you for that. He'll come around. But even if he doesn't, no need to worry. He won't be harmed."

Marcus willed his panic to subside. He needed to think clearly. This person knew him and his son. So, someone in the inner circle. It had to be. But who? Almost all had been killed in the recent poisoning attack. Who was left? And what did they want with him? Was this an attempt at revenge, or something else?

"Can't you tell me your name? Our conversation would feel much more civilized if I could address you by name."

There was a low chuckle. "Good try. I'll tell you who I am when I'm good and ready. If I ever become good and ready, that is. In the meantime, let's talk about how you're going to help us."

"I told you, I—"

"Yes, yes, I know. You only have a few dollars in your pocket. That's not our interest."

"Then what is?"

"Cryptocurrency."

Marcus stilled. Several thoughts flew around his head. None of them pleasant.

"It's simple, really," the voice continued. "We know you've manipulated the markets to your advantage. We know you have one of the largest, if not the largest, holding of cryptocurrency in the world. Clever of you to push so hard for cryptocurrency to become the only legal tender of the country. I understand you hoped to extend that goal worldwide. Too bad you didn't accomplish your initial goal before the current circumstances created such chaos. Had you done so, you could literally have bought the position of Leader. Who could have denied you? But alas, such was not to be."

"So you're responsible for all the deaths?" Marcus's voice displayed his bitterness.

"Quite the leap of logic. But no. Neither I, nor my associates, are responsible for what's being called the Great Purge. We're as curious about who's behind it as everyone else. But that doesn't mean we aren't willing to seize the opportunity the situation offers. And our biggest opportunity is the fact that whoever was behind it messed up with you. Your lucky escape is our golden ticket."

"What do you mean?" Marcus knew the answer before he heard it.

"We want you to transfer all your cryptocurrency holdings to us."

"So it turns out that you're the equivalent of a street mugger. Perhaps a sophisticated one, but a mugger nonetheless."

"That's rather harsh. Mugging implies violence."

"And taking me off the street and bashing me in the head wasn't violence? Holding me prisoner?"

"Sorry about the bonk on the head. Couldn't be helped. But I still take offense at being labeled a mugger."

"A thief, then. Whatever. I can't help you. I don't have the information on me to access my wallet to make the transfer."

"Wallets, Mr. Hubbard. Wallets. We know you have several. Don't think we'll be satisfied with just one."

"I still can't help you."

"Don't lie. It's well known you have a photographic memory. You've even bragged about it. I've heard you recite long complicated passages after just a brief glance. You and I both know you can easily recite the wallet codes."

Marcus was about to object again when he realized the mistake the speaker had made. If the person had heard him recite things from memory, then he was certainly part of the inner circle. He didn't indulge in the party trick except when with those he hoped to impress. But the voice indicated the speaker was young. An offspring, then, of one of the circle members. But which one? He wasn't familiar enough with the families of those he courted.

"I can't help you," he repeated.

"Pity. Things would have been so much more civilized had you complied. I'm afraid you won't be going home for a while. Troy will begin to worry about you. He might even think about trying to find you. The streets aren't safe right now. You know that. Do you really want him wandering about on his own?"

"He wouldn't go out. He's smart enough to know better."

"But if he was convinced you were in danger, he might think differently, wouldn't he? Rich kid like him. He wouldn't have the first clue how to protect himself, would he?"

"Leave Troy out of this!" Marcus shouted.

Silence greeted his outburst.

"Hello? Are you there?"

Realizing he was alone again, Marcus slumped in his chair.

47

The afternoon merged into the evening. No one had come beating at their door. The small boarded-up house was simply ignored. Somewhere in the mid-afternoon, Carson had begun peeking through the small holes of the boards covering the windows. He'd watched as crowds of men and boys moved through the streets kicking at garbage and laughing when someone's foot was covered with more than rotten food.

"I don't think we're in any danger," he said to the group inside. "Everyone looks like they just don't know what to do with themselves."

"For now," his father cautioned. "Things will change if the power isn't restored soon, and order brought to bear. They'll begin to realize something bigger is going on. When the easy supplies are depleted, desperation will set in. That's when things will get ugly."

"Then we'd better hope that whatever is going on is soon contained," Shannon said softly.

Carson looked at his dad. "Maybe one of us should go out and talk to those roaming around. Maybe they've heard something we haven't."

"No. There's no telling how they'd react to someone asking questions. Particularly if they don't know the person. They'll look at everyone with suspicion. We can't risk it."

Carson knew his dad was probably right, but it didn't still his need to do something. Anything. Anything but staying hidden in the house like some mouse avoiding the neighborhood cat. Any action was preferable to this never-ending waiting.

"I can avoid them. I know every inch of this neighborhood."

"No. I forbid it."

Carson smiled sadly. "Dad, I'm not a child. You can't use the same words and think I'll just slink into my bedroom."

Frank sighed. "I know, son. I'm just afraid for you. I can't lose you like I've lost my wife and your brother."

"They're coming back! You'll see!" Carson kept his voice controlled as to not scare the young girls in the room, but there was no missing his emphatic belief that they'd find their family members.

Shannon's mother stood, went to Carson, and placed a hand on his arm. "It's good that you believe that. I did, too. But my husband has been gone for over a year. We still don't know any more than we did when he was taken. You need to be realistic."

Carson shook her off. "No! We'll find them. Maybe something big is happening out there. Maybe the government has completely collapsed. That might be exactly what is needed to find and release those who were taken."

"Or more of us will be taken. We need to wait it out, Carson. At least until we have more information." Frank's voice was firm, but soft.

"We won't get any more information sitting here."

Shannon interrupted. "I'm afraid I must agree with Carson, Mr. Jacobs. The only way we're going to get more information is to get out there and find it." She looked at Carson. "I'll go with you."

"No!" Shannon's mother pleaded.

"Mom. We know the neighborhood. We know a lot more than that. And we know the people who can give us the information that we need. You must trust us. We'll be okay."

Frank sighed, recognizing the inevitable. "Don't split up. You'll be stronger together. And please be careful."

"Frank!"

"They're right. We need more information. And they're uniquely capable of getting it."

Frank got up and walked to his son, enfolding him in a strong hug.

"Be safe," he whispered in Carson's ear.

"I will, Dad. I promise."

Carson looked at Shannon. "It'll be dark in another hour or so. We'll leave then. It'll be easier to remain unseen. Get ready."

Shannon nodded and went into the room she shared with her mother to get her things together.

48

The young man read the message on his laptop. Glad he had power and could keep the thing running, he quickly typed a reply.

The response was not what he expected.

Things were quickly escalating. His contact indicated the military would soon be engaged if the rest of the plan wasn't implemented immediately.

Military.

He thought they were safely tucked away in the wilds of the country. How did they suddenly become an immediate threat? He must have missed something. Or was deliberately left out of the loop. Neither of those thoughts were good. He needed to pay more attention. He'd need to check in with his network of informants.

Closing his laptop, he stood and stretched. It had been a long day. Now it seemed like it would be a long night. Best get to it. But first, he'd have a bite to eat.

The sound of a door closing roused Marcus. He was stiff, hungry, and had bodily needs. He was also trying to decide if he were angry, scared, or defeated.

"Ah. I see you're awake."

"Look. I need to use the facilities. You can't keep me here like this. It's been hours." Marcus's voice was a harsh croak. He'd tried to convey strength, but knew he'd failed miserably.

"Sorry for your discomfort. Perhaps, if you cooperate, you can soon be in the comfort of your own home."

"I told you before. I can't help you."

"And I told you. I know you have the capability to do so."

Marcus heard noises and tried to figure out what they meant when the voice spoke again.

"I'm all set up. Just a few codes from you will end this. It's an easy ask."

Marcus remained silent.

"I've got the time. I've eaten, I'm free to use the bathroom when and if I wish. I have a bottle of water next to me. Do you?"

At the mention of water, Marcus leaned forward and sucked on the straw. An empty sucking sound greeted his efforts. His glass was empty. The knowledge of that increased his feelings of thirst tenfold.

"You believe in torture to get what you want?"

"Not sure I'm comfortable with that word, but if it speeds the process without resorting to the extremes of ripped-off fingernails or broken bones, then so be it."

The words were said casually. So casually Marcus didn't doubt for a minute that things could get extreme if he didn't cooperate. He reflexively pulled at his restraints. They didn't give a fraction of an inch. He sighed. He thought of Troy. Would his son stay in the house? Would that even keep him safe? He thought of all the effort he'd put in to become part of the inner circle. He'd never made it. Had always been a hanger-on. The failure ate at his ego.

On the other hand, that same inner circle was no more. All had succumbed to the poison purge. All but him. Perhaps being on the fringe had been a blessing.

But who was running things now? The youthful voice goading him couldn't be the mastermind. He had to be just a cog in the machinery. Others must be above him. Instructing him. What was their goal? Could he become one of them? Join in whatever their plan was? He was certain the plan involved taking over the government. He could help. He had knowledge. He needed to sell this idea to his captor. Arrange to meet with someone higher up the food chain.

His natural arrogance returned. He made his demands.

As he felt two pricks on his upper back, the last thing he remembered hearing before passing out from the jolt of electricity that entered his body was that annoying chuckle.

49

It was late. Very late. Troy was worried. The power hadn't returned. The house was getting uncomfortably dark. His father still wasn't home.

Troy had spent most the day on the couch in the living room. He'd tried to read a favorite adventure story but found he couldn't concentrate. At one point he'd reviewed the reports he had, figuring he'd give trying to decode them one more go. But his interest soon deserted him. The silly code words still annoyed him, and without some kind of guide, he knew he'd never crack the real meaning of the reports. Disgusted, he tossed them in the corner of the couch.

He stood and paced. With no television, and his electronics quickly losing all power, he felt isolated from the world.

A knock on the door roused him from his lethargy. He contemplated whether he should answer. But the knock sounded again. More insistent.

Reluctantly he moved to the door.

"Who is it?" he called out loudly, hoping the person could hear him.

"It's Dr. Jones. Troy, open up."

Troy stepped back in surprise. To his knowledge, he didn't know any Dr. Jones. But the name was generic, so maybe that's why it didn't ring any bells in his memory.

Then he hesitated. It was almost too generic. Like when articles don't want to mention real people and simply say John Smith or something similar. But the biggest surprise was that the man knew his name. How?

As his hesitation stretched, the knocking sounded again, with another demand to open the door. Reluctantly, Troy did. Dr. Jones stepped through quickly and closed the door behind him. Troy wasn't sure, but he thought he saw someone else on the doorstep. Before he could ask, Dr. Jones spoke.

"Is your father at home?"

"No. I'm sorry. If you need to speak with him, you'll have to call or come back. I'm not allowed to have people here when he's not home."

Not strictly true, Troy still said the words with authority. He was becoming more and more concerned. Something didn't seem right. He instinctively stepped back as the man moved toward him.

"Don't be nervous, Troy. It's actually you I came to see."

"Why? And how do you know my name?"

"Your father speaks highly of you. He's very proud of you, you know."

Dr. Jones' voice was soothing. Not the least threatening. Troy relaxed slightly but still tried to keep his guard up.

"How do you know my dad?"

"We've worked together on several projects. Some more successful than others, but Marcus has always been supportive."

As he spoke, Dr. Jones moved slowly towards Troy. So slowly Troy was unaware of how close the man was until his arm was grabbed and he felt a slight sting.

"What did you do?" Troy demanded, rubbing his arm.

"Nothing for you to worry about. Just relax and let the drug take effect."

"What drug? What are you talk—"

Troy's legs gave way, and as he sank towards the floor, Dr. Jones was there to ease his landing.

"Don't worry. You'll be fine." Dr. Jones' voice echoed in Troy's head, the tone designed to sooth and comfort. He gently stroked Troy's face.

Troy's body jerked as he made one last effort to fight the effects of the drug. But it was a losing battle, and soon his eyes closed. He fell into a deep sleep.

Dr. Jones quickly checked his breathing and pulse, then stood and went to the door. He opened it and motioned the two men standing outside to come in.

"Hurry. Let's get him into the car. Be careful. No injuries."

Without speaking, the men rushed to comply.

50

Carson and Shannon snuck out the back door of the house and navigated around the corner to face the street. Not that they could see anything. The darkness was too complete.

Hugging the wall, they inched their way forward until the only choice they had was to cross the open space between the house and street. They stood quietly, listening for any evidence that the crowds were on their street.

"I think we're good," Carson whispered. "Where do we go?"

Shannon pointed. Carson could see a flickering glow a few blocks away and knew it to be the result of a large bonfire. He wondered if Shannon intended to join the crowd that was sure to be congregated around it.

"You sure it's safe to mingle with them?"

"It's the only way we can see if anyone has any information. We might know some of them, which will make it easier to blend. Unless you have a better idea?"

Carson didn't. They stealthily moved forward. When no one challenged them, it didn't take long to gain confidence and walk briskly towards the fire.

They arrived at the end of the block in question and stopped in surprise. First, the gathering was much larger than they anticipated. Second, almost everyone was seated in an assortment of kitchen or lawn chairs. A few stood, apparently not having handy access to a chair. There was no grumbling or yelling. It almost looked like a neighborhood block party.

In the extended glow of the fire, Carson and Shannon exchanged glances.

"You really think it's as friendly as it looks?" Carson's voice was still pitched as a whisper.

"Only one way to find out. Can you see anyone you know?"

"Can't tell from this distance. You?"

Shannon stared intently at the group. She shook her head. "It's too far and too dark. C'mon. Let's join them."

Carson put a hand on her shoulder. "We need to approach slowly and give them plenty of warning. No telling what they might do if surprised."

"Agreed."

They covered half the distance before Shannon called out.

"Hey! Hello? Can we join you?"

Someone at the edge of the crowd heard them and turned. The general murmuring ceased as several turned to look in their direction. Soon the entire crowd was silent. Carson suppressed a shiver of apprehension.

"Who are you?" a voice called out.

"We live a couple blocks away. We saw the light." Shannon called back, keeping her voice light.

A person stepped from the crowd. "Shannon? That you?"

"Tim? Yes. I'm with a friend. Can we join you?"

There was an exchange of words between the first person that addressed them and the person that had recognized Shannon. The longer they spoke, the more nervous Carson became.

"You sure?" he murmured to Shannon.

"Yes. It will be fine."

"Doesn't look fine."

"Shhhhh."

"Yes. Come join us," Tim called out.

Shannon and Carson approached slowly. When they got close enough, Shannon held out her hand to Tim who reached out and shook it. They exchanged quick greetings before Tim turned his eyes to Carson. Shannon introduced them.

The first person spoke again. "What are you doing here?"

"Saw the light. Got tired of sitting in the dark." Shannon replied nonchalantly. "There's a lot of people here. Seems to be a bigger gathering than just this local neighborhood."

"What of it?" was the aggressive response.

Tim interrupted. "Jeez! Tone it down. I know her. She's all right."

He studied Shannon for a minute. "It is larger than the locals here. We're making plans."

"Plans?" Shannon quizzed.

As the other man looked to object, Tim put a hand on his shoulder and shook his head. The man subsided, but angrily shook off Tim's hand, turned, and walked away.

"Don't mind him," Tim apologized. "He's just a bit jumpy from all the enforcement squads milling around. Several of them are here with us. Quinn doesn't trust them.

"Can't say I disagree with that opinion." Carson murmured.

Tim glanced at Carson. "They're fine. The ones here never wanted to be part of that whole thing. Circumstances and necessity. We all do what we must to survive."

"True," Shannon said. "But you mentioned something about plans. What's that all about?"

Tim glanced over his shoulder, then back at Shannon and Carson. He lowered his voice.

"There are several groups like this. There's going to be a coordinated attempt to resolve this stalemate on who's governing our country."

"What do you mean?" Shannon and Carson spoke the same words at the same time.

"People are tired of this general lack of focus to fix things. And they're tired of being told what to do by a bunch of billionaires who don't care about the likes of us." He smiled grimly. "Although, the number of them have recently decreased, which helps. They're too busy worrying about what's going to happen to their wealth to pay attention to what's going on right under their noses."

"And what's going on?" Carson asked, a feeling of dread forming deep inside.

"Revolution, insurrection. Call it what you will. But the people are ready to take back the government that was formed by the people for the people. A government that worked for everyone. Not just a few. Before all this corruption took hold and everything went topsy-turvy."

"And just how do they plan to do that?" Carson was convinced that whatever happened, there would be a lot of deaths. Unnecessary deaths, he thought. But then again, change of the status quo always brought with it great risk.

"Join us and find out," Tim said shortly. "Or take this opportunity to return to wherever you came from." He paused. "And I'd suggest you stay off the streets."

An uncomfortable silence followed his words. Carson and Shannon exchanged a long look. Suddenly Shannon leaned forward and gave Tim a hug.

"Stay safe," she said as she released him and stepped back.

Tim understood her decision. While he looked disappointed, he nodded his acknowledgement. He looked at Carson, who shrugged and held out his hand.

"Good luck."

Without further speech, Carson and Shannon turned and walked in the direction they'd come. Tim watched them go. Before the distance increased too much, he called out softly.

"If you change your mind, we'll welcome you."

51

"Ready to cooperate?"

The voice roused Marcus. It took a few seconds for him to remember what happened, that he was a captive, and what was being demanded of him.

"I told you, I—"

"Cut the crap!" The voice was harsh. "This is your last chance. Give us the passcodes or recognize that your death will cause your vast wealth to be lost to the ether world. Your son will not benefit. Unless, of course, he has them. Perhaps we should have taken him instead of you. He might have been more eager to please. To avoid the pain."

"Pain? What are you talking about?"

Marcus had barely spoken before something heavy and solid came down on the top of his shoulder. The unexpected, instant pain almost made him black out. It took him some time to recover enough to formulate words. And those words were pleading.

Another blow on the opposite shoulder forced a scream from his lips.

"Stop! Please stop!"

Marcus's mind was so numbed by the pain, he didn't realize how, in that moment, his captor was close enough he might have seen him if he'd turned his head. By the time he did realize it, his attacker had moved back into the protected space he'd previously been in.

After a brief silence, the voice spoke. "Have you reconsidered?"

Although both shoulders throbbed and the pain radiated down his arms, Marcus recognized that no bones had been broken. He was certain he'd have significant bruising, but he could live with that.

Live. He was beginning to understand his arrogant assumption about surviving this situation might be misplaced. He'd thought that if their true objective was his money, then they'd know they wouldn't get it if he died. That gave him leverage.

But the roughness with which he'd just been treated gave him a new appreciation that the space between life and death could be filled with immeasurable amounts of pain. And he didn't doubt for a minute that Troy could be in danger. They wouldn't believe the boy didn't have the passcodes. The idea that they would capture and torture Troy was too much for him.

"I'll give you what you want."

"Excellent. I knew you'd see reason if given the proper incentive."

Marcus had developed a deep hatred for the voice that taunted him. He promised himself he'd find his tormentor and serve up the justice the owner of that voice deserved. His satisfaction with that thought was interrupted by the voice speaking again.

"I'm ready. Let's begin. Recite the first passcode, please."

Marcus did. He heard the tap of keys as he said each letter and digit. There was a pause, and he thought he heard a murmured 'perfect' but he wasn't sure.

"Next one," the voice commanded.

This went on for several minutes; Marcus reciting a string of letters and digits, the tapping of a keyboard, and an affirmative noise followed by a demand for another code. Finally, Marcus declared in a defeated voice that he'd given up every account he owned, even those he'd set up in Troy's name. The total amount was valued at well over four billion dollars.

"I actually believe you," the voice replied. "Your talent for accumulating wealth is quite impressive. I thank you for your cooperation."

"What happens now?" Marcus asked tiredly.

"I'll see that you're returned to your residence unharmed. Thank you, again, Mr. Hubbard. Your financial assistance to our cause is greatly appreciated."

"And just what is your cause?"

Silence greeted his question and Marcus realized he was again alone in the room.

A few minutes later he heard the door open and heavy footsteps. He was about to ask who was there when a hood was pulled over his head and his world went black again. This time he didn't struggle when two sets of hands released his restraints, stood him up, and re-secured his wrists behind him. He allowed himself to be led away and ultimately put in the back seat of a vehicle.

Neither he nor his escorts spoke on the journey back to Marcus's home. He was walked up the sidewalk and assisted into the house. He felt his wrists being freed just as someone kicked the back of his knees. He barely got his hands in front of him to stop his face from smashing into the floor. He stayed still as he heard the door close.

Slowly he pulled the hood off his head and looked around, relieved to see the familiar sites of his home's entryway.

"Troy?" he called out. His first attempt was hardly more than a croak. He cleared his throat and called again.

"Troy? Are you here, son?"

No response.

"Troy?" Marcus's voice now held slight panic. He awkwardly got to his feet, continually calling out his son's name. Each time became more insistent.

He finally accepted that Troy was not in the house. He wandered into the living room looking around listlessly. He first saw his son's phone sitting on an end table. He processed the thought his son wouldn't leave his phone behind if he'd left the house. Willingly left the house, that is. Then his eyes found a pile of papers piled messily in one corner of the couch. He went to them, reached down, and picked up what looked to be a bound report.

His eyes widened in alarm as he recognized what he was looking at. He quickly checked the rest of the stack. Each report he picked up increased his panic. Underneath the reports was a hand-drawn chart. He immediately understood its purpose and the relationships revealed.

He allowed himself to sink slowly onto the middle cushion of the couch. As he sat staring at the floor, holding a report in one hand and his son's chart in the other, a memory came to him.

Your son. How old is he?

Marcus trembled. He let the items he held fall to the floor. In a near trance, he stood and walked to the bookcase in the corner of the room. Pulling two large leather-bound volumes from one of the shelves, he reached into the open space and removed the small handgun hidden there.

Understanding the significance of his son's absence, and given his current financial status, he knew his son was beyond his reach and power to help. He raised the gun to his temple.

Just before he pulled the trigger, he whispered his regret into the empty room.

52

"Learn anything?" Frank asked as Carson and Shannon slipped into the house through the back door.

"Only that something big is about to happen and that if we don't join in, we should stay inside and off the streets," Carson responded.

"What's that mean?"

"I think there's going to be massive riots. No telling how all that's going to turn out."

"Do you think the people taken will be released? Maybe those rioting will understand these folks are victims and should be rescued."

Carson looked at his father. Saw the hope in his eyes.

"I don't know, Dad. Maybe. But even if they're released, how safe will they be if there are violent riots going on? And we don't know where they are. They could be miles from here. Possibly in a different state."

"Or they could be close enough to easily make it home."

Carson sighed. He very much doubted it. But he didn't want to destroy the last of his father's hope.

"Well, right now there's nothing we can do. It's late. We should all go to bed. Tomorrow will bring what tomorrow brings."

"You're right, son."

Frank looked at everyone in the room and repeated Carson's words about going to bed. Shannon helped her mother shoo the girls into their room, then followed her into the room they shared. As she closed the door, she heard Carson whisper to his father.

"I'm scared, Dad."

"I am, too."

~

Sometime in the early morning hours, the power was restored. The unexpected humming of the various appliances woke Carson. He rolled over and looked at his father sleeping in the twin bed across the room.

"Dad? Dad. Wake up. The power's on."

"What?" His father's sleepy voice replied.

"The power is on. C'mon. Let's see if there's any news on the television."

Father and son got up and crept into the living room. Carson turned on the television and kept the volume low. Frank went into the kitchen and started a pot of coffee. The aroma soon filled the house with a welcome cheeriness.

Carson flipped through several channels that were nothing more than blank screens with static. He felt a presence next to him and turned his head. Shannon and her mother were staring intently at the television.

A working channel suddenly appeared. Frank joined them, sipping on a cup of coffee as he offered another to Shannon's mother. The four of them watched the screen. Each had a different expression on their face.

Shannon's was curiosity. Her mother's was alarm. Frank's was thoughtful. Carson's uncertain.

"They've got the power back on. That's a plus for them," Shannon commented. "I wonder how they got the media to get this on the networks. Must have taken over the stations. Well, at least this station. The others were all blank. Probably had an inside contact. Or, more obviously, this media outlet was part of the resistance movement all along." She half-smiled. "Maybe we should take the opportunity to charge our phones. They may still not work, but you never know. At least they won't be completely dead."

"But look at the videos of armed conflict! This will just make things worse for all of us. And how can you possibly think about charging your phone when you see this?"

Shannon's mother was nearly in tears. Shannon put an arm around her to comfort her.

"Look at that!" Frank exclaimed. "They've found one of the settlements! They're releasing everyone."

"Yeah." Carson agreed, as he quietly plugged in his phone. Shannon's comment made sense. He wouldn't waste the opportunity. "And it looks like they're rounding up those they're fighting and pushing them into the place at gunpoint. Seems a fitting reversal. But I rather agree that all this might make things worse for everyone. What if martial law is declared to get everyone under control? What then?"

Frank looked at his son. "You've got to have a military to declare martial law. Ours was disbanded, remember?"

Carson stayed quiet. He had no proof. Just something his contact let slip once. And his conversation with Shannon a while back. He didn't know how it could be accomplished, but he had a feeling the military was still in place. Hiding somewhere. How something like that could be kept secret for so long was an interesting puzzle. He shrugged. If billionaires could take over their country in every way from cultural to economic, perhaps they could also have figured out how to take over the military. The thought was sobering. But not completely out of the question. Particularly in the socio-political environment they'd been living in.

"Dad?" Shannon spoke hesitantly. Everyone looked at her, thinking she was addressing Frank. But her focus was intensely directed at the television. Her mother looked at the screen, then muffled a scream with her fist.

Instinctively, Shannon turned and took a step toward the door. Carson grabbed her arm.

"Wait. We don't even know where that is! There's nothing you can do right now."

"But I need to get out there and find him! He'll need help!"

At that moment, gunfire erupted on the street outside their house. Everyone hit the floor in an instant survival mindset. Shannon's little sisters ran from the bedroom shrieking. Shannon hurried to them, pulling them to the floor next to her. She murmured comforting words.

When she next looked at the television, the scene had changed, causing her to wonder if she'd really seen her father. But she remembered her mother's reaction and knew she had. He was out there somewhere. Alive. She promised herself she'd find him and bring him home. If it was the last thing she did.

Everyone flinched at the sound of explosions. Carson was the first to recognize the noise came from the television. He watched in horror as several homes in a residential area went up in flames. He wondered if what he was seeing was intentional or an accidental result of some other action.

Either way, the scene was frightening. If ordinary homes were being destroyed, how safe were they in this one? The gunfire outside suddenly ceased. Rather than feeling more secure, the silence added to the tension.

"Grace? Carson, look! It's your mother! Where's Eddy? Do you see Eddy?" Frank was staring at the screen.

The video showed a large group of people being shepherded to an area away from the buildings of the settlement they'd seen earlier. Some were helping others, but all seemed relieved to be outside the fencing. Carson didn't like the idea those guiding them had guns, but then again, there was no obvious indication of hostility. On the surface, it looked to be a rescue.

He now better understood Shannon's instinctive move toward the door. He was fighting his need to jump up and run outside. The problem was, they still didn't know where the settlement was. He watched and listened intently, hoping for some clue as to the location. He was also looking for his brother, who hadn't been with his mother.

"There!" he almost shouted, as he pointed to the television. "There's Eddy! They're both alive!"

"Thank God," Frank muttered repeatedly, as he covered his face with his hands and openly wept.

Carson and Shannon looked at each other. In that moment, they both knew that nothing would stop them from retrieving their family members. Somehow, they'd figure it out. Before Carson could gesture to Shannon that they should move to another room to plan, more loud explosive noises came from the television.

All stared as the camp that had once held their loved ones disintegrated in front of their eyes. Something or someone had caused a massive explosion. There was no question about anyone inside having survived.

Sounds of wailing and crying came at them from out of the television. Those on the floor, who'd rearranged themselves from prone to sitting positions once the outside gunfire had ceased, watched as the group who'd been earlier freed were moved further away towards trucks that were sitting in the distance.

"They're taking them somewhere. We need to find out where. Do you think they'll announce it?"

Carson spoke his thoughts aloud, not realizing he'd done so.

"If the goal is to protect them, it's doubtful," Frank responded. "Is there any way you two can get that information?" He looked to Carson and Shannon.

The two glanced at each other, then back at Frank. Both shrugged their shoulders.

"I don't know," Carson verbalized their uncertainty.

"You've got to try," Frank said softly, urgently. "I know you have contacts in that world. Please. You've got to try."

Carson looked at Shannon again. An unspoken commitment passed between them. Carson reached out and put a hand on his father's shoulder.

"We will, Dad. We will."

53

The riots went on for days. At times, it was questionable if they could accurately be called riots or whether an all-out war was being waged. Thousands were dying. Yet every hour more and more of the population joined in the resistance.

Two additional news channels came on the air, offering slightly different perspectives of the situation. Those not on the street fighting, hovered in their living rooms and watched the carnage unfold before them on their television screens. Their one goal: survival.

For those on the street, the goal was reclaiming their government. The problem was that many weren't even sure what they were reclaiming or who they were reclaiming it from. The only thing they were sure of, was they were tired of being hungry, feeling forgotten, or considered expendable. Even as they questioned their reasons for joining the resistance, they continued to fight, caught up in the excitement and mob-like thinking that pushed them forward.

Not since the 1861 Civil War, lasting four years, had countrymen fought countrymen with such viciousness and convictions of righteousness.

There would be an end. There's an ending to every story.

How long it would take and what it would look like was yet to unfold....

54

EPILOGUE - DAVID

"You secured the funds?" the voice over the phone asked.

"Yes." David replied. "I told you he'd be an easy mark. This was the final transfer. It's unfortunate the others were killed before we could get access to their holdings. Very poor timing. I told you it was too soon. We're lucky we got his before the poor sod shot himself. Not sure why he did that. Do you know? Had to be more than just financial ruin."

"No, I don't. As to the others, it had to be done. Where did you transfer the funds to?"

"My account."

Over the angry objectives coming at him, David assured the caller the situation was only temporary.

"It was the quickest and most efficient way. Calm down. I'll move the funds as we agreed."

"You better. This unrest is getting worse. Quite brutal in fact. What's the plan?"

"Not to worry. Things will be under control soon. How's the research going?"

"My colleague seems happy enough. But he's asking for more funds. I told him not to be concerned. His work would continue to be funded."

"It will be. Everything else ready to go?"

"Yes. But I don't see how we can go forward with all these riots going on."

"Let me worry about that."

There was a brief silence. Then the voice, sounding confused, spoke again. "Hold on. Someone's at the door. I'm not expecting anyone."

"You should answer it." David said softly. "I'll wait."

David listened intently. He heard his caller open a door, then a surprised exclamation followed by two gun shots. He assumed the next noise he heard was the phone hitting the floor. He waited.

Another voice spoke. "It's done."

David disconnected without speaking. He stared at his phone for a long moment. Then tapped a number in his contacts, identified only by a flexed-arm emoji, and waited for his call to be answered.

55

EPILOGUE - ROWAN

Major Rowan picked up the secure line with a feeling of dread. "Yes?"

"It's time. We need order and we need it fast."

"Are you sure you want to take this step? We may not be able to undo it."

"A couple of days should take care of it. A week at most. Your counterparts are ready to go. A coordinated effort. Then things will get back to normal."

Rowan grunted. "What's normal?"

"You know what I mean."

"I'm not sure that I do. I have your word that if we do this, fair elections will be called, and the people will have the right to choose their next government?"

"Yes. We all want to return to what we had, or thought we had, before this last administration took hold. The old ways may have been inefficient, but for the most part they were balanced. Perhaps this time around, we can get things right. Or at least better."

Rowan hesitated. He wasn't convinced he could completely trust the young man on the phone. While the man, and his group of supporters, had financed the continued existence of the military for the past two years, what would stop them from forcing the military's complicity in yet another corrupt takeover?

"Major?"

"Yes. I'll give the order. But hear me on this. And hear me well. If you double-cross us, I can't be responsible for the outcome."

"Is that a threat?"

"No. It's a statement of reality."

The silence stretched. Finally, Rowan heard the voice say harshly, "Just get it done."

"I'll give the orders."

Rowan hung up the phone. He hoped what he was about to do would bring a bright beginning and not a cursed ending to his beloved country. He also wished the earlier purge of the upper ranks hadn't happened. It left him, as a mere Major, the sole holder of responsibility for what was to come.

56

EPILOGUE - JIMMY

Jimmy stood with his arm around his mother. It was obvious she was exhausted. He tried to keep her spirits up. They'd been waiting in line for hours. He could see the end was in sight. Only a few more people were between them and the gate.

"Stay strong, Mom. We're almost there. It won't be long now."

His mother smiled tiredly. "You've such a kind soul. I'm so proud of the person you've become. I hope we've made the right decision."

"We have. You'll see. Everything will be so much better. Even if we struggle a little to get settled. Even if I'll still face some of the same prejudices. I can handle it. Ultimately, we'll be happier. And safer."

The line shifted and they shuffled forward. Neither said anything more as they continued their wait.

An hour later they were facing the immigration officer, answering questions and presenting documentation. After all the time in line, Jimmy was amazed at how quickly the actual process was accomplished.

The man smiled as he stepped aside and gestured them through the barriers that he'd pushed away.

"Welcome to Canada. From sea to sea. The true North strong and free."

57

EPILOGUE - CARSON

The family continually hugged each other. They would stop what they were doing and randomly turn to each other for the physical contact. Tears of joy always mingled with expressed fears of what was to come.

Light streamed in through the windows. The coverings had been removed. Thankful his family unit was together, it was clear his younger brother was traumatized. With loving support, he hoped the boy would turn back into the happy-go-lucky kid he used to be.

Shannon, her mother, and sisters had gone back to their own house. Carson hoped Shannon would soon share the same family blessing. Her father still hadn't returned. While not certain, they had strong reason to believe it was just an administrative mix-up. They'd been assured that everything would be resolved soon. The same couldn't be said for the other family in their neighborhood who'd been taken. They'd simply disappeared, and no one seemed willing or able to figure out what happened to them.

Military rule had been declared. All the declarations of the military having been disbanded was disinformation at its highest form. Initially, it seemed better than the alternative they'd been experiencing, but Carson still had concerns. There were murmurings of elections being arranged, but so far nothing appeared to be happening. While the military acted completely in charge, Carson knew someone was directing them. No one knew who.

Food, water, and other supplies were being delivered to preset distribution points and passed out with minimal disruptions. It was safe to walk the streets, although Carson thought it was still safer to avoid unnecessary journeys outside.

He stood in his open doorway and looked down the street. Not completely free of garbage, significant inroads had been made in cleaning things up. The sports court was almost back to functioning in its original form. Hopefully he'd see kids playing there soon. Just like when he, Troy, and Jimmy used to play there.

He still missed Jimmy. When alone, he would pull out the happier memories and indulge in them. He'd stopped by the mother's house, but she was no longer there. Carson didn't know what had become of her. He hoped she'd survived the violence and was as happy as she could be, having lost her one child.

As for Troy, he hadn't seen or heard from him since before the uprisings. He'd gone over to the house once, but it was boarded up with a for-sale sign in front of it. He'd tried calling but had received a disconnected number announcement for his efforts. Carson still had some small hope, but he wondered if he'd ever see or hear from Troy again.

He thought about the reports Troy had given him. He'd never read past what he'd skimmed when at Troy's. Subsequent events obliterated any priority of them in Carson's mind. He'd passed them along to others and quickly forgotten them. As he stood on his doorstep, he briefly wondered at their significance, or lack thereof.

He stepped back and closed the front door. He heard laughter behind him and turned to watch Eddy triumphantly resolve some conflict in a video game he was playing. Carson smiled and walked toward the couch.

"Room for another player in that game?"

58

EPILOGUE - TROY

Troy opened his eyes. His view consisted of a rectangular picture of a blue sky with a puffy white cloud in the middle of it. He felt pressure on his forehead and tried to lift his hand to investigate. That's when he realized he couldn't move his hand. Or his arm. Or any part of his body.

As his brain tried to comprehend the situation, it also registered a slight tugging sensation. Down there. Where his privates were. Consistent. Not gentle, but also not hurtful. If he were honest, it felt rather pleasant. He gave into the pleasure and let his mind drift to sexual thoughts.

It didn't take long for the inevitable to happen. As his brain and body absorbed the orgasmic release, he felt a pressure in his arm. He quickly drifted into a euphoria initiated by the administered drug.

But just before he lost complete consciousness, he thought he heard a voice say something about a successful harvest.

OTHER BOOKS BY THE AUTHOR

ABOUT THE AUTHOR

Naiditch has had a varied professional career that includes hospital administration, practicing attorney, director of a multi-million-dollar nonprofit organization, adjunct college professor, and Human Resources professional. She also holds a 6th Degree Black Belt in Shaolin martial arts, as well as a Black Sash in traditional Shaolin Kungfu animal forms. Retired from her various day jobs, she fills her days in New Hampshire with teaching the martial arts, yard work, bicycling through her annoyingly hilly neighborhood, and of course, writing.

Website:

https://clnaiditch.com

Contact:

Naiditchreads21@aol.com

Facebook:

https://www.facebook.com/naiditchreads21/

ACKNOWLDEGEMENTS

Thank you for reading my stories. Word-of-mouth referrals is the greatest gift you can give an author. Leaving a rating or review allows you to do that with little effort. Should you make that effort, know that it is humbly appreciated.